T0277181

met North beautifully fractures the veil between genres, weav-
g a kaleidoscopic journey of identity, love, and the choices that
ake us. This is a multiverse where both tender and painful
ildhood memories echo through the dark matter of adulthood
d find their way to post-apocalyptic gardens of the dead. An
sured and wildly imaginative debut that never loses its heart in
y of its realities."

—Sequoia Nagamatsu, bestselling author of
How High We Go in the Dark

aring, brilliant, and revelatory, *In Universes* scatters its char-
ers' stories across the multiverse, showing us every one of the
inite lives we might live. It's a miracle of physics and art, filled
h wonder and grief, hope and regret, survival and romance
loss. By its end, we know: the best of all possible worlds is this
where we get to read Emet North's writing."

—Julia Phillips, bestselling author of *Disappearing Earth*

Universes has a wondrous way of taking the full expanse of
heart (vast! unending!) and collapsing it into a jeweled beauty
can hold in your hands. This novel is brainy and surprising
—in a cartwheeling, star-spinning way—completely real."

—Ramona Ausubel, author of *The Last Animal*

a feat of narrative structure both dazzling and convincing,
et North gives us deep and emotionally complex access to
human being's journey across the multiverse, makes us think
ly about our own unchosen doorways, redefines realism as
kick its ass. *In Universes* is a wonder of a novel."

—Pam Houston, award-winning author of
Deep Creek: Finding Hope in the High Country

Praise for *In Univers*

"*In Universes* is an explosion of creative beauty
North is a massively talented writer arriving rea

—Nana Kwame Adjei-Brenyah, *New Yo*
author of *Ch*

"Bafflingly good. *In Universes* is an exhilarating
ulist extravaganza to which we can only, and ha
it is also, secretly—and brilliantly—kind of a
the melancholia of science fiction itself."

—Jordy Rosenberg, author of

"Beautiful and surreal, *In Universes* is a tenderly
brims with emotion—despair and regret, lov
wrestles with the endless seeking of self and
define a life."

—Fonda Lee, World Fantasy Aw
of

"*In Universes* is a dazzling and inventive explo
people we might become, the possibilities we
the heartbreak we can't run from. This nov
introduction to a brilliant new voice."

—Danielle Evans, aw
The Office

IN
UNIVERSES

IN UNIVERSES

A NOVEL

EMET NORTH

HARPER

An Imprint of HarperCollins*Publishers*

IN UNIVERSES. Copyright © 2024 by Emet North. All rights reserved. Printed in the United States of America. No part of this book may be used or reproduced in any manner whatsoever without written permission except in the case of brief quotations embodied in critical articles and reviews. For information, address HarperCollins Publishers, 195 Broadway, New York, NY 10007.

HarperCollins books may be purchased for educational, business, or sales promotional use. For information, please email the Special Markets Department at SPsales@harpercollins.com.

FIRST EDITION

Library of Congress Cataloging-in-Publication Data has been applied for.

ISBN 978-0-06-331487-0

24 25 26 27 28 LBC 5 4 3 2 1

For anyone who has chased genius because they thought happiness wasn't made for them.

To suspend the future, radically, may be to enter a kind of freedom that we do not readily know or even want to know. . . . It means to queer our worlds. And to queer is not to respond to the law of desire or its illusion of scarcity: it is to have no fixed idea of who or what you are or might become, and to find this an extraordinary pleasure.

—Shannon Winnubst

* **I** *

Deformation Catalog

Here is what I remember most about the months I spent searching for dark matter: there are some things in the universe you can only find by looking away from them. It was how the professor who ran the lab greeted me on my first day, and I remember thinking, yes, of course, and the thought was a revelation because this was a time when nothing about the world made sense to me. Later, sitting at my desk at midnight or nodding my way through some incomprehensible explanation, I would repeat the words to myself, try to re-create that first frisson of—what? Joy, almost. Hope. The feeling that the universe itself was something I might take hold of if only I kept reaching. Even now, worlds away, the words have a certain magic to me.

I spent my days at the lab removing stars from vast pictures of the night sky. They were too bright, too loud. They hid the smaller changes we were looking for, the slight bending of light that would indicate the presence of dark matter. This was not my job, precisely. I was meant to be constructing the two-point correlation function for certain galaxy clusters. Every time I thought I understood what this meant, it became immediately clear I did not. So I sat at my desk for ten or twelve hours at a stretch, using my mouse to draw lopsided red circles around problematic stars. At the desk next to me, the other new research assistant was developing a computer program we could feed my cleaned data into. We had our own corner, three computer screens each, a nickname: the NASA girls. We were the only women in the lab.

Before beginning this job, we had emailed, proofread each other's grant applications, discussed housing arrangements. I thought of us as friends until our first day, when two things became immediately clear—that for me a yearlong grant from NASA was an apex, and for her it was only a stepping-stone. She was the real thing, had the sort of brilliance I was only pretending to have. I think she understood this as well as I did, which I respected and resented. No matter how many times I told her to call me Raffi, she kept reverting to Raphaela, which was the name of my great-grandmother who'd died in the camps. Nobody called me that. She had dark, greasy hair that fell to her shoulders and a perfectly white center part. When she spoke, I would stare at the part and will her to run her fingers through her hair. She never did.

After staying at the lab each day as long as physically possible, I walked the twelve blocks back to the sprawling, decrepit house where I lived with most of a men's intramural rugby team. The room I'd rented was up in the attic, half the price of anywhere else I'd found, with a single narrow window and sloping ceilings I crashed into once or twice each day.

Up there with me was a curly-haired rugby boy named Graham, who had a new injury each time I saw him: a split lip, ragged stitches beneath one eye, a wrist so swollen it hurt me to look at. He seemed too delicate for such a violent sport, but I knew violence was not proportional to mass, latent as it was in something as small as an atom. He'd grown up in northern Montana, close to where my great-aunt lived. This, along with his immediate and unflagging belief that my job at the lab meant I was a genius, created a warmth between us. We slipped into a strange domestic orbit, in spite of our utter lack of similarity, in spite of my boyfriend, Caleb, who was working at a start-up across the country, and the rugby boy's girlfriend, Kay, whom I'd met briefly when she helped him move into the house. She'd worn cowboy boots and a flannel, had the sort of walk that made boys whistle. Measured against her, I found myself lacking. This made it more satisfying when the rugby boy ignored her calls so we could finish dinner.

Our intimacy was not physical, or was no more physical than the way our shoulders tilted together as we watched terrible movies on the couch late at night, or the way he sometimes fell asleep with his head resting against my thigh. Our intimacy was two children playing house. The way he paid for our groceries with cash he'd stockpiled in his sock drawer from selling weed, waving off my gestures of refusal—though in reality I was perpetually a paycheck away from overdrawing my bank account. The way he had water boiling on the stove in the attic's tiny kitchen when I got home from the lab, the way I tilted the cheap box of pasta into the water without a word. We ate straight from the pot, no matter what we cooked, so as not to create more dishes. Our intimacy was forks occasionally clinking into one another, flecks of pasta sauce staining our skin and clothes.

It was, above all else, the mutual willingness to see only the best in one another. It's a shame you don't want kids, Raffi, he said to me once. As if my DNA were so valuable that not passing it on was some kind of loss for the world.

I'd gotten the job at the lab by pretending I'd worked through all my difficulties with physics—a lie I still hovered on the edge of believing. The job was a doorway, a wormhole that would lead me to the life I wanted: acceptance to a PhD program, a prestigious postdoc, research papers and discoveries and the inner workings of the universe revealed. I'd emailed the professor who ran the lab during my last year of college and begged him to take a chance on me. True, my transcript was unimpressive, but what I lacked in pedigree and proof, I tried to make up for in conviction. *Dear Professor*, I wrote, then listed all the extra math courses I'd taken *to give myself the necessary background for rigorous research.* This, I told him, was what I wanted to do with my life, and I would put in whatever work was necessary. Even in spaces less public than emails, even in the dark corners of my brain that admitted no visitors, I held entirely to this rhetoric. Some part of me must have known that my conviction was a construction that had no capacity for flex, that unlike a skyscraper built to sway with the wind, any gust at all would be enough to cause collapse.

When I wasn't pretending to be an astrophysicist or a housewife, I was hanging around a sculptor named Britt, pretending to be an artist. I'd come across her work in a gallery I'd wandered into on one of my first days in the city and recognized her name— we'd gone to the same high school, lived down the street from one another, though we hadn't been friends. Coincidences in those months felt imperative. My work, after all, was tracking the ways in which seemingly random alignments were proof of invisible, underlying structure. I asked the gallery owner for Britt's business card, sent an email before I could convince myself not to. *I think we might have gone to the same school*, I wrote. *I came across one of your sculptures, the one where the girl is breaking open her rib cage and inside there's a whole galaxy. I can't stop thinking about it.*

We met at a coffee shop that served their lattes deconstructed on wooden boards: a shot glass of espresso, a tiny pitcher of steamed milk, a vial of lavender or hibiscus or cardamom essence. *So you're a physicist*, Britt said. *That's cool.* She had half her head shaved, the other half long. Graceful tattooed lines crisscrossed one arm. For an instant, I considered telling her how deeply miserable physics made me, as if I could tie us together with a confession.

You're an artist, I said, instead. *That's cooler. I wish I were creative like that.*

It's not like physics, she said. *If you want to do it, you can just do it. Come by my studio sometime, I'll show you.* She was the kind of person who was perfectly at ease in every situation. She could've been sitting naked in the middle of the freeway and the cars would've been the ones to feel out of place. I would've done anything to spend more time with her except ask.

And then there were the days I didn't go to the lab or Britt's studio, the days I spent lying in bed, the weight of all the bones in my body insurmountable. My personal gravity had become erratic. I hadn't figured out the formulae that would let me predict its rhythms, so I woke each morning with a sense of foreboding and waited to see how difficult it would be to lift myself from the bed. I was getting heavier as the months at the lab passed. Not larger, just denser. More tightly held to the ground, so that remaining upright required a tremendous effort. I began to look longingly at sidewalks while walking the twelve blocks to the lab, imagining what a relief it would be to stretch my body out on the ground and sleep.

I called Caleb on one of these walks, who said, *I'm at work, are you okay?* I described my fluctuating gravity. *What are you talking about, Raffi? Isn't Earth's gravity a constant? And shouldn't you be at the lab?*

It's the dark matter, I said. *Inside me.*

I think you should talk to a therapist, he said, not for the first time. *But I've gotta go, I have a design that needs to be filed by noon.*

Caleb and I had met the fall of my sophomore year, during a period I remember as a brief flicker of light. For once, my physics and math classes were going well. Understanding them made me feel invincible. On the weekends, I went with friends to the campus dive bar, where a library card could function as a fake ID, and temporarily became a person who could go out on Sunday and show up for Monday classes with their work done. A girl that boys like Caleb bought drinks for at bars. By the spring, this illusion of competence had dissolved—I couldn't understand anything, I was failing to prove to myself whatever it was I needed to prove—and some part of me was convinced Caleb never forgave me for that initial well-being, the way it had tricked him into thinking I was someone who knew how to be happy in life.

At the studio with Britt I tried to sculpt my heaviness, but it only looked like a lump of clay. I imagined asking her how to sculpt a black hole, the deepest gravity, exhaustion that eats whole days. I imagined her hands on top of mine, crushing the clay until it was dense enough to warp the weave of spacetime. In theory, any mass could become a black hole, if it was compressed tightly enough. In theory, inside a black hole space might flow like time, and time might stretch like space, and the law of causality might become mere suggestion.

Across the room from me, Britt was kneeling next to a statue of a horse so lifelike I kept startling at the sight of it. A girl was draped across the horse's back, her body melting into the animal's body. Britt was using a tiny scalpel to carve detail into one of the horse's hooves. She was wearing overalls with a sports bra and no shoes, though the floor was littered with scraps of clay and plaster. She had her bottom lip pinned under an incisor, hair plaited down one side of her head in a messy braid. I pictured myself wearing the same clothes, tried to bite my lip identically. I had read studies that showed forcing a smile could induce happiness. Maybe if I could mimic Britt's expression, I would feel whatever it was that she was feeling. But no matter how I arranged my lips, all I felt was tired. I was moving my mouth in weird ways when she looked over. She quirked an eyebrow, held my gaze for two heartbeats that I heard in my ears, then turned back to her work with a half smile. I looked down at my hands. I'd squashed my black hole; the clay was squeezing out from between my fingers. It was an improvement.

At the lab, I was left largely to my own devices, and I wondered if my bewilderment was perceptible, measurable in my endless red circles. I had thought nobody understood dark matter, that it was, fundamentally, an encapsulation of all we did not know, but it turned out that other people's lack of understanding took the form of complex theories, mathematical equations, computer programs that turned impenetrable data into different impenetrable data. Other peoples' confusion was a castle you could live inside, a whole architecture of the unknown. Once, at the lab, I called dark matter hypothetical, and the professor said, *I might be biased but I think hypothetical is a little much. We can measure its effect, we can detect it astrophysically, we just haven't identified it in the lab yet.* After that, I tried to avoid calling dark matter anything at all.

Another evening, the professor stood behind me, watching me circle stars. *Don't feel pressured to do all the data cleaning yourself,* he said. *We have undergrads who help with that sort of thing.* I told him I didn't mind, that I enjoyed working with the raw data, that I found the pictures of the sky inspiring. I had no idea what I was saying, but he smiled. *I know exactly what you mean,* he said.

I had time before I had to present my research. I had time in which anything might happen.

When I felt particularly despairing about my work at the lab, I let Graham and the rugby boys drag me out to the nearest bar. Anytime my glass of beer started to empty, they filled it from the pitchers in the center of the table. Soon my head was buoyant, though the rest of me stayed earthbound. This had always been the sort of belonging I'd found easiest to come by, not one of the boys, but not exactly a girl either. When someone from another table tried to talk with me, the rugby boys puffed their chests out and chased him away, tripping over one another to defend me. *Fuck off,* they said, *Raffi doesn't go home with strangers, she's not like that.*

What was I like? I wondered. How could these boys—these drunk and happy people I barely knew—have the answer? I felt I ought to be annoyed but instead was grateful. I was too tired to talk, too tired to pretend to be anything. Whoever the rugby boys thought I was, they seemed to like her. I tried to imagine what

Britt would think if she were here, but she would never be here. I let the rugby boys take turns piggybacking me home.

Caleb and I were communicating mostly via email, a fact that I didn't let myself interrogate too closely. Often, by the time he left work it was late enough on the East Coast that I could plausibly have been sleeping. Caleb's emails told me about the marathon he was training for, about the office dog who had his own line of raincoats. My emails were mostly run-on sentences about how I would never understand anything and what was the point of trying so hard. I often regretted these emails once I'd sent them.

You're doing this to yourself, he wrote back once. *Why are you so determined to do something that clearly makes you miserable?*

Dear Caleb, I wrote. It was late in the afternoon on a Saturday, and I was lying in my bed, a twin-size mattress on the floor, staring at the peeling paint on the ceiling. I had been half asleep, listening to the clatter of the rugby boys doing who-knew-what downstairs, when his email arrived. Now I felt an electric current of energy run through me, propelling me into a sitting position amidst the blankets.

Dear Caleb, what could be more worth making oneself miserable over than understanding the whole universe?

Dear Caleb, I want to be able to control everything, particularly time.

Dear Caleb, I need to prove to myself that I'm capable of anything if I work hard enough.

Dear Caleb, maybe I'm incapable of being happy, but what does that matter if I can be a genius instead?

Dear Caleb, why does genius always belong to men?

Dear Caleb, maybe if I understand dark matter and the night sky I will also understand how to get out of bed in the morning.

Dear Caleb, dear Caleb. I deleted all my answers, electricity draining out of me. I lay back down. I didn't respond.

I loved Caleb like a part of my own body, not something I'd compose odes to, but difficult to imagine life without. I felt certain of two things: he wouldn't leave me—if he was going to, he already would have—and he loved only certain parts of me. Maybe it is more accurate to say I loved him like my left hand, without which it would be difficult to tie my shoes or chop an onion. But I would still be able to make circles around stars.

The days I woke to find myself weightless were rare enough that I wished I could hoard them, bind them like atoms into some new molecule—an effortless week, a bearable life. Since I couldn't, I tried to shield them from any interference that might cause collapse. So when I woke one morning hours before my alarm with my mind so crisp and clear that a part of me wanted to head straight to the lab, I ignored the urge. Instead, I texted Britt, the only person I trusted not to ruin it. *Breakfast?* I asked. When I arrived at the diner nearby, she was sitting in a corner booth, hands wrapped around an enormous mug. She'd dyed her hair magenta since I'd seen her last.

You're vibrant this morning, she said, and I thought of Caleb, saying to me on a good day: *You're luminous, I love you when you're like this.* How all I could hear was the inverse.

Tell me about your sculpture, I said. *I keep seeing it, but I never want to interrupt your work to ask.* I was talking too fast. I stole her cup of coffee and took a sip to stop myself.

She told me about rescuing a horse from an auction when she was a kid. *It was a ridiculous thing to do*, she said, her family already living below the poverty line. Britt's face went soft as she spoke. *I think we overlook the importance of nonhuman relationships*, she said.

The grief I felt when she died, I've never felt a grief like that for a human. It was as though she was a part of me, like the boundaries of what I considered to be myself had expanded, or even dissolved. That's the feeling I'm trying to capture in the piece.

She wanted to hear about my work in return, and I told her how some invisible thing was changing the behavior of galaxies, making them spin together instead of fly apart. I told her about searching for gravitational lensing, that it was impossible to detect from a singular piece of data. *Distortion is a matter of relation*, I said, feeling a thrum of comprehension move through me for the first time. I was talking too fast again and stopped, blushing, but Britt smiled. After breakfast, she walked me to the lab, her arm looped through mine as if it were nothing.

Inside, computers were humming and people were clicking and the other research assistant was not yet sitting at her terminal next to mine, but soon she would be. I could feel the weightlessness seeping out of me. The professor walked past my desk and thanked me for a write-up I'd sent him the week before. *Good work*, he said, and it occurred to me that perhaps he meant it. I had spent so many years worrying about someone realizing I was a fraud. For the first time, I considered the opposite. My confusion might remain hypothetical, unidentified. I might be able to spend the rest of my life sitting at this desk, wishing for the lightness of nonexistence.

Sometimes Britt invited me to things—a gallery opening, a poetry reading. I always said yes, though I wondered if I ought to say no periodically to make it seem like I had a life.

One night we went to a lecture by Britt's favorite architect, called "Impossible Design." *Who decides what is possible?* the architect asked, standing onstage in a corona of light. *It's tempting to frame it as an objective characteristic. The laws of physics, a teacher of mine once said, tell us as architects what we can and cannot do.* I felt Britt smile at me. *But that is an oversimplification and one that conceals myriad considerations that are far from objective. Possibility is always changing. New materials are developed that are stronger, lighter. Advancing technology allows us to render and test designs with increasing accuracy and complexity. On the most fundamental level, physics now suggests the act of measurement alone alters the fabric of our universe. Possibility is not objective, in other words, it is created.*

Outside, afterward, the wind whipped leaves into gyres, the air cool and damp. *Isn't she incredible?* Britt asked. I nodded, wanting to match her enthusiasm, but what I felt was a specific, habitual despair: a recognition of brilliance that was inextricably linked to an understanding of my own deficiency. *Is it true, that each time you throw a ball at a wall it might go straight through? That measurement alone can be enough to create a new universe?*

She's talking about the many-worlds interpretation of quantum mechanics, I'm pretty sure. And quantum tunneling.

Even the words are great, Britt said. *Can you give me the lay-sculptor's version?* I tried to come up with even the vaguest explanation, but all I could think of was the physics professor, who, when I'd suggested writing my thesis on branching universes, had said, *People hear multiple universes and get ridiculous ideas about alternate lives, but we're here for real science, not science fiction. Better leave interpretation to the philosophers.*

I can't understand any of it, I said, choosing honesty for once. *I'm failing.*

You're doing research for NASA.

It was what I'd always wanted from physics—indisputable proof of my own capability. And yet. *I barely made it through undergrad.*

What does that mean? That you got Bs? She laughed when I

didn't reply. I made an excuse to leave, shook off her offer to walk me home.

I called Caleb, once I was far enough away that she couldn't see me, but when he picked up, I realized I had nothing to say. *What's up?* he asked. *What's wrong?*

The leaves are changing, I said, *and my chest aches.* Soon the conversation was more pause than talk, and he had to run, goodbye, talk later.

When I got home, Graham was drunk and looking for his car keys. They were sitting in plain sight, but I slid them into my pocket, let him keep searching, tell me about how he'd agreed to meet up with a woman who'd slipped him her number at the bar. I didn't say, What about Kay, your girlfriend? I didn't say, What about me? I didn't say anything. I waited for him to notice my quiet. He filled the silence, didn't look at my face, didn't ask what was wrong. I thought about keeping his keys hidden—out of hope or vindictiveness, I wasn't sure—but when he stumbled over to me, I held them up. *I'll drive you,* I said. His car was new and expensive, and I drove ten miles under the speed limit. When we got to the house, he wrapped his arms around me then disappeared. I drove home, parked his car carefully, placed the keys on the counter where I'd found them.

Falling asleep was often a prolonged game of cat and mouse, but one night I closed my eyes straight into sleep and when I opened them, I was arm in arm with Britt, walking down a dusty orange path beside a stone wall. The sun was high in the sky, the air smelled of citrus and sand. I knew, in the way of dreams, that we'd walked this path many times before. *Are you going to keep deleting them?* she asked, gesturing toward the sky, where the stars were somehow visible alongside the sun.

No, I said. *I won't delete a single one.* I felt a certainty that was entirely unfamiliar and I closed my eyes into the relief of it. When I opened them, we had stopped in front of a wooden gate. I rested my palm flat against the door and felt possibility flood into me, a feeling like falling in love, but with the whole world.

When I woke, I was crying. I tried to remember ever feeling a happiness like that in my waking life. I lay in my bed, staring at the ceiling until the room became light.

Here is what I know about dark matter. It is what holds galaxies together. Or the galaxies are holding themselves together and we don't know why. Dark matter is the answer to a problem, the implication of an equation. Dark matter deforms spacetime, so the light from distant stars bends and haloes. Or spacetime is somehow deformed, so we know something is there, even if we can't see it. Dark matter is not dark, it is invisible, intangible, inaudible. It is the transparent scaffolding for our luminous world. Or maybe dark matter doesn't exist at all. Maybe there's another solution waiting for someone to think of it. But that someone would not be me.

I left my position at the lab via an apologetic email. I came up with better reasons for my departure than a dream. *The research here has helped me realize I might be better suited to a career in philosophy*, I wrote. I knew how these stories were meant to go, life arranged like a math theorem, each moment leading to the next in an irrefutable chain, QED. But the truth is that time is neither a river nor an arrow. It is a dimension, and our lives stretch across it, each of us a four-dimensional shape, taking up some small space in the universe. All moments existing at once and forever.

I circled a final star, thanked the professor for his time. Began researching PhD programs where I could study the multiverse, branching universes, infinite possibility. I stopped going to Britt's studio. Didn't answer her messages, asking if I was okay. I packed up my room, let the rugby boy carry my bags down the stairs. I would never see Graham again, nor the professor, nor Britt, though for years I would think of writing to her.

Dear Britt, I might write, *even now I close my eyes and see your thumbs shaping the hollows of a horse's skull.*

Dear Britt, have you ever felt one dream shiver straight through the center of another, gone to sleep in a familiar universe and woken up somewhere entirely new?

Dear Britt, when I was thirteen years old, I stood behind a tree and watched you ride your horse in circles around your yard and felt something I had no words for and instead of saying hello, I fled.

Dear Britt, I am studying the way universes branch and fracture, whether a person's consciousness might slip like a drop of water from one branch to the next.

Dear Britt, I am trying to imagine new possibilities.

Dear Britt, maybe in some universe I said hello.

Dear Britt, a professor once told me there are some things in the universe you can only find by looking away from them.

Isn't that a beautiful, ridiculous thing to say?

CHAPTER TWO

A Universe Where
I Said Hello

Raffi stares into Britt's eyes and thinks *apple apple apple apple*. The apple in her mind is green with a pinkish tinge. It's tart and crisp and the skin is a little waxy. *Apple apple apple*. Her head hurts, that's how hard she's concentrating. Britt's eyes are a warm, deep brown with yellowish flecks in them. Her front tooth is chipped and her cheeks are round and rosy and freckled. Raffi wishes she had freckles. But no, her thoughts aren't allowed to wander. *Apple apple APPLE*. Britt shakes her head, breaking eye contact.

Nope, she says, *nothing yet*. Britt refuses to guess. She's fourteen, a year older than Raffi, and decisive. *When it works it'll be obvious*, she says. But when it's Raffi's turn to listen for Britt's thoughts she doesn't know what *obvious* means. Thoughts pop in and out of her mind, and any of them might be Britt. Her brain feels porous, not entirely her own. She doesn't know if she likes the sensation or not.

What if random people are putting thoughts in my head? she asks.

That's not how it works, Britt says. *You have to know someone. Inside and out. There has to be a Bond.* From the way she says it, it's obvious the word gets a capital letter.

* * *

A few weeks earlier, Raffi doesn't know that Britt exists. She's living in her own world, which is mostly unpopulated. She's new to town, new to the little pink house with one bedroom and almost no furniture where she and her dad live now. She gets the bedroom, her dad sleeps on the couch. In the fall, she'll start seventh grade, but before school is summer: sticky days so devoid of activities that each one feels endless. Raffi's parents, newly divorced but a unified front for once: "How about summer camp?" But Raffi knows they do not have The Money, so she says she hates summer camp, hates bug spray, hates fruit punch, etc. She says she is old enough to stay home alone during the day, and her parents, barely staying afloat in the ocean of their own problems, give in.

The truth is that Raffi is afraid of the empty house. So instead of going to summer camp, she goes on walks. She wakes up in the morning and pours herself a bowl of the Lucky Charms she'd never been allowed to eat and reads the sticky notes her dad leaves on top of the orange juice. The stickies have terrible giraffe riddles on them, things like "Why did the giraffe get bad grades?" and on the back, "Because she had her head in the clouds!" Raffi saves every one.

After cereal, she pulls on khaki shorts and her favorite T-shirt— tie-dyed and starting to smell from being worn too many days in a row—and locks the pink house's door with the key she wears on a lanyard around her neck. She knows she is unbearably uncool, but at least this summer there is no one else to notice.

The first time Raffi sees Calypso, she stops and stares. The horse is grazing next to a run-down house. She's a gray so dark it's nearly blue, with snowy dapples and an elegant white face that shades back to gray around her nose. She gleams in the sun, her tail swishing.

A few feet from where the horse is whuffling her nose across the scrubby grass, an old couch steams in the morning's heat. Raffi's never seen a couch outside before. Rusted toys and single shoes peek out of the weeds. It makes Raffi's skin crawl. She imagines begging her dad to let her rescue the horse, promising to get a job. It's hard to imagine him saying yes, but this is her made-up scenario, so she doesn't let that stop her.

A screen door slams, and a girl appears: auburn hair in a pony-tail, denim cutoffs hugging her legs. She whistles at the horse, who perks up her ears and ambles over. The girl runs her hand down the horse's neck, saying something Raffi can't hear, and the horse nudges the girl's shoulder, and watching the two of them together makes Raffi flush. She slips away before the girl can see her.

Raffi meets Britt for real at a barbecue on the Fourth of July. Raffi is certain she and her dad would both be happier staying home, microwaving Lean Cuisines and watching *The Princess Bride* for the hundredth time. But her dad says, "We don't want your mom thinking you don't have any friends here." One of Raffi's many fears is that she will be made to live with her mom, so off they go.

The woman hosting the party works at the same aerospace engineering company as Raffi's dad, and she insists on introducing Raffi to the other kids. Raffi looks at her dad pleadingly, but he quirks his mouth and shrugs, so she follows the woman. Her hands are sweating, she's wearing the wrong clothes, she forgot to brush her hair. But when she's introduced to Britt, she forgets about clothes. She almost blurts out *I've seen your horse*, but this seems too close to saying *I was watching you and your horse*, or, *I saw you but you didn't see me*, which both sound creepy. She catches herself in time. Instead, she says *hi* then turns red and sidles away, wishing she could turn into a bowl of potato salad and get eaten.

Raffi sits under a tree and opens the book she brought with her, which is called *Time Travel in Einstein's Universe*. Its neon-green cover caught her eye at the library, and when she flipped open the book, she read: *What would you do if you had a time machine? You might return to the past to rescue a lost loved one. You could kill Hitler and prevent World War II.* If Raffi killed Hitler, probably her grandparents would never have met and she wouldn't be born, but that seems like a fair trade. She can't focus on the book though. She watches the other girls at the party, hanging out in a cluster and swinging Hula-Hoops in endless circles around their hips. Britt's not with them. She's sitting on the grass with her siblings off to the side of the yard, her baby sister perched in her lap. She airplanes potato chips into her sister's mouth and drinks Coke and laughs at something her brother is saying.

When the sky darkens, Raffi finds a spot alone on the grass to watch the fireworks. The adults are drinking beer and talking in too-loud voices, as if they've been replaced by weirder versions of themselves. She pretends not to notice when Britt sits next to her.

So when did you move here? Britt asks.

Last month, Raffi stammers, hating herself.

I heard your parents split up, Britt says, and Raffi thinks *rude* but she doesn't say anything. *My parents suck too*, Britt says, nodding her head toward two adults arguing with each other by the grill. Raffi shrugs, still feeling awkward, but the sense of camaraderie prompts her to say, at last—

Do you have a horse?

Britt's whole face goes soft. Later, Raffi will know that this is the look of love, but at the time all she thinks is that when Britt smiles like that she becomes, suddenly, pretty.

Her name is Calypso.

* * *

Raffi's summer changes just like that. Before, it was the summer of the empty pink house, the summer of divorce, the summer of long walks. But with a few sentences, it becomes the summer of the horse. The summer of *apple apple*. The summer of Britt.

Britt's house is the opposite of the pink one: cluttered, noisy, overfilled with people. She has four siblings, shares a room with her younger sister who's two and a half. Britt's mom is always losing things and shouting for someone to find something dammit. She hardly seems to notice the presence of an extra body, but when she does, she smiles and says "Oh hi, Rachel, honey" or "How's it going, Ramona?" Britt grimaces, but Raffi doesn't mind. Her own mom needs everything to be perfect, finds endless flaws in Raffi's behavior. She forces Raffi to wear a dress and go to synagogue and sit right, eat slower, stop fidgeting, why is your room such a mess? Britt's mom doesn't yell at them for talking with their mouths full or having dirt on their jeans.

They spend most of their time in the big backyard with Calypso. There's never much food in the fridge at Britt's house, so Raffi brings the lunch her dad leaves her each day, and they split it sitting under the trees. Raffi asks her dad to buy baby carrots, and she and Britt feed them to Calypso. *Like this*, Britt says, flattening Raffi's palm so the carrot sits atop it like an offering. Raffi is afraid at first, but Calypso is gentle and the hairs on her nose tickle Raffi's hand.

Britt loves her horse more than anything in the world. She says it like that sometimes: *I love you more than anything else in the world*. It isn't enough to say a thing, Raffi knows that. But she also knows everything Britt's done to have Calypso: babysat for a rich family a town over every week since she was eleven; convinced her older brother to help her build a shed out in the backyard; researched horse care and no-fee-rescues at the library, and photocopied all the info into a giant binder she used to give her mom an hourlong presentation. (Halfway through, according to Britt, her mom said, "For the love of god, girl, I get the point.")

Next year I'll be old enough to get a real job, Britt says. *And then I'll be able to buy Cally anything she needs.* She tells Raffi about the money she keeps in a secret place—*maybe I'll tell you where one day*—for vet bills and the horse dentist. About the time the family she babysits for went away for a month, and she couldn't afford to buy Calypso's grain. *I could see her ribs*, Britt says, *it was so awful. But soon Cally will have the best of everything.* Raffi believes her.

To Raffi, the smell of horses will always mean this: summertime, Calypso following Britt around, the crunch of carrots, the faint racing of Raffi's never-quite-at-ease heart.

They're braiding Calypso's mane one afternoon when Britt suggests they play a game. It's hot and Raffi's T-shirt is stuck to her skin and she has a rubber band between her teeth to tie the braid off with. She spits it out. *What kind of game?*

Britt puts her comb down and kisses Calypso on the nose. *Come with me*, she says.

She leads Raffi to the back corner of the yard where there's a cluster of trees that's mostly hidden from the house and a tiny pond whose water gleams golden when the sun hits it right. *Sit here*, Britt says. She points to a patch of grass, and Raffi sits. Britt drops down across from her, close enough that their knees are almost touching.

I'm going to think of something, she says. *An object. You try to see what it is.*

She stares into Raffi's eyes. Raffi blinks. *How?*

Just clear everything out of your mind and wait for it to appear. Like a pebble tossed into a lake.

I'm the lake?

You're the lake.

Okay, Raffi says. But her mind doesn't feel like a lake, not even a choppy one. She wonders if Britt can tell. If, in the center of her pupils where there's supposed to be a lake, Britt can see something else. Raffi's mind feels like outer space: dark sky and explosions, collisions and loneliness. She thinks *lake lake lake* and sees nothing unless some of the gazillion thoughts careening around outer space belong to Britt.

It'll take practice, Britt says. *But I believe in us.*

There's a piece of hay in Britt's hair, and Raffi plucks it out without thinking. *I do too*, she says.

Sometimes Raffi doesn't think about apples. Sometimes she breaks the rules Britt has laid out for the game—*think of one specific object, something simple*—and tries to send her sentences. *You're the best friend I've ever had*, Raffi thinks. *I hope one day someone loves me as much as you love Calypso.* She stares hard into Britt's eyes. Usually Raffi hates being looked at, but this feels different. *I'm afraid you're going to get sick of me. I'm afraid I'll do the wrong thing. I'm afraid if we can't form a Bond, you'll find someone else.* But sitting across from Britt, their fingers intertwined, she doesn't feel so afraid.

Every day they sit in the grass and practice. *It's how learning to ride Calypso was*, Britt says. *At first everything is impossible, and then you keep trying and boom, one day it isn't anymore.*

You really think it'll work? Raffi asks. It's an overcast day and they have been staring at each other for what seems like hours and Raffi keeps thinking she feels raindrops.

Britt looks at Raffi with an odd expression, like she might sneeze. She leans forward, her face close enough that Raffi can smell SunnyD on her breath.

I've done it before, she whispers.

Raffi's insides go funny, hot and cold and trembly. *With who?* she asks.

Britt doesn't answer, just closes her eyes. She's smiling like a jack-o'-lantern carved by a six-year-old. Over Britt's shoulder, Raffi sees Calypso walking toward them, her ears flicked forward. *Tell me something you want her to do,* Britt says, without opening her eyes.

Raffi feels like Britt is playing a trick on her, like the time one of the popular girls at her old school invited her to sit at their lunch table, and as soon as she did, everyone got up and walked away.

Well? Britt says.

Tell her to spin in a circle.

Calypso stops walking and pivots, her front legs crisscrossing. She spins 360 degrees, then stops. Her shadow stretches over them, the bones of her face prominent so that she looks skeletal, menacing.

All the hair on Raffi's body stands on end. She pushes herself to her feet. *You should have told me,* she says. She doesn't know what she's upset about—it being true or it being a trick or something else altogether. *I have to go,* she says.

Go where? Britt asks. She stands too, her jack-o'-lantern smile vanished.

Raffi shakes her head. *It's creepy,* she says. She sees the words hit, Britt takes a step back. *I have to go,* she says again, and this time Britt doesn't say anything.

Raffi's never walked away from Britt before; she's only ever left when she had to go home for dinner. She doesn't let herself look back until she's at the fence. Britt has her arms around Calypso's neck. She might be telling Calypso what a freak Raffi is. She might be crying.

At home, Raffi sits on the floor in her room and runs her hands back and forth across the carpet until her palms tingle. She wonders whether Britt is mad at her, and the thought makes her itchy to rush back and explain herself. But she stays on the floor, trying not to notice the room getting darker around her, trying not to see shapes in the shadows, waiting for the sound of her dad opening the front door, home from work at last.

The next day is a Saturday, so Raffi stays home with her dad. They make a pile of pillows in the living room and lie on top of it and read books together. Raffi asks her dad whether he believes in time travel, and he says, "I believe there's a lot we don't know yet about how the world works."

For lunch, he makes raspberry pancakes. He makes her a snowman, then a dinosaur. "What about a horse?" she asks, before remembering that she's trying not to think about Britt and Calypso. The resulting pancake looks like a dog with chubby legs, though, and Raffi laughs and eats the legs off one by one. "I wish you could stay home every day," Raffi says, and her dad says, "Me too, Giraffe."

By Monday, Raffi's feeling better. She thinks about the fact that the game is real and Britt wants to play it with her. She feels light as she puts on yesterday's T-shirt.

When she gets to Britt's, Calypso is alone in the yard. Raffi's stomach squirms. Britt is always outside waiting for her on the days she doesn't have to babysit. *It's okay, it's okay*, Raffi thinks, like repetition can make it true. She knocks on the front door. She's afraid one of Britt's siblings will answer, but it's Britt who opens the door a crack.

I have to do some stuff with my mom today, Britt says.

Do you want help? Raffi asks. She wants to say she's sorry, but she can't figure out how. *Or should I come back after?*

No thanks, Britt says, as if she's talking to a telemarketer.

Raffi wanders around the neighborhood, but she's forgotten the trick to being alone. A dog snarls at her, the crows overhead scream. She goes back to the pink house, but she's afraid of all the emptiness inside, so she sits in the yard and plucks puffball mushrooms and squishes them between her thumb and forefinger, and thinks at each one *your fault, stupid, bad* and the mushrooms send up tiny apologetic clouds and she doesn't feel any better.

Raffi makes a plan. Over dinner a few nights later, she tells her dad that Britt's mom has agreed to give her weekly riding lessons. "It'll be even better than summer camp," she says. Her pulse is racing, but her voice is steady.

"I don't think we can afford that, Giraffe," her dad says, but when she tells him that Mrs. Mason only wants ten dollars a lesson, he relaxes. Raffi's guilt is overshadowed by excitement. Now she has a reason to call Britt, a way to show how sorry she is. Now she has something to give Britt that Britt needs.

For real? Britt asks, when Raffi calls with the news. *He wants to pay me to teach you?* She doesn't mention Raffi leaving, or the fact that they haven't seen each other in days.

For real, Raffi confirms. She wonders if lying will get easier, if she will learn to do it as easily as adults do. *But are you sure it's okay for me to ride Calypso? You could teach me like, on the ground. Like how tack works and stuff.*

Britt laughs—with Raffi or at her?—and then there's a moment of silence while she thinks. Raffi tries to listen for Britt's thoughts, but she doesn't hear anything except the static of the phone line. *I trust you*, Britt says, at last. *We'll do things where I lead you around. And once you get better, we can put you on the lunge line. Cally's good at that.*

Raffi doesn't know what a lunge line is. But she does know that Britt is talking as though the lessons will last for a long time.

The next morning, Britt is out in the yard waiting. Raffi's heart bounds forward like a golden retriever. *We'll start with parts of the horse*, Britt says, businesslike, and Raffi worries that Britt isn't her friend anymore, just her teacher. But when Raffi calls Calypso's withers her thithers, Britt laughs until her eyes run. She rests her head on Raffi's shoulder. *That's so good*, she says. *From here on, it's thithers forever.* Raffi laughs too.

When Raffi can name all of Calypso's parts, they take a break and sit in their clearing, sharing the lunch Raffi brought. Raffi gathers her courage. *Should we play the game?* she says.

You sure? Britt asks. Raffi nods so emphatically she cricks her neck. Britt scoots into position across from her. *Okay. You send first.*

Apple, Raffi thinks, *apple apple.* This time she pictures a Red Delicious like something out of *Snow White. Apple I'm sorry apple sorry APPLE.*

It's only a few minutes before Britt shakes her head. *I think we need to know each other better, for the Bond. Tell me a secret.*

For once, Raffi's mind is a perfectly flat lake. *Um*, she says. Britt watches, not smiling or frowning.

It's my fault my parents got divorced, Raffi says, the only secret she can think of. *I used to sit at the top of the stairs and listen to them argue. All their fights were about me.* Britt's face stays quiet and the lack of response makes it possible for Raffi to keep going. *They'd fight about things like my dad checking on me at night, when I got scared of the dark. My mom said he was spoiling me, that I was being manipulative. She said he didn't care about her anymore. That she wished they'd never had a kid.*

Britt rests her hand on Raffi's knee. *You wanna know the real reason I got Calypso?* she asks, and Raffi feels like she's passed a test.

Not the horse rescue and the presentation?

Yeah, I mean, all of that. But that isn't the real real reason. I walked in on my mom having sex with someone. Not my dad. It was awful. I just ran out of the house. And then a day later my mom and dad sat me down and said I could get Cally.

Raffi sucks in her breath, then wishes she hadn't. She tries to make her face quiet like Britt's. In case Britt can hear her thoughts, she thinks, *that's so fucked-up.*

It was weird, Britt says. *It was the happiest moment of my entire life, finding out I could get her.*

Your parents stayed together even after that?

Yeah, it's stupid. They hate each other most of the time. I wish they'd just split like yours.

Raffi tries on the notion that her situation is something to be envied. It feels strange but not bad, like wearing someone else's clothes. Still, she thinks about the half-empty houses, the new school, the extra hours her dad is working and how tired he looks all the time. She doesn't feel like she can say any of that though.

Okay, let's try again, Britt says, and Raffi thinks, *apple.*

The first time Britt helps Raffi mount Calypso, Raffi realizes she is terrified of riding. From the ground, Calypso is dainty, like a glass figurine of a horse, but being on top of her changes everything. The ground is so far away that falling off becomes Raffi's number one fear in the world.

What if she runs away? Raffi asks, interrupting Britt's instructions: *relax your legs, eyes up, heels down . . .*

She won't, Britt says. *I'm holding on to her.*

But you're so much smaller than she is.

The trick with horses is that you've got to believe you're in control. And as long as you do, they'll believe it too.

But it's not true, is it?

It is as long as you both believe it.

To calm her fears, Raffi spends her time atop Calypso sending the horse quiet missives: *I'm sorry for sitting on you, please don't kill me, I promise I'll bring you carrots later, don't you like carrots?* It's not that she thinks she has a Bond with Calypso, but she figures, who knows how horses' brains work? Maybe if you're a horse you can hear everyone's thoughts.

Britt is a good instructor, patient and precise. Raffi feels immature in comparison, but when she thinks about how Britt's expected to take care of her baby sister, it makes sense. Maybe this is what Raffi wants: to be a member of Britt's family, someone Britt is required to love. She imagines them as twins, able to read each other's minds since the womb, sleeping in the same bed at night so they can share each other's dreams.

The new routine is *apple apple, lake lake*, then secrets.

My mom is so angry she scares me. But when I told her I wanted to live with my dad, she cried.

Once my sister wouldn't stop screaming and I pinched her so hard she got a bruise. My parents never figured out how she got it.

After my great-aunt died, I couldn't sleep with the lights off for a year.

Sometimes when I'm running out of money for Calypso, I steal cash from my parents' wallets. They said if I can't pay for everything myself, I have to sell her.

The girls at my old school left a note in my locker about how weird I was. I think my best friend wrote it.

A boy I was friends with locked me in his basement and wouldn't let me out until I took my shirt off. He told everyone we hooked up.

I'm so scared of dogs that once my mom forced me to pet one and I threw up.

Whoever is talking, the other person's only job is to listen. Britt's impassive face makes Raffi feel like she can say anything at all.

Raffi's favorite part of the lessons is their end.

What do you think? Britt asks. *Enough for the day?*

Raffi understands that because of the money, these lessons are a Serious Thing. That if she were to say *That's it?* or, *Not yet!* Britt would keep walking her in circles. The knowledge makes her uneasy, but she feels safe with this new version of Britt, who can't get tired and send her away.

Always, though, she says, *Yup!* Or, *Better not make Cally work too hard!* Then Britt stops Calypso and loops the reins over her neck. For a terrifying moment Raffi is alone on the back of the horse who is unattached to anything, before Britt's hands are reaching up, steadying Raffi as she drops to the ground, swaying with relief.

Then Britt swings herself onto Calypso's back, landing in the saddle as light as spun sugar. Raffi settles onto the step of the mounting block to watch her ride, and it is as though Britt and Calypso come into focus and everything in the background softens.

Don't you get tired of watching me? Britt asks, and all Raffi can say is *no*.

Weirdo, Britt says, but her voice is warm, and she's smiling in a wide-open kind of way.

The first time it works, Raffi is trying to be a lake. The water is calm, more or less, like it's supposed to be. And then—the thought *pretty* pops into her head, like a bubble.

I thought we were supposed to think about objects! Raffi says.

Britt stares at her, and then her face breaks into a smile. *I cheated.*

Raffi thought if they succeeded, there would be shrieking, jumping up and down, a flurry of hugs. Instead they sit still, not breaking eye contact, Britt's grip tightening on Raffi's hands, the air between them electric, the bubble floating inside Raffi's porous brain, and for a moment it seems possible that it will float there forever.

I wish we were going to the same school, Raffi says while she grooms Calypso before a lesson. Summer isn't endless anymore; August is almost over.

Not my fault you're going to the rich kids' school, Britt says.

It was my parents' choice, Raffi says. *If it were up to me, I'd go to school with you. And the only reason I can go is 'cause my great-aunt Zlata died and left money for my parents to spend on schools and stuff.* She feels anxious to convince Britt that they are the same, though she understands this is not entirely true. *Besides, you're the one with the horse.*

Promise me we'll still be best friends once you start school, Britt says.

Of course we will, Raffi says. *Best friends, best friends*, she thinks. *You promise?*

Raffi touches Britt on the shoulder and thinks, *I promise*, and Britt smiles.

The weekend before Britt goes back to school, she invites Raffi to spend the night. Raffi is afraid of sleepovers. Always, after the other girls fall asleep, Raffi lies awake imagining something will happen to her dad while she's gone—a car crash, robbers, a heart attack like the one that killed Aunt Zlata—and she will never, ever see him again, and she ends up sobbing until he comes to pick her up. ("Stop coddling her with this nonsense," her mom said, the third time this happened.) But this is different; this is Britt. Raffi gives her most enthusiastic nod, and Britt squeals and hugs her, which feels like proof Raffi made the right choice.

Her dad walks her to Britt's house, even though Raffi has done the walk a million times by herself. At the door, he kisses the top of her head and says, "Call if you need me," and Raffi hugs him and feels like she might cry. But she packages her fear into a ball and squashes it down by her toes.

Britt makes them microwave veggie burgers that she bought for Raffi with her own money. She doesn't make a face when she tries hers, either. She touches Raffi's hand and thinks, *not bad for beans*, and Raffi thinks something back that is a jumble of: *thank you for getting them—for not acting like they're gross—for having me— sorry for the trouble*. Britt raises her eyebrows, and Raffi turns red.

After they eat, they go out into the backyard. The moon is close to full and it's bright enough that they can see without flashlights. Calypso is silvery with moonlight. She nickers when she sees them. It's so lovely that Raffi forgets to be afraid.

Britt convinces her to get on Cally bareback. *I'll hold on to you,*

Britt says. *I won't let you fall.* Without a saddle, Calypso's back is slippery as silk, but before Raffi can get frightened, Britt climbs on behind her. She wraps her bare arms around Raffi, and it feels as though they are blending together, so it's not only her own happiness she's feeling, it's Britt's too. So the thought *all the bad stuff is worth it to be here riding Calypso in the moonlight* could belong to either one of them.

When they get too tired to hold themselves upright, they slide back to the ground and go up to Britt's room. *I convinced Bailey to sleep in Mom's room tonight*, Britt says. She yawns, and Raffi feels the familiar panic tingle in her fingers and toes. Soon Britt will fall asleep and Raffi will be left alone in the dark. She puts a finger on Britt's shoulder, thinks, *I'm afraid.*

Let's get into bed and share secrets, Britt says. The bed is small enough that when they lie on their sides facing each other, their noses are only a hand's width apart. Britt's pillows smell like Herbal Essences shampoo. Her face across from Raffi's looks almost the way it does when she's around Calypso.

I'm scared of the dark, Raffi thinks to Britt. *I have nightmares.* She closes her eyes and the images are there waiting, shadows twisting themselves into creatures with hungry, golden eyes, some with teeth and some with claws, coming for her dad, for her, for everyone she loves. She feels tears welling and swallows. Britt squeezes her shoulder, and the shadows recede until it's just the two of them again.

I'm scared too, Britt says. *Not of the dark, but of other things.* Raffi doesn't ask what things, though later she will wish she had.

Raffi's new school feels like a fresh start. From kindergarten through sixth grade, she'd gone to a small Jewish school where her grade had only twelve students and she got free tuition because her mom worked in the office. Sixth grade had been a bad year for Raffi—everyone knew her parents were getting divorced and she got a write-up for whispering with her best friend when they were supposed to be praying and her best friend became friends with the most popular girl at school and stopped talking to her. But Raffi has a new best friend now, and seventh grade will be different. Her dad takes her shopping and buys her a whole new outfit even though it's expensive. Raffi brushes her hair and puts on strawberry ChapStick. But when she gets to school, everything she's wearing is wrong. The cool girls here wear polo shirts and carry designer purses. Raffi tries to will herself into invisibility, but this is difficult when she has to keep introducing herself to the class.

"Do I know you?" a girl asks, in biology. "Weren't you at that Fourth of July party at the O'Learys'?" Raffi nods. Jacqueline is chatty and friendly and has most of her classes with Raffi. At lunch, she waves Raffi over to her table, and Raffi feels the knot in her stomach loosen a little.

It's not until the third day of school when Raffi is finally starting to relax that she mentions her friend Britt who has the most beautiful horse in the world and—

"You don't mean Brittney Mason, do you?" Jacqueline asks. "You know she's like, a huge lesbo, right? Oh my god, did she ever come on to you? You guys aren't, like, girlfriends are you?"

"What?" Raffi says. "No! No, I just rode her horse, I didn't even know—I don't know—" It feels like the time her mom slapped her, leaving a handprint on her cheek that stunned them both into silence.

Jacqueline is staring at her, a half grin on her face. The other girls are watching too. Raffi imagines saying *I know all Britt's secrets, if that were real I'd know*, but that would only make things worse. And besides—is it true?

"It's not like that," Raffi says. "I'm not into that. My dad was just paying her to give me some riding lessons. 'Cause I love horses."

"Oh yeah, that makes sense I guess," Jacqueline says. "Anyway, I heard she got caught making out with a girl behind the tennis court last year."

"Her sister's a total slut too," someone else says. The girls are all leaning in now, elbows on the table, swapping stories they've heard about Britt and her family. "I heard her mom fucked Janine's dad." "Have you seen that couch in their yard?" "Gross." "They're such trash." Raffi tastes bile. She breathes through her nose, swallows hard. She thinks, *I'm sorry I'm sorry I'm sorry.*

Raffi stops going to Britt's house. She's afraid that even without going near, Britt will hear her thoughts. Maybe that's why Britt hasn't called or dropped by.

She doesn't tell her dad she's stopped taking lessons. She puts his money in an envelope. In school, she sits with Jacqueline, who bombards her with a stream of gossip so constant that Raffi doesn't have to say anything. Sometimes they get together outside of school, but mostly Raffi pretends her dad is too strict. "That makes sense," Jacqueline says, her favorite phrase. "It's probably 'cause your mom left him. Probably he's afraid you will too."

When Raffi has $110 in the envelope—riding lesson money plus all her own savings from babysitting—she shoves it into her pocket and pulls on her tie-dye shirt. Britt is cantering Calypso in circles when Raffi shows up. No shorts and flip-flops this time, she's wearing tan breeches and tall black boots, her spine ramrod straight. The boots are worn and there's a hole in the knee of the breeches, but still—if the girls from school could see Britt now, they wouldn't be able to call her trash. Raffi feels extra shabby. She thinks about leaving before Britt can notice her, but at the thought, Britt looks over. She doesn't smile.

Raffi sits on the grass outside the wire fencing and watches Calypso's floating gait. She hopes Britt will keep riding forever. But eventually Britt's circles slow and then she's walking Calypso over to where Raffi is sitting. She doesn't say anything, just looks down at Raffi from so high up.

All the words Raffi wants to say are ricocheting around her chest. She thinks them—*I'm sorry I haven't been around, I'm sorry I didn't defend you, is it true what they said?*—and hopes Britt can hear, even though they're not touching. She holds out the envelope. It trembles in the space between them.

Britt takes it. Raffi looks at Calypso so she won't have to watch Britt. *Do you hate me too?* she thinks to the horse, who blinks at her.

Are you kidding me? Britt says. She throws the envelope back at Raffi, but it's too light, it drifts gently to the ground.

Raffi shoves thoughts of Britt and Calypso and apples beneath the surface of the lake and freezes the water solid. She goes to school, impresses her new teachers, comes home, and reads the section of the time travel book that talks about going back in the past to save someone you love. "As far as we understand today," it says, "this can only be accomplished if the many-worlds theory of quantum mechanics is true. And if that is true, then there is already a parallel universe in which your loved one is okay now. That's because all possible universes exist. Unfortunately, you are in the wrong one."

* * *

It's the middle of October before Raffi sees Britt again. She's doing homework with Jacqueline at the pink house. "It's too empty in here," Jacqueline said the first time she came over, but Raffi's dad had gotten a table by then, so there was a place to sit and do math problems, and no siblings to bother them.

When someone knocks on the door, Raffi startles so hard she drops her pencil. She can't remember anyone ever knocking on the door before. It's already dark outside and she wishes her dad were home. She thinks of the SS pounding on people's doors in the middle of the night. She doesn't move until Jacqueline asks, "Aren't you going to answer that?" Without the prompting, maybe Raffi wouldn't have. But she gets up obediently.

Britt is so disheveled Raffi barely recognizes her. There's dirt on her face, sweat stains under her arms. She smells like horse manure and BO. Raffi shifts to block her from Jacqueline's view. *What are you doing here?* she asks.

Raffi, Britt says, pushing hair out of her face. *Raffi, I need the money. I'm sorry I threw it back at you.*

What? Raffi says. *Why?* Her brain is moving too slowly, she's still existing in the moment before Britt knocked, still sitting at the table trying to solve for x.

Cally, Britt says, and she starts to cry, hiccupping sobs that make it hard for Raffi to understand her, loud enough that she knows Jacqueline can hear. *Cally's colicking. I don't have enough money for the vet, and it's colic, Raffi, it happens so fast, I don't have time, you have to help.*

Snot glistens on Britt's upper lip, and Raffi is frightened and furious. Why couldn't Britt have taken the money when she offered it?

"Raphaela?" Jacqueline says from behind her. "What's going on? What's *she* doing here?" Raffi doesn't say anything. "Are you asking her for money?" Jacqueline says to Britt, and Britt looks at Raffi, just looks at her, and like a bubble popping into her mind, Raffi sees Calypso, eyes wide and panicked, nostrils flaring, kicking at her own stomach, her beautiful stomach, gray coat lathered with sweat. Raffi's anger vanishes. She thinks to Britt, *Of course I'll help you, the back door's unlocked, the envelope is under my mattress, you're my best friend, I love you*, but Britt doesn't stop crying, her face shows no relief, she stands there, icicles of snot stretching from her chin, and Jacqueline says, "I think you should go," and Raffi watches as Jacqueline shuts the door in Britt's face. She doesn't open it back up, doesn't run to her room for the envelope, doesn't respond to whatever Jacqueline is saying. She stands there, facing the closed door, and she thinks that if there is a parallel universe where everyone you love is okay, then there must also be one where everyone you love is already gone, and she wishes herself there, to the place where there is nothing left to fear.

CHAPTER THREE

What Is Left
to Fear

Raffi stares into the grizzly's eyes. They are molten gold. Alien, appallingly beautiful. *Come on*, she thinks to the bear. She has spent her life cowering before the great vast nothing of death, but, *Come on, what are you waiting for?*

The bear stands on its hind legs and looks down at her. Immobile, as if harmless. As if it hadn't, only moments before, torn through the planks Raffi had nailed over the windows of the house where she grew up with her Aunt Zlata. The same house where she and Graham had constructed their little life together, not the life Raffi had once hoped for, maybe, but a life nonetheless. Until the bear came and swiped a paw across Graham's face so effortlessly it could have been a lover's slap, but for the cracking of bone. Raffi watched him crumple and what she felt was not devastation—it was a zeroing. Her life a list of subtractions until here, at the end of everything, everyone was gone.

Come on, Raffi thinks again to the bear, though she knows it's a fool's errand to send one's thoughts out into the world and expect a response. The bear stares and stares and then it drops back onto four legs and pads silently out of the house, leaving Raffi alone with Graham's body.

She walks to the basement door—calmly, as though she's been waiting for this moment, and maybe she has. As she climbs down the stairs, she has a flash of certainty: Graham will be waiting for her there, sifting through his old rugby gear, searching for a helmet. A helmet will solve their problems.

The basement is full of the detritus of their life, but it is empty of Graham. Raffi finds his rugby helmet anyway and slips it on before grabbing the sled she came for. Back upstairs, she hefts Graham's body onto the sled, shoulders her backpack, and unlocks the front door for the first time in months onto a frigid Montana morning. It's July—or maybe August?—but there's snow on the ground. And thank god for the broken climate, for the slickness of snow that lets the sled's runners slide over the frozen ground.

The streets are, of course, deserted. Paradise, Montana. Population 184 before the world ended. Paradise, where Raffi moved when she was fourteen, shedding childhood like snakeskin, refusing to call home because if she heard her dad's voice she'd have to return to him, and if she returned she'd have to face Britt. Paradise, where she'd moved in with her great-aunt Zlata. Who'd had the foresight to die before all of this.

Raffi hauls Graham's body through the empty streets and waits for the animals to come for her. No one comes. She walks and she thinks about how she has survived every loss she'd imagined unsurvivable. She has survived and her survival is a miracle and the miracle is a cruelty. A cruelty, how a body can endure, how the heart circulates blood and the lungs suck in air and the whole machine keeps running, regardless.

She walks and her heart pounds and her lungs inhale the cold, bright morning. The padding of Graham's helmet cradles her skull. She is walking toward a house a few miles outside of town, where the person who had once been her closest friend might still be living. Might still be alive. *We're heading to that place my mom used to clean. The one with an electric perimeter*, Kay had said a few months earlier, when the animals had just begun to change. The statement had almost been an invitation. Almost, but not quite. *Good luck*, Raffi had said. Like life was a game of tennis. Like good or luck still existed. *Good luck, good night, goodbye.*

Raffi walks until her arms and back are throbbing, until each step feels impossible. Until she sees Kay's husband, Buck, in the distance. Then she sits down on the hard ground and waits for him to find her.

Buck is a hunter, who's never seemed to find any irony in the deer he shoots or the cuts of venison he used to store in the freezer. Even from a distance, Raffi can see the AR-15 resting on his shoulder, and she thinks what a joke it would be, after all this time, to die by startling a man with a gun. She starts laughing, and she can't stop. When Buck gets to her, he takes in the situation at a glance, throws Graham's body over his shoulder, and carries it off. Raffi stays where she is until Buck returns and throws her over his shoulder too. He delivers her to Kay like one more body.

"Hi," Kay says. "You made it to the taxidermy garden."

The taxidermy garden isn't a garden. It's a chalet, all hand-hewn logs and woodstoves and floor-to-ceiling windows crowded with snowcapped mountains. The only plants in the taxidermy garden are bodies, and the bodies are not exactly taxidermied, but that is the closest word Raffi can find to describe what Kay is doing to them.

What Kay does is take the bodies down to the basement and empty them of their insides and fill them with new, longer-lasting substances. Before the world ended, she was a woodworker. Now she turns people's wounds into decorations the same way she used to take pieces of wood and seal their knots and whorls with shimmering teal enamel so that flaws metamorphosed into features.

She explains this as though she expects Raffi to understand. And Raffi does. What else is there to do with their dead? With their remaining days?

The bodies lounge on couches, sit at the dining room table, lie in perpetual slumber in the chalet's many beds. They aren't what Raffi would call lifelike—their angles are too strange, their stillness not at all like that of sleep. But this makes them somehow more lovely, the way they wear their own death as an adornment, like a diamond necklace, like an elaborate and absurd peacock-feather hat. When Raffi looks at her old neighbor whose leg is now made of concrete, it pours out of him so naturally that it is difficult for her to remember that once he had a leg made of flesh, before the mountain lion tore it off and he ended up here. If it were less beautiful, she thinks, it would be easier to remember how things used to be.

The taxidermy garden wouldn't exist if the animals—the mountain lions and bears and coyotes and so forth—acted like real animals. If they ate their prey, if they dragged it off to dens or into the underbrush, if they stripped flesh from bone, there would be nothing left for Kay or Buck to find and haul back to the chalet. Then again, if the animals acted like real animals, there wouldn't be any need to have a taxidermy garden at all.

Kay doesn't ask Raffi what happened to Graham. Doesn't ask how she's doing. Doesn't hold Raffi in her arms and say that she's glad

Raffi is still alive. She explains the workings of the taxidermy garden and then she disappears down the basement stairs. There are bodies waiting for her. Graham among them.

Raffi spends the day wandering the taxidermy garden, greeting its many inhabitants. The bodies belong to people Raffi knows. It feels good to see them again. *I'm sorry*, she thinks, to the neighbor she hated, to Graham's father, to her aunt's hospice nurse. *I'm sorry that you're dead and I'm alive.*

At dinner—venison, of course—Raffi sits at one end of the large dining room table, across from Buck and Kay, next to the woman who used to own the diner. The woman has gray hair that's coiled into a bun and a wide grin that's almost, but not quite, like the one she used to flash whenever Raffi slipped into the diner to splurge on a cup of coffee or a plate of pancakes. The wrinkled flesh of her neck slips seamlessly into wood now, a smooth, varnished oak that disappears beneath the collar of her shirt.

They eat in silence until Raffi can't bear the sound of her own thoughts anymore. "How do you keep the electric fence running?" she asks.

Buck launches into an explanation about solar power, like she'd known he would. About the creatures that have slipped through, his system of patrolling. Kay pushes her foot against Raffi's leg under the table, and Raffi feels the contact through her whole body. She's only half listening when Buck mentions the grizzly.

"Lurking in the trees," he's saying. "Unnatural."

Raffi makes a noise, interrupting Buck's monologue. *It's my fault the bear is here*, she could say. But Kay's foot is warm against Raffi's leg and she is tired to her bones. So instead she asks the pointless, ridiculous question "Why do they hate us?"

Buck shakes his head. "The aliens don't give a fuck about us.

They just kill because they're living inside the animals, and that's what animals have always wanted to do."

"You think dogs have always wanted to kill people?" Raffi asks. Kay pushes her foot harder against Raffi's leg. Raffi takes it to be support, but it might be Kay's way of telling her to shut up.

"They're descended from wolves, aren't they?"

Raffi thinks about the Siberian husky she and Graham had. After the animals changed, Graham took him out into the yard and came back alone. She woke in the middle of the night to the movement of him sobbing next to her. "That's bullshit," she says now. "The aliens aren't mindless. There's a logic to all of this."

"There's a logic to a hawk eating a rabbit," Buck says. "That doesn't mean the hawk is the next Einstein."

Kay nudges Raffi harder under the table. Raffi could tell Buck how Einstein once made a list of rules for his wife to live by: do my laundry, bring me food, renounce all expectations of intimacy. How he wrote, in a letter to the cousin with whom he was having an affair: *I treat my wife like an employee whom I cannot fire.* But what would be the point? Raffi grabs Kay's foot with her hand and doesn't say anything else, only holds it there and watches the bloodred sky fade to orange, then indigo. The evening star appears, bright on the horizon. Electricity ceding brilliance to the stars again, here in the aftermath of the end of the world.

The first time Raffi saw the aliens up close was before they were in the animals, back when they were still just liquid. Her aunt was dying from one of the new tickborne illnesses, and as she often put it, "one of the perks of dying is that everyone has to do what you want."

The pools had been around for a few decades by then, longer than Raffi had been alive. Long enough for biologists to deem the extraterrestrial microbes both inert and innocuous, long enough for general fascination to fade. The government still monitored the larger pools, but there were too many of them appearing and too many other ecological catastrophes unfolding. Million-acre wildfires, F5 tornadoes, earthquakes spawning seismic waves. An unending list of record-breaking disasters. Everyone in Paradise knew there was an unmonitored pool in the caldera a few hours away.

Raffi drove her aunt over the winding mountain roads, hands sweaty on the steering wheel, creeping around the turns like a tourist. They had to hike out to the pool, and Raffi was afraid that it would be too much, that they would make it halfway and her aunt would keel over and Raffi would be left alone in the mountains with no way to fix anything. If Kay hadn't left for college, she would have come with them. The trip would have been an adventure instead of an ordeal. But Kay was gone and Aunt Zlata wanted this, so Raffi would try to help her have it.

It was a fall afternoon and the air smelled of snow and the sky was slate gray. Aunt Zlata held on to Raffi's arm, and together they walked up the path, one step and another and another. She was breathing hard, her grip on Raffi's arm growing heavier, but she smiled each time their eyes met. Every ten minutes they stopped to rest. "Did you ever study them?" Raffi asked, on one of these breaks. Her aunt had been a chemist, though she'd retired before Raffi moved to Montana.

"I would've liked to," she said.

The pool sat in the very bottom of the caldera, maybe fifteen feet across. The aliens looked like water, if the water were laced with golden dust. Aunt Zlata didn't say anything, only unlooped her arm from Raffi's and stripped off her clothes. She walked into the water without a pause, without a shiver, and Raffi felt as though there were a fist clenching her voice somewhere deep inside her. She could only watch, could only wait for her aunt to turn around and come back to her.

Weeks pass, and Graham doesn't appear in the taxidermy garden. Sometimes Raffi thinks of Kay, in the basement, running her hands over his body. She wonders if Kay talks to him while she works, wonders what Kay might say. She wonders if Graham feels haloed by Kay's attention, like Raffi once did.

Raffi doesn't know if the delay is because Kay has a large backlog of bodies and Graham must wait his place in line, or if something about him is difficult to repair, or if Kay is trying to do a particularly good job for Raffi's sake. Or maybe she's just buying Raffi some time before she has to look his death in the eyes.

Regardless, Raffi is grateful for the reprieve. Instead of living in the universe where Graham is dead, she is living in the one before she knew he existed. She has found her way back to those first years in Paradise, back to the time when her life was a small snow globe with Kay at the center. There had always been something untouchable about Kay. It was both the foundation for their friendship and its outer limit. It was what made the moments of contact so sharp, so bright.

When they're together now, Raffi finds herself thinking about how they used to go camping as teenagers. Even in the summer, their Walmart sleeping bags weren't warm enough for the deep chill of Montana nights, and Raffi would wait for Kay to suggest zipping their bags together. Wait for the boundary between them to blur until they became a tiny, singular enclave of heat amidst so much cold.

* * *

When Buck tires of the bear's looming threat and suggests going after it, the three of them are in the kitchen butchering a bighorn sheep. Kay and Buck stand side by side in front of the butcher block, the shape before them looking strange and diminished without its skin. Raffi sits at the kitchen table next to Buck's old hunting friend. Kay has replaced the eye he is missing with a glittering hunk of mica, and anytime Raffi glances over he appears to be watching her skeptically.

"I know," Raffi says to the hunter's body, "you could do better. Too bad you can't take over." Raffi was a vegetarian before, and now Kay gives her simple tasks with clear instructions. She cuts things into slices, she salts or cures or debones. She listens to Kay and Buck talking quietly as they disassemble the sheep.

". . . if I can't kill the bear in our territory, then I'll follow it into its own. Catch it sleeping and put a bullet in it." Buck's voice is uninflected, as though he is talking about building a fire or cooking dinner.

Kay's butcher knife clatters onto the block. "No," she says, "absolutely not." Her hands are bloody; there is a crimson smudge on her forehead. The blood shimmers golden.

Buck doesn't look up, only shrugs as he methodically saws off one of the sheep's legs.

Raffi is sitting in a window alcove when she sees Buck walk away from the house with a rucksack over his shoulder. "A rucksack might mean anything," she says to her dead neighbor, but even the dead can tell she's lying. She pushes herself to her feet. Buck is walking quickly, but she could go after him. She could at least try. Kay is in the basement with the bodies. Raffi is the only witness. She walks to the front door, but her steps are slow and by the time she gets there, Buck is out beyond the electric fencing. A small shape disappearing into the distance.

That night, for the first time, Kay climbs the narrow staircase to Raffi's bedroom in the attic. She knocks on the doorframe and Raffi thinks: *Is this why I let him leave?*

Raffi moves over to make room for Kay on the bed, and Kay sits, pulling the comforter over her knees.

"Do you think he's okay?" Kay asks. Raffi nods, although she is trying not to think at all. "I can't believe he went out after it. Or I can, but I don't want to."

"He's always been persistent."

"Remember when that coyote kept hanging around the house and I was afraid it would eat the kittens and he didn't say anything, just presented me with the pelt like it was a bouquet of flowers?"

Raffi remembers. Raffi remembers Kay and Buck's entire courtship, how unthreatening he had seemed at first, so quiet and focused on killing things. It had seemed impossible that someone like Kay would fall in love with a person like that. That someone like Buck could take Kay away from her.

"If only we'd seen this coming," Kay says. They look at each other, silent for a moment, then burst out laughing. They're close enough that Raffi can feel Kay's laughter, and she leans into it. Who would have known that the end of the world would feel so ridiculous?

Raffi doesn't talk to Buck about it, but secretly she is convinced that the aliens are saving the planet. What bigger threat is there to Earth's survival than humans? What more destructive force?

When she thinks about the polar bears and tigers and bees dying, about the glaciers melting and the oceans warming, the Great Pacific Garbage Patch and whales washing up dead on the beaches, when she imagines the mountain landscape she loves so much teeming with life, decades or centuries in the future, she can feel something that is not so far from relief.

Buck comes back from hunting the bear a day later, not victorious, but alive, which feels like nearly the same thing. While he was gone, the taxidermy garden held its breath: the dead, waiting to see if their number would grow; Raffi, waiting to see the extent of her culpability; Kay, waiting.

When Buck unlocks the door and shoulders his way in, there is a sense of exhalation. They take the day off from their typical pursuits—killing and preserving and talking to the dead. Kay opens some of the dusty bottles of liquor that sit behind the bar, irreplaceable now. She pours them each elaborate, personalized cocktails in glasses so delicate it seems preposterous that they still exist. Raffi finds a cardboard box of Christmas decorations in a closet and drapes the living room's bodies in tinsel and silvery baubles so they can feel included in the celebration despite their inability to imbibe cocktails.

They drink until they forget about the bear, still pacing outside the chalet. Until they can't remember they ever lived another life. They try on each other's personalities so that for a while Raffi is the stoic hunter and Buck is the taxidermist. "Do me," Raffi says to Kay in Buck's gravelly monotone, and Kay says, "Very accurate," raising her eyebrows suggestively, which makes Raffi not want to be Buck anymore. Kay-as-Raffi drapes her legs across the lap of a woman who'd only recently moved to town and says, "Tell me all your secrets." They drink until the bodies aren't bodies anymore, until they're people who can talk and laugh and respond to questions. They drink until the room spins, and Raffi imagines it spinning fast enough to shake off all the animals lingering outside it. At some point, they fall asleep, and when Raffi wakes later, Kay is nestled into the crook of Buck's arm, and the room is cold. She pushes herself to her feet, staggers back to the attic. Better to be alone if she's going to be alone.

The bear disappears for a few days after Buck's excursion. Then it returns: heavy paw prints in fresh snow, coarse fur tangled in fencing. Raffi feels the bear's presence, tugging on her. It has become the pole of her personal compass. At dinner, she looks up and the bear is just visible beyond the electric fencing. Its gold eyes glint in the dusk, emitting their own light. Raffi turns away, but Buck's already noticed her gaze.

"You should leave it be," she says to him, unsure whom she is trying to protect.

"So it can find a way in and kill us while we're sleeping?"

"So you don't get killed yourself."

Buck doesn't respond, but Raffi knows the inside of his mind is a gun.

Raffi is an excellent shot. When she moved to Montana, she begged her aunt to take her to the range. She wanted to be someone other than who she'd been before; she wanted to be fierce, powerful. She hadn't understood then, or hadn't considered, what the sound of gunshots might mean to her aunt. But her aunt didn't try to dissuade her, just signed her up for classes. The first time at the range, Raffi startled at every report; her back was sore for days. She loved it. Loved feeling afraid and doing it anyway.

Loved being the only girl in the class and the way the boys looked at her differently after she hit the bull's-eye six times in a row, like she was someone to compete with, someone to respect.

Kay had teased her, asking if she planned to join the ranks of the valiant deer slayers—their name for the boys who spent lunchtimes bragging about the size of the rack on their latest kill. Years later, when Kay started dating Buck, Raffi wanted to remind her of those conversations. To say, *if that's what you want, you already have it—why do you need him?*

Raffi is sitting in the smallest bedroom when Kay comes to say she's finished working on Graham's body. "Do you know where you'd like him to go?" Kay asks.

Raffi has a pile of her aunt's old letters on her lap. She'd found boxes of saved correspondence after her aunt died, kept a stack of them in the backpack she'd brought to the taxidermy garden. She shrugs without looking up from the letter she's reading.

"Do you want him up in the attic with you?"

Raffi feels a surge of anger that Kay no longer knows her well enough to intuit the answer. She reads the same sentence over and over.

"Raffi," Kay says, an edge to her voice. "Will you please answer me? What do you want?"

What Raffi wants—other than a million things she can't have—is to linger in limbo, Graham's body neither present nor gone. "Not in the attic," Raffi says.

Sometimes Raffi pretends the bodies belong to different people. They're empty vessels now, they don't mind. Sometimes the woman in the smallest bedroom is Aunt Zlata, napping. The elderly man by the window is Raffi's dad, gray-haired now. In the living room, a small girl reads a book with her knees to her chest, and Raffi touches her shoulder, thinks *apple apple*. She wonders what the chances are that Britt is still alive. She wonders if Britt has forgotten her, whether being forgotten is the same as being forgiven.

Raffi finds Graham in one of the taxidermy garden's most luxurious bedrooms, stretched out on the king-size bed. He is reading a book of poetry, one that she and Kay once read aloud to one another in a tent in the woods at night. Raffi wonders if this is a gift Kay is trying to give her, this version of Graham endowed with their shared memory. Or maybe she's forgotten.

He's some of Kay's best work, the crevasses in his face filled with a gold substance that is the exact color of the animals' eyes. Seeing him is like seeing a stranger wearing Graham's skin. It makes the space behind her sternum ache with loneliness, the pain deep enough that she pushes a hand against her chest. She climbs into bed with him, rests her head on his shoulder. It is hard beneath her cheek. They lie like that, not talking, the light gradually shifting in the room. Graham reads the same poem endlessly—*Tell me about despair, yours, and I will tell you mine.* Raffi tries to imagine they came here together, that they are on a prolonged version of the world's weirdest double date. She can't do it. Imagining Graham alive means imagining the possibility of losing him a second time. She watches him read. She used to pester him to read more, spend less time playing video games. She used to wish that he was someone slightly different than the person he was.

"I'm sorry," she says. "You deserve better. You deserve someone who loves you the way you loved me."

Graham says nothing.

"It made my aunt so happy, seeing us get married. Knowing I wouldn't be alone after she died."

Graham says nothing.

"I'm sorry," Raffi says.

And nothing.

Raffi visits Graham every day. She brings him new things to read— murder mysteries and legal thrillers she finds in the study, a selection of her aunt's most interesting letters, an old newspaper meant to be kindling. She tells him about her secret name for the chalet.

"Do you remember that store, the House of Discounts? The one my aunt used to call the House of Discontent?" Raffi could swear Graham smiles at the name. They'd both loved the misnomer. English was Aunt Zlata's fifth language after Yiddish, German, Czech, and Hungarian. "Can you imagine a more discontented house than this one?"

She describes the chalet to him. In her descriptions, each room is an alternate universe. Each body a person, just visiting.

At night on her way to the attic, Raffi overhears Kay and Buck arguing behind the closed bedroom door. She tells her feet to keep walking, but they disregard her directions and move closer—muscle memory from childhood. It is mostly Kay's voice she hears, the cadences of it familiar. Though Raffi can only make out a handful of words, she knows what they are saying. That the taxidermy garden must be protected, that the risk is unnecessary, that they each want the other to stay alive, that they are furious with this desire.

Back when Kay and Buck first got married—only a year or so after Kay finished art school and came back home—Raffi waited for Kay to call and complain. Raffi stored her discomfort to share later: how awkwardly she wore the word *wife*, how she wished it were possible to have some other version of this life with Graham, one not predicated on marriage, on romance. She waited to see her own discomfort mirrored and thereby diminished, waited for their similarity of circumstance to return them to the intimacy they'd had before Kay left and Raffi stayed. But Kay didn't complain. She slipped into married life like it was a bespoke jacket sewn perfectly to her measurements. She flourished, developing a name for herself making beautiful furniture for rich people, content with Buck's stolid affection.

Raffi wants to push the door open, tell them that it is too late, now, to be arguing. But she doesn't. She listens until their voices grow soft, and then she leaves.

The next morning, the taxidermy garden is uncomfortably quiet. Raffi roams from room to room, checking in with the various inhabitants, until she finds Kay in the master bedroom, sitting on the floor at her mother's feet. Kay's mother is wearing a silk robe, reclined in a wingback chair with one leg crossed over the other. She looks more elegant than Raffi remembers her, and more distant. Raffi sits on the floor beside Kay, the carpet so plush it feels like sinking into a pillow.

"He's gone again," Kay says. Raffi thinks, *of course*, thinks, *my fault*, but she doesn't say it, just puts her arm around Kay's shoulders. Kay slumps into her. "He left a note. Said he'd be back in two days, that he'd only stay out the one night."

Raffi wants to comfort her, but she can't think of anything to say that is both comforting and true. "He just wants you to be safe," she says, at last. Kay shakes her head, pressing the palms of her hands into her eyes in the way that Raffi knows means she's fighting not to cry. When she lowers her hands, Kay looks up at her mother's calm, lined face.

"She was the first one I did," Kay says. "Did I tell you that?" She traces her finger over a seam that runs down the back of her mother's leg. "I had no idea what I was doing. I was out of my mind. Buck tried to take her body away, but I screamed and screamed. I woke up the next day and couldn't remember why my throat hurt. I couldn't bear the thought I'd never see her again."

"Here she is."

"It was Thanatos that got her, while she was sleeping. Isn't that the world's worst joke?" Thanatos was a Siamese cat Kay and her mother had found at the cemetery after Kay's dad died. "I wanted her to get rid of him back when the animals first started killing people, but that was when it still seemed impossible to believe. And she loved that cat." Raffi thinks about Than's lambent blue eyes, his resonant purr, the way he'd follow Kay's mom around the house. About the particular devastation wreaked by loving and being loved. "I should've pushed her harder."

Raffi shoves her shoulder into Kay. "Stop it. None of this is your fault."

"She used to clean this house. We joked about what a fucking tourist the owner was, having an electric perimeter in Montana."

"Didn't save him in the end though, did it?"

"Can't say as I feel too sorry. He was always a dick to my mom."

"Now she's got the master bedroom," Raffi says.

"She sure does."

Instead of going down to the basement, Kay says, "Let's make popcorn on the woodstove. There's only one bag left, but if Buck's going to take off like this, he deserves to miss out." The kernels

pop and jump, and the smell of movie theater butter is so strong
Raffi can almost taste it. Probably this is the last popcorn Raffi
will ever eat. She tries to savor it.

"Remember how we used to sneak into double features?" Kay
asks, and the question is enough to dislodge the memory: the two
of them kneeling between rows, trying not to catch each other's
eyes so they won't laugh and give themselves away. And alongside
that memory, so many others that Raffi locked away after Kay
left, because this is the only way she has ever known to deal with
loss—quarantine the memories, discipline her thoughts to never
look in certain directions—so that now, so many losses later, there
is nowhere left to look.

They finish the popcorn. Raffi feels queasy with the unfamiliar richness, but licks her fingers anyway. She waits for Kay
to leave, but Kay says, "Let me read some of your aunt's letters."
They lie on opposite ends of the couch, their feet touching under
a blanket.

The windows darken to mirrors. "Can I come and sleep up in
the attic?" Kay asks, and Raffi feels a surge of ruthless happiness.
It doesn't care what sacrifices have been made at its altar.

Sometimes Raffi can't help but wish that she could climb into
Kay's skin with her. Sometimes she wants to press their bodies
together, hold Kay so tight that their boundaries dissolve. Sometimes she wants to say, when we die—tomorrow or next month—
can you taxidermy all of me inside all of you so that I never have
to be alone again?

They lie side by side in Raffi's little bed, both of them still in
jeans and sweaters, touching at the hips and shoulders. "I'm having

doubts about the taxidermy garden," Kay says, and Raffi understands that Kay needs to think about something that is not Buck,
that it is her turn to create for Kay a world where Buck is not somewhere in the darkness with golden eyes watching him.

"What kind of doubts?"

"Not doubts so much as nightmares. The bodies keep talking
to me."

"What do they say?"

"They want to tell me everything, all the details of their lives
and what it's like to be dead and how it was when the animals
killed them. They talk and talk and talk and when I wake up
I'm so tired." Kay tilts her head so that it rests against Raffi's, and
Raffi leans into the closeness. Fights the urge to pull Kay closer
still. "They tell me about the things they miss most: red velvet
cake, a favorite song, television on a rainy day. It's never what you
think it'd be."

Raffi matches her breathing to Kay's.

"What do you miss most?" Kay asks.

Raffi tries to recall. It is like looking for a word in a language
she has mostly forgotten. How long has it been since it all began?
Less than a year, Raffi thinks, though she's lost track. The first
attacks, the comprehension that blossomed like a bruise. *Before* is
a dream.

Before Raffi's aunt got sick—before the aliens were in the animals, before the end of the world—Raffi and Kay were going to
leave together. Raffi was the source of this ambition; she'd had to
convince Kay, who planned to stay in Montana and find an ap-
prenticeship close to her mom. Kay's mother had sided with Raffi
though, and gradually the plans took on life, became a shared
dream. Raffi didn't want to go back east, so they'd go west, to

Oregon or Washington, somewhere they could have the mountains and the ocean both, only a day or two's drive from Paradise. Kay would go to school for woodworking and Raffi would study physics and philosophy, turn her lifelong obsession with parallel universes into real research.

When Aunt Zlata got sick, and Raffi realized she couldn't leave, she assumed that without her impetus, Kay's plans would revert to their earlier shape. Kay wouldn't leave her, not with her aunt dying, so it didn't feel dangerous for Raffi to insist Kay should go. Of course she wouldn't.

Raffi avoided Kay's calls, after she left. Because she was hurt, but it was more than that. The dream had felt so real that even once it was dead, Raffi could close her eyes and see the little apartment they would have shared. Could almost transport herself to that universe, physics books piled on a table, Kay's tool bag sitting by the door. Could almost smell the sawdust on Kay's skin. Each time Raffi talked to Kay, the ghost of that other life faded a little further, color draining out of it until Raffi could hardly see it at all.

Buck doesn't come back the next day, or the one after that. Raffi tries to feel for the bear's presence, but all she can feel is worry for Kay, a wailing alarm that drowns out all other sound. Kay hasn't returned to the basement. She sits on the couch, staring out the window. She doesn't brush her teeth or change her clothes. Her hair tangles and the shadows under her eyes deepen and she smells of sweat and anxiety. She is so still that Raffi watches for the movement of her chest, waits for her to blink. She is afraid that if she stops willing Kay to be a person, between one breath and the next she will transform into another body. Raffi is afraid she is watching something in Kay break that she will never be able to repair. The sensation pulls her back through time to that night, so many years ago, when Britt knocked on her door, sobbing. The sensation says: this is what you do to the people you love.

Raffi wakes in the watery light of dawn on the fourth day of Buck's absence, resolute. She climbs out of bed, careful not to wake Kay, and tiptoes down the stairs. She doesn't let herself turn for a final glance at Kay, doesn't even let herself think the word *final*. She pulls on her boots in the mudroom. She has a few strips of jerky in the pocket of her coat, one of Buck's guns slung over her shoulder.

It's a bluebird day, the air sharp, the sun bright, and Raffi feels something that is almost joy as she walks away from the house. She will fix what she has done or she will join everyone she's lost. She's halfway to the fence when she hears a bang behind her and spins, fumbling for the gun, heart leaping.

Kay is standing outside the house. Raffi gathers the pieces slowly, it was the slamming of a door she heard. Kay is ablaze with morning sun and fury. They stare at each other across the empty space, a silent argument, and it's Raffi who caves and walks back to the house.

"How could you?" Kay asks, her voice so taut it vibrates. In all the years they've known each other, Raffi has never seen Kay like this. "At least Buck told me he was leaving."

"I'm going to find him for you," Raffi says. She's shaking.

"You're going to die and leave me here waiting for ghosts," Kay shouts. Raffi wants to tell Kay that she deserves more credit than that, that she's a good shot, that she has survived many things. She wants to say, *you're the one who left me, you're not allowed to be mad*. She wants to rewind the movie of their lives until they're sixteen years old, zipped into a sleeping bag cocoon, and pause there. But before she can say anything, Kay slackens, sits hard on the ground, buries her face in her hands, and starts to cry.

Raffi is there, at once, kneeling beside her, saying, "I'm sorry, Kay, I'm so sorry. Don't cry, I'm here, I'm sorry." Kay relaxes into Raffi's arms and Raffi holds her, smoothing her knotted hair, whispering soothing nonsense.

"I was so scared," Kay whispers.

"I'm sorry," Raffi says again. "I just wanted to fix it. It's my fault."

"What are you talking about?"

"The bear followed me here. I'm the reason Buck's gone."

Kay tilts away from Raffi so that she can meet her eyes. "Raffi, the bear was stalking the taxidermy garden for months before you arrived. It's a house full of dead bodies."

"What?" Kay's words bead like condensation on the surface of Raffi's mind, she can't absorb their meaning.

"Oh Raffi." Kay sighs. "You want so badly to be responsible for everything."

They decide they will go together. Kay tells Raffi she needs to put things in order in the basement, and Raffi doesn't ask what things. She walks through the taxidermy garden, says her provisional goodbyes. The sun streams in through the windows, reflecting off bits of metal and glass, polished wood and leather so that Kay's creations gleam. The strangeness of the taxidermy garden settles over Raffi, as though, in preparing to leave, she is able to see it clearly for the first time. But its beauty is more undeniable than ever.

In Graham's bedroom, she climbs onto the bed, rests her cheek on his shoulder, the same way she fell asleep so many nights. She feels her heartbeat steady. "I miss you so much," she says to him.

So many rooms, so many bodies, but eventually Raffi finds

herself back in the mudroom. This time, she and Kay lace their boots up together. Kay is calm now, a backpack slung over her shoulders. "I brought a tent and sleeping bags," she says, and Raffi remembers her earlier wish, can almost imagine this is the universe's answer. "Plus some portable electric fencing I rigged up a while ago."

Raffi opens the door, cold and light pouring in. "Ready?" she asks, and Kay nods. They walk away from the taxidermy garden hand in hand. Like children in a fairy tale. Heading into the woods, where the bear waits.

"It feels like we're going back in time, doesn't it?" Kay says, echoing Raffi's thoughts like she always used to. "Like we're going camping, again."

Raffi thinks, then, of a different sort of fairy tale: of time as a fourth dimension stretching before them, so that with each step they get younger. She keeps her eyes wide open, she's looking for a gap in the trees, she's looking for footprints, paw prints, the gleam of gold eyes. She's looking for the doorway to another universe, for the ghost of that other life, the one she never got the chance to live. "Here we come," she says—to the bear, to Buck, to her many dead, to the younger version of herself, who has never stopped hoping.

CHAPTER FOUR

The Ghost of That Other Life

B efore they found the bodies in the hotel's cistern, those bodies left submerged so long they'd become something other than the bodies of women, become creatures of the water, too gruesome to print in the newspaper, before the news could reach backward in time and desecrate those days Kay and I spent together—before that, I fell prey to hope. It had been ten years exactly since Kay and I packed her old Corolla to overflowing and left Paradise for college, and though I tried hard to be someone serious, practical, I was, at heart, a romantic and I believed this synchronicity might mean something. I didn't ask Kay if she remembered the anniversary, only asked if we could spend a weekend away, and when she agreed, I made a reservation at a hotel in Utah, the same one we'd stayed at all those years ago. It was too far, really, for a weekend trip, but as we drove south through Idaho, the windows down and the music up, I felt the ghosts of the girls we'd been in the car with us, I felt filled up with the past and present, the wind on my face and Kay singing off-key next to me. It was close to midnight by the time we arrived at the hotel and still, astonishingly, 110 degrees, and we laughed at the heat, like kids seeing snow for the first time, and stumbled through the sweltering darkness into the bright, cold lobby, and Kay left her arm around my waist. *Brimful.* That was the word for what I was feeling.

The woman at the front desk didn't smile at our approach, didn't greet us, she wasn't hostile, but she was a shade of polite that was nearly indistinguishable, saying *I'll need your friend to sign this pass for her car,* and I said, *my girlfriend,* though this wasn't a label Kay and I had ever used—*what's your friend's license plate?—my girlfriend's license plate,* because I wanted to hear the word said aloud, because I was trying to imagine my way into a new life—*your friend—my girlfriend—*and so on, until Kay sighed and said *would you let it go* and so I did. As we walked away from the desk, I apologized but she was frustrated, I could tell, and by the time we got to our room with its two queen beds instead of the king we'd requested all the delight had drained out of the moment and there didn't seem to be any way to put it back in.

I fell asleep with Kay's head on my shoulder, but woke to a too-familiar absence, one that had somehow followed us down all those highway miles, Kay's body a shadow on the other bed that could have belonged to anyone, could have been an axe murderer for all I knew, but I just closed my eyes and willed whatever future was coming to hurry, I was tired of waiting for it. The absence reminded me that Kay was Buck's girlfriend, not mine, that he was the one she'd chosen to live with, the one she drove home to late at night after slipping out of my apartment, though I'd once overheard him say, his voice tinny through the phone, that he didn't mind if she spent the night at my place. He'd never been threatened by the intimacy between us, never cared about the two of us having sex, never taken us seriously enough for it to matter.

The next time I woke, the sun had shouldered its way into the room through the crack in the curtains, and Kay was missing from both beds. I flung myself out from under the covers, prey to the panic that had stalked me since childhood, the voice saying, *at any moment, anyone you love might disappear.* I found her in the bathroom, holding a half-empty glass in one hand, her phone in the other—she must have been texting him—the sink still running. *There's something wrong with the water,* she said. *What do you mean wrong?* But even my voice was wrong now. Sometime in the night the balance of anger had shifted so it belonged to me, I had become the one who needed to be appeased and she had to do the appeasing or be angry in turn, in which case this trip might offer a different clarification than the one I'd been hoping for. But she only gestured her beautiful, haggard face toward the water and said *touch it* and she sounded tired and afraid and so I did.

The water was only water at first, cool against my fingers, exactly the right mix of hot and cold. Kay had a knack for balance—her relationship with Buck sitting easily next to whatever our relationship was, work ceding to leisure at 5:00 P.M. sharp—and I lacked this knack entirely, tending always toward extremes, my ambition an organ whose function I controlled no more than I did my own heart, but then the sensation in the water became impossible to ignore and I forgot about the rest. If you have never existed as a woman in the world you might have been able to wash your hands and feel nothing, not a skittering up your arms, not a clenching in the pit of your stomach, not a crawling on the back of your neck—not a hundred other clichés that are clichéd precisely because of their exhausting relevance, but there it was: that entirely recognizable feeling of being prey.

Strange how a bad thing can make everything else better, so that I met Kay's eyes and saw my own fear reflected there and it made us the same again, reminded me we didn't have to keep passing our frustration back and forth, we could set it down and walk out of the bathroom, which we did, the water still running in the background and the sound of it becoming soothing, like an ambulance going to someone else's home. Between the two queen beds,

Kay reached for me. She was shorter than I was, a fact I tended to forget unless we were standing like this, my arms wrapped around her, so that the recollection itself was an intimacy and brought with it the familiar urge to protect her, to make my body into a shield or safe haven or alternate timeline so that I was constantly disappointed when it was only a body. Disappointed too by how frequently Kay turned to Buck for protection, though I understood he was a large man with several guns, and how could I compete with that, particularly when it was the very fact of my presence, of our togetherness, that might incite violence. But Buck wasn't here. *I drank it*, Kay said, her voice small, and I kissed her, to let her know that whatever she had done, I would do with her. She returned the kiss, leaned into it, and I let myself forget the water, Buck, all the things I'd come here to say, and instead I thought back to the first time she'd kissed me, at a college party, the two of us drunk, her a little more so, and it had been a performance, or at least it had begun that way, the boys near us whistling and hooting and urging us on, they were all a little in love with Kay, but it had shifted, the kiss hooking something deep in my stomach so that I pulled her toward me and spent the rest of the night wondering if that had been a violation of the rules of the game.

The kiss opened a doorway and I followed Kay through it, as I'd followed Kay to so many places over the years, let her pull me onto the same bed she'd defected to in the night, kissed her and tasted dirty metal and begged my brain to quiet, to let me be here, only here, but it was no use, I felt myself fracture. A part of me was on the bed with Kay, knotting my hand in her hair, digging my nails into her back, all of it a little too hard—did this violence belong to me or to whatever was in the water?—and a part of me was watching from a slight distance, wondering how this compared to the sex she had with Buck, whether I was destined in all areas of my life to live in the shadow of men, and a part of me was thinking *how can I possibly leave her*, and a part of me was thinking *how can I possibly not?* It was this feeling of fracture, of superposition, that had led to the research which now, if I let it, would lead me away from Montana, away from Kay. If the universe was multitudinous, infinitely overlaid, a thousand thousand branching possibilities, why was it that we experienced life as singular? This was the question I'd spent my PhD trying to answer, and finally the professors who'd once laughed at me were saying they'd always thought my research had promise, and an offer had come, for a position at a university 2,500 miles away.

Kay's hand lingered at the waist of the boxers I'd been sleeping in, *do you want to?* she asked, a question I never knew how to answer, though I understood desire was meant to be audible, legible, mine never was, when I listened for it all I heard was an echo: *want to, want to, want to?* It was easier, in a way, sleeping with men, who were less likely to ask these sorts of questions, whose desire was often loud enough for the both of us. I wanted Kay's desire to be like this—implacable, resonant. If I flipped her over, pinned her arms over her head, ran my fingernail down her stomach, could I make her stop caring about what I wanted?

More than sex, I loved what came after, the lethargy of satiation, skin sweat-stuck to skin, and Kay's smile, radiant, so the hotel room brightened and became beautiful and I felt certain I'd made the right choice coming here, that this would be the place in which I could say to Kay, *I got offered a postdoc in Boston*, in which I could say, *tell me not to go*.

But I had always been a coward where Kay was concerned. I settled for the first clause, for the facts alone, *I got offered a postdoc in Boston*, and I watched Kay's face, desperate for even the slightest hint of sadness—if I saw it, I would say the rest. She looked delighted. *That's wonderful*, she said, *I'm so proud of you*.

I don't know if I'll take it, I said. It was the best I could do.

Of course you will, she said, *you're too ambitious to walk away from an opportunity like that.* I realized, then, something I'd known for a long time. Familiarity, history, they didn't mean someone knew you. They could function, instead, like a scab over what was raw and real. Kay looked at me and the person she saw was a compilation of my past selves, and not only selves, but all the lies and omissions I'd ever told her. How I'd pretended the University of Montana was the only grad school I'd gotten into, rather than admit I wanted to be close to her, how I'd never said that Buck's amused tolerance of our relationship felt more demeaning than generous. If I wanted Kay to see me, it would require violence. I would have to rip off the scab. It would be easier to be known by a stranger.

And besides, she said, *why would you stay?*

For you, I said; I imagined saying; I might have said. If I were a different person, a braver version of myself. If Kay's phone hadn't vibrated then, from the bedside table, so that she rolled away from me, the cold air tracing a map of her absence across my skin. *You mind if I take this?* she asked. It was the sort of question that had only one answer, but I didn't want to give it, I knew who was on the other end of the line, knew that his presence, even at a distance, would rupture the moment's carefully constructed intimacy, so I said, *I'm going to take a shower*, and waited for her to remember the water and tell me not to go, but she only nodded, still looking at her phone.

It was a relief to pull the bathroom door closed and be alone, a relief until I turned on the shower and the water spattered the linoleum with flecks of darkness before it ran clear. Fluorescent light cast hard shadows and my skin puckered into goose bumps, I wished I could open a window, let the day pour its heat and sun into the room, but there were no windows, it was only me and the water, guttering like a candle flame so that I knew it was a bad idea to step beneath it but did so anyway. I watched my body in the mirror, this body that had always felt closer to a list of inadequacies than an actual body, so that I saw not my eyes but the circles beneath them, not my hair but the way it lay lank and limp on my shoulders, breasts too small, ribs jutting, bowlegged, knobby-kneed, skin splotched with eczema, and I still don't know why I stepped into that water, but this was a part of it and so was Kay's laughter, barely audible through the door, and the way she'd said *I'm so proud*, and the fear, that was a part of it too, I wanted to refuse it, I wanted to punish the fear or Kay or Buck or the stranger I saw in the mirror. I watched as she stepped into the shower but then I wasn't a stranger anymore, I was there, in the water, and it was on my skin, in my mouth, the fear flooded in, fear like footsteps in a dark hallway like a door slamming open in the night like a man who can hold you in place with no effort at all, fear that drowned out the sound of the water and I sank to the floor and pressed my lips together and closed my eyes, but I could still see them. The women sat beside me, one on either side, their bodies bloated, barely recognizable, their knees and hips jostling against mine.

Later, the story would make headlines: DEAD WOMEN FOUND IN UTAH HOTEL CISTERN—GUEST COMPLAINTS LEAD MAINTENANCE WORKER TO GRUESOME DISCOVERY—ROTTING BODIES FOUND IN UTAH HOTEL'S DRINKING WATER—AUTOPSY RESULTS INCONCLUSIVE IN UTAH HOTEL MYSTERY—MURDER OR MISTAKE? WHAT WE KNOW SO FAR ABOUT DEAD UTAH WOMEN—COUNTY HEALTH OFFICIALS SAY NO HEALTH RISK FROM CONTAMINATED WATER—EX-BOYFRIEND SUSPECTED—HOTEL WORKER SUSPECTED—TAXI DRIVER SUSPECTED—SEXUAL ASSAULT SUSPECTED—ACCIDENTAL DROWNING SUSPECTED—WOMAN FROM UTAH HOTEL'S SORDID PAST REVEALED—MENTAL ILLNESS CITED BY AUTHORITIES AS SIGNIFICANT FACTOR IN UTAH WOMAN'S DEATH—DISTURBING VIDEO DISCOVERED IN UTAH HOTEL MYSTERY—and on and on until the women's names became shorthand for all the ways there are for a woman to disappear. Later, I would read the news and understand that these women carried their own histories, had their own lives, that it was a kind of solipsism to look at them and see only versions of Kay and myself.

But we hadn't gotten to any of that yet. The women's names still belonged to them. I sat in the shower and the women sat with me until Kay said my name from the other side of the door and then I turned the water off. I scrubbed myself with a towel until my skin glowed red, until I stopped shaking, I didn't want Kay to know what I had seen, I wanted to be able to offer her at least this small protection, this last window of time before the news broke.

Were you going to say something before the phone rang? she asked, but the words I'd come here to say, the confession I'd wanted to make, all of it seemed irrelevant now. There, in the shower, with the women, I'd thought of my aunt, of the fight we'd had when I'd told her I wouldn't leave for college while she was sick. *I'm going to die one way or another*, she'd said. *People are always dying. An education, at least that you can count on.* The women weren't a revelation, only a reminder. A person is a fragile thing to build a life around. A woman even more so.

So I said to Kay, *it was nothing*. I did one better: I unsaid everything I'd said thus far. We like to imagine that cause and effect are linear, that while the past can affect the future, the future is powerless to change the past. But I have always believed that this—like our experience of a life that is singular, rather than infinitely branching—is a matter of perception, a limitation of our consciousness, not a reflection of reality. So I undrove the miles, unplanned the trip. What had balance bought me but mediocrity, half a relationship, half a career? I unenrolled from the University of Montana, unmade each of the small anniversaries I'd hoarded until Kay and I had never even met. Until I was a kid again, watching Britt come undone at the loss of her horse, promising myself I would find something indestructible to love. Reading books about time travel, quantum mechanics, parallel universes, each of them making the same promise: genius over fear. Until I could see it, laid out in front of me, a life where I wouldn't have to hurt or be hurt, a life as clean and unassailable as a philosophical proof. Undoing and undoing until all that was left of the weekend were the women, who would not be undone, who would stay with me across every branch of my life.

CHAPTER FIVE

Proof

W hen my mentor calls to tell me he's nominated me for the award that, each year, plucks two dozen people from the teeming masses and designates them that hallowed thing— a genius—I think, *here it is.* The moment I have been waiting for. Working for. Forty-some-odd years of effort was all it took. I wait for euphoria. I keep waiting. *Raffi*, my mentor says, *are you there?* I nod into the phone, then remember to say it out loud. *I'm not supposed to tell you any of this*, he says, *so mum's the word, eh? But I wanted to let you know so you could keep up the good work. Officially it shouldn't matter, but, you know.* I assure him I know. *Stay the course*, he says. *Stay the course*, I echo. We hang up. It's a Friday and I'm meant to be teaching a graduate seminar on the concept of self-continuity in the multiverse. Instead of heading to the university, I email my students and instruct them to spend the class looking at themselves in the mirror.

I tell myself I'm celebrating. I tell myself I will use the free afternoon to work on my second book, a draft of which was due to my editor two months ago. I go so far as to open the document, nod approvingly at the first pages. *The Fractured Self: An Exploration of Identity in the Quantum Age.* The epigraph is Whitman, a little overused but still serviceable: *Do I contradict myself? / Very well then I contradict myself, / (I am large, I contain multitudes.)* After the first two pages, things go downhill.

I close the book, click over to my browser, which is open to the rental section of Craigslist. A new habit of mine, browsing random locations: San Antonio, Lincoln, Sacramento. Nowhere I have any connection to, no goal in mind except a direction to move that isn't forward. I click on a listing for a room in Vermont, whose Craigslist isn't even divvied up into cities. A few sentences, two pictures, $300/month. Four hours from where I am meant to be *staying the course* in Providence. I send an email, get a reply in minutes. *Yes it's still available, are you interested?* I am.

I don't know why I think that Vermont will have the thing I cannot name but must find if I am going to continue doing the activities that together constitute life: brushing my teeth, writing papers that no one will read, greeting my colleagues when we pass in the halls. It is true that I have sometimes wished not to exist (*il n'y a qu'un problème philosophique vraiment sérieux: c'est le suicide*, etc., etc.), but always if some other human asked *how's it going* I would reply *good, thanks, how about you.* This is how I knew I was fine—I could pretend to be fine. Not even could—had to, the way your knee jerks when the doctor demands it, regardless of your wishes. But all my reflexes had gone dormant. When a student asked whether branching universes meant that his dead mother was still alive somewhere, I asked if it made a difference. When one of my TAs walked into my office and found me holding my penknife up like a question, I didn't joke about contemplating Occam's razor. This apathy frightened me—not the knife, but the way I couldn't make myself care about the person I'd spent my whole life trying to be.

I sublet my attic loft with its sloping ceilings and bountiful sunlight at a discounted rate to the first person I can find. He's a student at a nearby art school—a puppet artist, he tells me unprompted, and I don't ask what that means, only picture the apartment filled with dancing Pinocchios. I leave everything as is—mugs of coffee blooming into mold terrariums, books crumpled next to the walls they were thrown at. On my desk, an old paper titled "Quantum Immortality: A New Framework for the Ethics of Suicide in the Multiverse," across which my mentor had scrawled, *Let's talk.* (*Look Raffi, the arguments are compelling and not something I've seen before*, he said, *but I don't know . . . do you think it'll look good in your tenure dossier?*)

Driving away from fourteen years of relentless effort feels like driving to the store. It feels like sleeping, or what I have been calling sleep: hours unhinged from time, when I am neither conscious nor unconscious. A text pops up—*where the hell are you?*—but I swipe it away. *I'm nowhere*, I could say, but I let my absence say it for me. Snowflakes fall onto my windshield, tiny crystalline architectures that melt into fat drops of water and roll down the glass. The other cars on the road are a mirage of blinking yellow lights. I put my hazards on too, out of solidarity. We are all moving through the hazard together. How nice it is, to have company and still be perfectly alone.

When I arrive at the house, hours later, I knock on the door gently. It opens the smallest crack, revealing a sliver of a woman's face. *I have a lot of dogs in here*, she says. *Great*, I say, and it's like a password, she opens the door wide enough for me to slip in. The hallway is thick with huskies. The woman tells me her name is Alice and this is her dogsledding team. They all want to press their bodies against mine. *Back*, Alice says, *get back, all of you!* They don't listen to her, they're overwhelmed by their desire to meet me, and I'm gratified. I kneel down. *Hello*, I say, *hi, hello, hello.* They throw themselves into my greeting, and I let them topple me so that I'm lying on the carpet looking up at a tangle of dogs. They shove the cold of their noses into my neck, they lick my face.

Alice shows me the room I have rented. It is small and square. It has a bed, a closet, a lamp. The kind of minimalism that manages to look like style rather than mere emptiness. *Great*, I say, *perfect*. Alice tilts her head. *What did you say you do?* I hadn't, and I feel reluctant to, as though acknowledging my real life will invite it to accompany me, but I need time to prepare lies, so I tell the truth: *I'm a professor*, I say. *Isn't it the middle of the semester?* she asks. *Well, yes.* We both pause. My phone buzzes as if to make Alice's point. *Snitch*, I think, and power it down with one hand. *I'm on sabbatical*, I say. I have not prepared, the lie won't hold up to interrogation. *A ski sabbatical*, I add, though I don't know how to ski. Alice doesn't interrogate. *We'll have to go out together sometime*, she says. She's maybe ten years older than me, in her early fifties I'd guess, and something about her feels familiar, comforting. I'd like to be one of her sled dogs. *I'd give you a key*, Alice says, *but there isn't one.*

In my new bedroom, I turn out the lamp and am astonished by the darkness. I wave my hand in front of my face—it's invisible. A kind of nonexistence; a perfect lack of observation. There was a time when darkness like this terrified me, but now I feel a rush of relief. I climb into bed with my clothes on, pull the comforter up to my chin. For the first time in a long time, I close my eyes and sleep like a normal person.

When I wake, the sun is shining. The dogs are draped across the couch, sprawled on the floor. Alice is cooking in the little kitchen. *Hash browns?* she asks, and I sit with the dogs and listen to the snick and sizzle of oil. Alice moves about the kitchen with the economy of motion that implies expertise. *Don't get used to it*, she says, handing me a plate of perfectly crisped potatoes. *I cook all day, so I'm usually too lazy to bother at home.* She's a chef at one of the local ski resorts, *the kind of place that charges twenty-five dollars for a burger*, she says, *rich people love it. You hitting the slopes today?* I nod, trying to infuse the gesture with enthusiasm, authenticity, as if I am someone who often hits slopes. A husky wanders over, and I'm relieved to have an excuse to stop nodding. His eyes are a warm, soulful yellow, and his ears are tufty, like an old man's. *Ishmael is a rescue*, Alice says, *he had a rough life when he was younger, so he's a bit of an introvert, but he seems to like you.* I pet him between the ears. *I like you too*, I say to Ishmael. He licks my arm once, then lifts his leg and pees on my foot. *Um*, I say to Alice. *Oh Ish, no!* she says, and he scuttles away, tail between his legs. *I'm sorry*, she says, *I guess he really does like you. He's marking his territory.* As I peel off my damp sock, I say, *I'm flattered.* I feel it too.

After Alice leaves for work, I lie on the floor with the dogs again. I tell myself I will stand up when the slant of sun through the window touches me. I tell myself the mountain is mandatory, that I need to have an answer when Alice asks me later how it was. My left elbow lights up, and I tell myself I will move when the sun touches my ribs. Before it can, Aros, the lead dog, walks over and stares down at me. He has the same eyes as my second grade teacher. *Okay, Mrs. Greenfield*, I say. When I've pushed myself to my feet, Aros nods approvingly and then drops onto the ground in the patch of sun, resting his head on his paws. Hypocrite.

By the time I put on every piece of clothing I brought, it's snowing again, lazy drifting flakes. They've figured out the secret to lightness, but they won't tell me what it is. I haul my heavy body toward the car and turn my phone on for directions. The rattlesnake buzz of it goes on and on, notifications filling the screen. When it stops, the message on top says *not sure what's happening, but we'll figure it out, just give me a call.* To restore my life: a phone call, a depressive episode, a few apologies. My brain offers: a car going sixty, a brief jerk of the wheel, the screech of metal.

I turn the phone off, back away from the car like it's a viper, hissing, lethal. My feet tangle with a buried branch and I half sit, half fall into the snow. I grab the branch, try to break it between my hands, but it's too thick, so I stand and hold it at an angle, slam my boot into it, stomp on it again and again until my hand is throbbing and it gives way with a loud crack. Satisfying, but only for an instant. I stomp the pieces into smaller pieces until all that's left are fragments, my hands bright red and splintered. I'm breathing hard, my eyes sting. I see the dogs watching me from a window, so I bury what's left of the branch in the snow and get back in the car. *Easy*, I say to it, imagining I'm talking to a spooked horse, *easy now*.

Leaving the phone off, I drive at random until I come across a used sporting goods store. Skis lean up against every wall, racks of winter coats look like huddles of strangers. I run my fingers down the skis' sharp edges, read the names and numbers written on them, as if this is a language I speak. *Parlez-vous ski?* I ask them. (*If anything exists and is comprehended, it is incommunicable*, my brain quotes at me, helpful as ever.) I buy a battered old snowboard for seventy-five dollars, a single object seeming more manageable than two.

I get back in the car and keep driving until I see a ski resort, which takes less time than one might think. At the ticket window, I purchase a season pass. It is stunningly expensive. I stand in the bustle at the base of the mountain and don't think about student loans or unpaid rent. People walk past me talking loudly, shouting to friends, skis propped over their shoulders. Chairlifts carry people up and away, new people speed down the slopes to replace them. My snowboard is camouflage, a passport granting me access to another universe. In that universe, surely I already know how to ski. But this is the problem with all my research into branching universes: real or not, they remain unreachable. I turn around and walk back to the ticket window. *I need a lesson*, I say. *What level?* the man behind the glass asks, gesturing to a laminated sheet that depicts levels zero (*never-ever!*) through five (*ripper!*). *Minus two*, I say. He looks at me and I look back. *Zero?* he says. *Sure.*

The shock of my body colliding with the snow is like a cold shower on an August day. I shift my weight, the snowboard responds, an edge digs into the snow, I plummet. I had never realized there were so many different flavors of pain: the nauseating, full-body throb of my tailbone hitting ice entirely distinct from the localized stab when my wrists bend too far back or the way my head against the ground rings me like a bell. I crash over and over, each time in new ways. I breathe through the pain until I can name it, then push myself back to my feet.

When I limp into the house that night, Alice hands me an old-fashioned ice pack. *Out of practice?* she asks. *Something like that*, I say. The ice pack is made of fabric printed with green stars; it has a thick white cap that unscrews so ice can be added. It is the Platonic ideal of an ice pack. Alice sits on the couch and drinks a beer and neither of us speak but this doesn't feel like a problem.

I fall into a routine: days spent crashing into the ground, evenings icing my body. The exhaustion turns my thoughts to molasses. I leave my phone turned off. Nobody knows where I am, another kind of inexistence. (*No one who possesses true friends knows what true solitude is.*) Most mornings, it isn't so hard to get out of bed. Most nights, Alice sits with me and updates me on the dogs' training— Aros is learning to gee, Hemi is thriving as wheel dog—or tells me about the people who were assholes at the restaurant that day. If there were too many assholes, she turns on a video game about zombies and hacks their heads off until she feels better. *It's a guilty pleasure*, she says. *My ex-husband used to play, and I teased him for buying into the American death cult, but here we are. You want to try?* I take the controller, but all I can do is walk into walls. The zombies eat me before I manage to turn around. Sometimes she asks me about my life in Providence and sometimes I answer. The best way to do this is to pretend I am talking about a stranger, which is near enough to true. They—that is, I—did have a partner, yes, but they were too focused on their career. They used to like teaching, but now it feels like walking the wrong way up an escalator.

Each night, invisible in the perfect dark of my room, my body so sore that stretching out between the sheets is a kind of painful bliss, I fall asleep at once. A small, repeating miracle.

The snow continues to fall. Neither of us believe in shoveling, so it lies unperturbed except for the paths we trudge from the driveway to the door. Every night new snow fills our tracks so that we must trudge them again in the morning. This stepping and restepping cradles me—every action is repeated, every action is undone.

My crashing accumulates into something new: I can make my way down the hill in slow, looping turns. I become brave; I ride the gondola to the top of the mountain, take the trail labeled EASIEST WAY DOWN. I only fall twice. If only every crossroad had one of these signs.

Back in the gondola, I watch two men in their twenties tell each other nonsensical jokes. They remind me of my students; they are clearly very high. The other woman in the cabin with us looks unamused. At the top of the mountain, we pile out, and one of the jokers says to me, *Hey, you wanna blaze?* I don't particularly want to blaze, but I don't not want to blaze either, and one of the boys is a near-perfect replica of the rugby player I lived with a decade ago so I follow them into the woods, wondering if they realize I'm over forty.

I prop my snowboard at a jaunty angle next to theirs in the snow—*make some friends*, I tell it, *stop being so antisocial*. We sit on the ground and pass around a joint. There are embers in my lungs and clouds in my head. They want to know who I am and where I'm from and when I tell them I'm a philosophy professor from Providence, they laugh uproariously. *What's the meaning of life?* not-Graham asks, and I tell him this is the problem, I haven't been able to find one. *A lot of the time I wish I didn't exist*, I say, the words floating out of my mouth like exhaled smoke. The taller one, who has blond hair down to his shoulders, nods, *yeah man, I know the feeling.* Some drawer inside me unlocks at his words.

I wrote a whole book, I tell them. *About how our true selves are spread across infinite universes, how the only reason we experience life as singular is because of the limitations of our consciousness. It's our tiny human brains*, I say, tapping my head. *But so what? What good are infinite possibilities if every single day feels impossible?* I realize I'm talking too loudly. I've spiraled us somewhere new, the boys are staring. *You haven't felt that way?* I ask. *This weed is some strong shit*, not-Graham says, sounding impressed. The joint is passed back to me, and I inhale once, twice, three times, holding my breath until I can't hear my thoughts anymore.

The boys are from Connecticut and Florida, respectively, and they go by the names Dragon and Leroy, although these are not their real names. *You need a name too*, Dragon says. *What's your favorite animal?* My brain goes entirely blank, this is one of its party tricks, I have never even heard of an animal. I close my eyes and see a bear, its eyes glowing golden. *Grizzly bears*, I say. *You're Bear Grizz, then*, Leroy says. *Professor Bear Grizz*, Dragon corrects. Later, I run into them at the base of the mountain. *Bear*, they say, *yo, Bear!* My head swivels. How quickly it has learned its new name, how ready it is to discard the old one. *Where'd you go?* Dragon asks. *We waited for you after the trail split. Oh*, I say. *I went the other way.*

At home, I tell Aros I have made some friends. Ishmael rests his head possessively on my foot, but Aros looks skeptical. *Okay,* I say, *perhaps friends is a bit strong.* I think about how I will package the day into an amusing anecdote for Alice, but she doesn't come home at the normal time. Even with all the lights on, the house feels dark, and I startle when the landline rings. *I'm running late,* Alice says, *could you feed the dogs?*

The dogs do not want me to feed them, which hurts my feelings, as I was under the impression that dogs were highly undiscriminating when it came to food. They each need to eat in a specific spot to avoid disagreements over what belongs to whom, but no one will go where they're supposed to. When I try to coerce Ishmael to his designated location, he shows his teeth and growls in a low grumble and it is only after I sit on the floor and sob that the dogs relent, but even this doesn't make me feel better.

For the first time since getting to Vermont, I contemplate the wreckage I've made of my carefully constructed existence. To repair my life: who fucking knows. I try to silence this thought by reciting the first twenty digits of pi. I explain Bell's theorem to the dogs. I say in ancient Greek, *all the good dogs to the paradise will go,* being careful to get the declensions right. I can't think of the word for *heaven*. None of it helps. I walk outside and wait for the cold to kill what's inside me. My brain suggests: a long walk into the woods, the river that flows too fast to freeze, a brief submersion.

I stumble through the snow to my car, don't let myself think about the car's destructive potential. I start driving south, toward Providence, though I don't think I'm going to Providence. If quantum suicide is true, every time you try to kill yourself you end up in the universe where it didn't work. Whether this is threat or comfort varies.

I pull my phone out of the glove compartment, veering toward the trees. The road glistens where the moonlight hits it. I hold down the power button. I have 14 voicemails, 136 emails, 34 texts, including one from my mentor saying, *are you out of your goddamn mind Raffi, what are you doing* and one from my landlord that says *???????* beneath a picture of a pile of bodies that I realize are puppets. Maybe I will drive to the place I called home and ask the puppet artist to make a marionette of me. I would be so much lighter if my parts were held together by string and wire. The puppet artist can pull the marionette's strings, send them to teach classes and write papers and drink cup after cup of black tea. Marionette-me reaches up and cuts their strings, collapses into a pile on the ground. I stop thinking about puppets.

Instead of looking at the email whose subject line is *DISCI-PLINARY ACTION*, I call my dad, who picks up on the first ring. *Giraffe*, he says, *I was worried*. My first thought is that this should have been the animal I gave to the boys, though on second thought it's obvious why I didn't. I tell him I'm having issues with my phone, but I'm fine, everything is fine. At least this one reflex remains intact. My phone vibrates again, it's a text from Alice. *I've got to run, research calls*, I say, *I love you. You know that, right?* The text from Alice says, *u ok? thx for feeding dogs.* I reply *home soon* and pull off at the next exit.

As a thank-you for helping, Alice invites me to come dog-sledding the next day. We load the dogs into dog boxes on the back of Alice's truck. *Up you go*, she says to them, hoisting them under their butts. *Up you go*, I say to Hemi, and give him a hoist. All the dogs want to go first, we are all very excited. When the dogs are harnessed and I am snug in the sled, Alice says, *Ready?* from her spot on the runners. The dogs are barking, howling, all talking over one another, so it is impossible to understand what anyone is saying. *Let's go!* she says, over the noise, and then we are flying forward in sudden, stunning silence. I laugh out loud, and Alice says, *It's the best, isn't it?* It is. I would like to stay in this sled forever, Alice shouting directions and encouragement, the dogs bounding forward as though life is nothing more or less than this perfect opportunity to run and run and run.

When I am pulling on my socks the next day, I notice that my right toenail is a lavender color with hints of indigo. *Interesting*, I think, and push my foot into my boot. I snowboard now with Dragon and Leroy and their band of woodland creatures: Hawk, Moose, Cougar. Boys, verging on men. Despite the age gap, I slip into the group easily. I have never known how to be a woman among other women, never mastered the knack of female friendship, which demands intimacy, disclosure. Too early, I learned the risks and have never been able to forget them. But this kind of camaraderie with boys or men has always been a skill of mine; it requires nothing of me.

I am not good at snowboarding, but I am fast. Learning to love the rush of air against my face, the adrenaline of impending crash. For so long I have treated my body like a suitcase for my brain, like something I could slice my way out of to uncover a better form. These days the dogs give me lessons in other ways to exist. *Speed*, they say, *muscle thrust, cold lungfuls, snowsnowsnow*. I collect injuries to confirm that my body is real: pop my shoulder out of the socket with a sickening shift, sprain my wrist, bruise my kneecap yellow against the ice. My purple toenail begins to loosen its grip on my toe. Each time I look at it, my stomach twists, so I refuse to take my sock off for a week. When I do, the nail comes with it. *My toenail fell off*, I say to Alice. I hold my hand up so she can see it sitting in my palm. *Oh yeah, that'll happen*, she says. *What do I do with it?* I ask. She shrugs. *Throw it away, or keep it as a souvenir, up to you. But the dogs will probably eat it if they get a chance.*

On the coldest day of my life, I snowboard in the trees for the first time. The sky is blue and the temperature lingers far below zero; motes of frost hang in the air and catch the sun, so everything glitters. I have learned that clear days are the coldest, that clouds are a blanket, holding in the warmth. The mountain is empty. After a few runs, Hawk says to me, *Should we hit the trees?* This seems like the worst thing to do with trees, but I nod. What's the worst that could happen is my favorite inside joke with myself. The trees feel like a different world than the wide-open runs, combed smooth each night by large nocturnal machines. Here, in the space between trails, it is possible to forget the fingerprints humans leave on everything they touch. I follow Hawk's ever-disappearing form, making tight, careening turns a breath away from too late.

I catch an edge and slam into the ground, lie on my back gasping, looking at the outline of branches against the bright blue of the sky. *Oh*, I think, *here it is. Here I am.* When we reach the bottom, I say, *again!* This time, I turn too slowly: my body is on one side of a tree, my snowboard on the other. My leg tries to go in both directions at once. Such a people pleaser. *You okay?* Hawk calls back to me. *Oh yeah*, I say, *I'm fine, it's fine. I'm just gonna take my time. You go ahead.*

This varietal of pain is binary. As long as I don't put any weight on my leg or try to turn, it is quiet, barely noticeable. When I break these rules, it is excruciating in an unfamiliar, insurmountable way. My body refuses it. My teeth are chattering, though my shirt is soaked with sweat. *You have to get down the mountain*, I tell my body, *there isn't any other option.* My brain says: *there is always another option.* I ignore it. When I teach undergrads, they try to avoid my hypotheticals. *I wouldn't divert the trolley or let it keep going! I'd knock it off the tracks / find the brakes / keep them all alive.* As a professor, I have mastered the art of gently reinforcing a lack of options. But as a person, here I am, trying to opt for neither/nor.

This is your fault, I say to the tree, but we both know that's a lie. I crawl out of the woods. I slide down the trail on my butt, directly under a chairlift. *Are you okay?* someone shouts. *No*, I yell back in a moment of unprecedented honesty. The chairlift carries my confidant away, my sore tailbone carries me to the base of the mountain.

On the X-ray, I'm made out of moonlight and darkness. *A stress fracture*, the doctor says, pointing to a place on my lower fibula where the moonlight intensifies slightly. *Typically caused by overuse*, she says, *though it seems like yours was exacerbated by trauma*. I think, *A little on the nose*, but out loud I say, *Can I still snowboard?* She shakes her head. *Not if you want it to heal. It needs rest. Four weeks at least, but six would be better. Listen to your body; if it hurts, more rest. Ice for twenty-four to forty-eight hours to keep inflammation down*. Her words sound like I am looking at them through the wrong end of a telescope. I stare at the X-ray. My insides are mist: I could walk through walls, I could lean into a shadow and disappear.

Are you all right? the doctor asks. *Are you in pain?*

I am not in pain, I am in nothingness. When was the last time I felt all right? On the day I found out I'd gotten tenure—a joint appointment in the physics and philosophy departments—I cried, and they might have been tears of happiness. But if I'd put the tears under a microscope, maybe I'd find exhaustion or relief or fear. What did I know of happiness? I thought of horses in the moonlight, joy as intense and undeniable as a stomachache, a memory so distant it hardly feels like mine. I leave the office with my leg cradled in a sheath of air and plastic.

Alice is killing zombies when I walk in, an IPA held between her knees. She raises an eyebrow when she sees my leg, and I shrug. I limp over to the couch, not bothering to get the ice pack. *How long you out of commission for?* she asks, and when I tell her, she whistles. *So much for your ski sabbatical. You going to head back to Providence? I had a friend of a friend ask about renting the room yesterday*. I don't reply at first, afraid of what my voice will give away.

I'm being replaced; I had thought I was a part of the pack. *I'm not on sabbatical*, I say. She turns to look at me and the zombies take advantage of the distraction to gnaw on her avatar. *Shit*, she says, turning back to the TV.

While she makes the zombies pay for what they've done, I tell her about leaving the university. About the irony of writing a book on how our lives are infinitely branching while my own felt more claustrophobic each day. *The afternoon I emailed you*, I say, *I was doing research for this DEI committee bullshit and I found a study about how girls start thinking of themselves as less smart around the age of six. How this correlates with fewer women being represented in fields that place a great deal of value on sheer brilliance. E.g., mathematics, physics, philosophy. You know what my undergrad degrees were in?*

Alice hands me the controller, and when I take it, she says, *I used to be an architect. Lived in the city, worked eighty-hour weeks.* I look at her and I can see that other version—sharper edges, faster speech. *I loved it*, she says, *or I thought I did. But it was like a beautiful house built underwater. I couldn't live there. I broke down one winter. My husband tried to help, took us to this beach house, like what I needed was a saltwater cure. I couldn't do it. I left him, left my job. Bought tickets to Svalbard, north of the Arctic Circle. That's where I tried dog-sledding. I was forty-three and for the first time it occurred to me I could stop trying so hard. Heads-up on your left*, she says, and I manage to shoot the zombie staggering toward me. *You know what I'd wish for my younger self? Less perseverance. Less of an ability to get by.*

I kill another four zombies before the horde takes me down and I pass the controller back to Alice. She takes it and says, *Your research is about alternate universes?* I nod. *If you meet me in another life*, she says, *remind me I can't breathe underwater, okay?* I try to imagine Alice at thirty and smile. *Only if you'll do the same for me,* I say.

We go to bed late, but I still can't sleep. My leg throbs at the edge of my awareness like half-heard music. After a while, I stand up and pull a coat over my pajamas. The dogs sleep piled on Alice's bed with her, but Ishmael comes to check on me. I kiss him between his soulful eyes, tell him not to worry.

Outside, I take a deep breath of frigid air, cough, take another. I am filling myself with the scent of snow and bare branches and frozen water. I make my way down the driveway. The illusion of Bear disperses like vapor, clouding the air around me. I am not Alice's renter, one-time-feeder-of-the-dogs, Ishmael's favorite. I am not a professor at a prestigious university, thinking thoughts that will change the world. I have lived so much of my life trying to be a certain kind of man—or to claim as a woman, these possessions of men. But in the deep dark of the woods, I am not a genius, not a woman, not a success nor a failure. What does it mean that I can define myself only in negation?

Soon I will have to take the ice pack off, thaw out, and evaluate the damage. But for now, I walk down the dirt road, my broken leg quietly disagreeing with each step, so that it is impossible to forget that I am here, alive, in this universe, in this body, which is still trying to protect me, in spite of the disregard I have shown it. Above me, the sky is busy with stars, but I don't look up. I have spent enough time with my gaze turned toward other worlds. I hold my hands up in front of my face and try to see the moonlight inside of them.

CHAPTER SIX

A Beautiful House
Built Underwater

R

In my memory, the sandcastle's lines would always be stark against a pink sky—the walls undulating like waves, the sand arcing outward then cresting into spires as though it had transformed into a new state of matter. But it was the middle of the night when I first met Alice, when I first saw one of her creations, and the castle's size was more evident and thus more breathtaking than its beauty. The castle was impossible. It should have collapsed. It should have required backhoes, concrete, a team of builders. But there was just Alice and a sandcastle tall enough to live inside.

I'd been walking along the beach, where the sand was damp enough to numb my feet. It was 2:00 A.M. in December and I was trying to think of nothing: not the fight I'd gotten into with Caleb, not the things I'd said to him, not the fact that it was Christmas break and the dorms were closed and I had nowhere to go. *Nothing nothing nothing nothing*, I recited to myself. This worked as long as I gave it my entire attention. I watched my feet so that I could match the nothing to the rhythm of my walking, and I might have kept going like this forever except that between one step and the next the sand gave way and I skidded into a deep pit.

"You've destroyed my moat," a voice said. I looked up to see the shadow of a small woman, and behind her, the shadow of an enormous castle.

"I'm sorry," I said. Then: "Can I fix it?" I was twenty and desperate to believe destruction could be undone as easily as it was wrought.

The woman stared at me for a moment. "Sure," she said, voice uninflected. "Why not?"

"Thanks," I said. "I'm Raffi."

"Alice," she said, then gestured toward where the ditch I was standing in stopped, a few feet to my left. "It's not finished." She turned back to the castle.

The digging was easier than it should have been, as if I were uncovering a path in the earth that had always been there, but soon my arms and back were throbbing. I didn't realize I was done until I hit empty space with my shovel and fell into the sand again. Alice climbed down into the moat beside me, somehow managing not to collapse the sand, then helped me out the other side. She walked away and I followed her, waiting to be told to leave. "I like to see them from a remove," she said.

We stood in silence, watching the castle emerge from the darkness. My arms wanted to float now that they weren't holding the shovel; there was a squashy blister on the skin between my thumb and forefinger. "It's a good one," Alice said, "thanks for the help."

I searched for a compliment that could fit the beauty and the strangeness and the gratitude I felt for being included, so sharp it made me want to cry. But before I could find the words, if they existed at all, a wave poured into the moat. Then another and another. The wall closest to the ocean gave way, and my stomach clenched. "I didn't make it deep enough," I said.

"For what?"

"To keep the water out."

"There's no fighting the ocean," she said. "No point in trying."

Then what was the point of any of it? I wanted to ask. What was the point of digging or building or getting out of bed or existing at all? Water splashed up the far side of the moat, drops of foam spattering the castle's closest wall. I couldn't bear it.

"I have to go," I said. Alice nodded, didn't tell me to stay—why would she?

I walked to my aunt's house without letting myself look back, and checked there was no one around before ducking inside. My aunt was dead. I didn't know who owned the house now. I had no right to be there. But it was winter break and I'd been uninvited from Christmas with Caleb's family and the key my aunt had given me a decade ago still unlocked the door. I slipped into the smallest room, the one I'd always slept in, and curled up in a ball on the unmade twin bed.

By the time I woke, the sun was setting again and my body was a tangle of pain and stiffness. I walked from the living room to the bedroom to the living room to the bathroom to the living room to the kitchen. I grabbed my phone out of the drawer where I'd hidden it next to the cutlery. It took a long time to turn on; it had 7 percent battery. I'd thrown out the charger at a gas station on my way to Long Beach Island so I wouldn't call Caleb. I'd lasted nearly three days. That had to count for something. I called his number. When he didn't answer, I called again and again. After a while, the phone started going straight to voicemail, and I knew he was ignoring my calls.

I could picture him, sitting on the floor in his living room playing Monopoly or Scrabble with his family, turning his phone over when he saw my name appear. There would be a fire going and an enormous Christmas tree bedecked in gold lights and silver baubles, perfectly wrapped presents stacked beneath it. Last year there had been ones with my name on them. Caleb's family felt like an exclusive country club. They all loved each other, and it was an impenetrable love. My own parents had separated when I was thirteen then reunited a year later, due more to resignation than reconciliation. I found it almost physically painful to be in the house with them. I was, in other words, desperate for admittance to the club. What had Caleb told his family about my last-minute absence?

I threw the phone onto the couch and walked back down the beach to the place where the castle had been the night before, but there was no trace of it. No sign of Alice. *Stupid*, I thought to myself. I walked closer to the ocean, until a wave hit my toes. The cold was so intense that it felt like heat, like burning. I took another step, until the water darkened the bottom of my jeans. And another and another, until the water reached my thighs, my stomach. Because I could. Because it was a bad idea. Because Caleb wouldn't answer my calls. Because I had no home that belonged to me.

I thought of my freshman-year roommate, who used to say *I'd rather walk into the ocean* anytime there was something she particularly didn't want to do—an orgo exam, a bad date—and I'd say, *Okay, Ophelia.*

I walked until the water lapped its way over my lips, my nose. Until it closed over my head. Beneath the surface, movement gave way to stillness, and I held myself there in the nothing and felt something not so far from joy.

A

Alice watched the girl walk into the ocean. It was the middle of the night, and she was sitting by the dunes, Henry's old Carhartt pulled tight around her bare legs, the seconds oozing by. She'd been out of the hospital for eleven days and nothing was real. The girl was a ghost, walking through the water rather than into it—a step—another sludgy second—another step—until she was gone and all that was left was the ocean. Alice took a breath and held it, sinking into the empty space at the center of her chest. Time paused. She noted the cold, the need for air, but they were outside of her. It was almost pleasurable, this ability to deny her body the things it wanted. Deny and deny until her lungs rebelled, her body insisting on its reality, and the girl surfaced, then, too. She began walking back toward the shore, but she stopped where the water was knee-deep and stood there, shaking, and at last Alice felt afraid.

She pushed herself to her feet, knees aching, and stumbled toward the water. As soon as a wave hit her feet, the world snapped into realness. Her vision sharpened so that she saw the girl's body go still at the sight of her. Then the girl convulsed with cold, and she looked so much like some half-drowned animal that Alice closed the remaining distance between them and wrapped the girl in her arms. It was like embracing the ocean. Alice was soaked, salt on her tongue, gripping the girl tightly enough to feel the wings of her shoulder blades. The shivers moved through them both. She was certain, all at once, that she was embracing her own self, the self she'd been a decade earlier, and she wanted to say, *keep going*, say, *someday you will get everything you want.* But on the other side of that reassurance was the despair of the present moment, and it was this despair, as much as the cold, that made Alice pull away.

She led the girl—Raffi—out of the ocean, the fear sharper now. That small, stubborn part of Alice perpetually determined to live. She pulled them across the dunes to the outdoor shower beneath the house her husband had rented. Raffi sank wordlessly to the wood-plank floor. Alice turned on the water so that it rained down on the girl's body, then sat next to her. Even lukewarm it felt scalding. Raffi leaned her head against Alice's shoulder, carefully at first, so Alice could feel the tension, then releasing the full weight of it, the scaffolding of their bodies shifting until the sliver of space between them disappeared. The canvas of Alice's jacket grew heavy, sodden; her right arm fell asleep, but she couldn't bring herself to move and disrupt whatever delicate equilibrium was holding the moment together.

They'd been silent for so long that speech had stopped feeling like a possibility by the time Raffi spoke. "Do you think Ophelia meant to kill herself when she walked into the water?" she asked, as though they were in the middle of a conversation, one that had used the language of body and landscape rather than words until now.

In the airless months of summer, Alice had trawled through message boards filled with people who meant to kill themselves. The users' lives were litanies of tragedies they listed off for faceless strangers. She couldn't relate to them. Her own life was a building she'd constructed as carefully as any of the elaborate homes she'd designed for her clients. At its foundation, work—coffee from Zabar's in the periwinkle hours of morning, Revit and blueprints and endless emails, meetings where people gestured wildly and waited for her to turn their movements into a home they could live inside. A continuous flow of problems, the continuous satisfaction of solutions.

It was all she wanted, and sometimes, without discernable reason, it became impossible. Time thickened, she couldn't move her body, couldn't string two thoughts together, couldn't face even one more moment in that glass-walled office. But it was equally impossible not to do those things. Impossible to destroy what she had worked so hard to create, impossible to fail her obligations.

It wasn't life she wanted to escape, it was the shrinking space between these two impossibilities.

Alice didn't have an answer to the girl's question, couldn't remember the details of the play. "Does it matter?" she asked. "Either way she ends up underwater. Either way she's dead." Raffi didn't respond, and Alice felt the real question pulsating in the air between them. "Did you mean to kill yourself?"

"No," Raffi said, so quickly that it sounded reflexive, practiced. Alice waited. "I wanted to feel in control of something. And it's quiet under there."

"It's fucking cold," Alice said. The girl laughed, a surprised hiccup that made Alice want to laugh too, but she thought then of her husband, asleep above them. At any moment, he might come to look for her, decide he didn't trust the note she'd left about going for a walk. Lately, his gaze had taken on a weight that crushed whatever it landed on. "I should go," Alice said. The girl stood immediately, as though she'd been waiting for dismissal.

"Me too," Raffi said. "Thank you." And she was gone.

R

In my dream the next night, Alice led me out of the ocean and into a castle on the shore. It looked like the drip-castles I used to make on this same beach in another life, the sand slipping slick through the cracks between my fingers. Inside the castle, thick rugs covered the floor and the walls were a regal shade of red. Light flickered out of sconces, warm on my skin. My clothes were dripping, and when Alice began to undress me, I felt an overwhelming relief that I would not ruin the rugs. I wasn't nervous to be naked in front of her. My body felt like a part of me, as undeserving of criticism as any animal's body. Then we were lying on the ground, and it was sand again and the castle was crumbling around us so that I could see the moon. Dream-Alice smelled like the honeysuckle bushes outside my childhood house, and I rooted into her, dug my face into the crook of her neck, pushed my body against hers. I woke with the thin comforter tangled between my legs, hot with need and shame.

I walked to the bathroom and splashed cold water on my face. When this wasn't enough to displace the dream, I slapped myself so hard my ears rang. My desire was like a feral cat, begging for attention one minute then hissing and showing its teeth the next. I blamed this capriciousness for the wreck I'd made of my relationship with Caleb. For months I hadn't been able to make myself have sex with him. I couldn't stand his sour morning breath or the white fluid that would gather at the corner of his lips overnight. My desire for him had curdled and neither of us understood why. Freshman year, his attention had felt like an aphrodisiac. I wanted him to want me—to love me—as badly as I'd ever wanted anything. We went on long midnight walks together and I straightened my hair and chewed cinnamon gum and when our hands brushed together my whole body thrummed.

Inevitably, we'd end up at the playground a few blocks from our dorm, where we'd sit on the swings and dig up stories from our pasts, laying them down like stepping-stones toward intimacy. This was a game I'd first played with Britt, and I felt grateful to have the practice, though it was a gratitude I understood to be morally bankrupt. I didn't tell Caleb about her. When he told me about his sister dying of brain cancer—how he'd wished, amidst the endless doctors' appointments, to be an only child, how he couldn't forgive himself for wishing her gone—I considered it. But I understood the gendered dynamics of confession: men were meant to admit to doing terrible things. Women were meant to confess the terrible things that had been done to them.

And besides, what was a dead horse compared to a dead sister? My silence had been rewarded: he'd kissed me for the first time. I'd wanted him to, wanted to sleep with him, wanted and wanted until one day, I didn't anymore.

I took my phone out of the kitchen drawer, turned it back on. Four percent battery. If only he would pick up the phone, I could find a way to fix things.

I called, and when he didn't pick up, I texted: *Did you know that the Atlantic in January is 35 degrees?* I walked to the top of the dunes and sent him a picture of the ocean. I texted: *It seems like that should be cold enough to kill you immediately, but it isn't.* I texted: *Did you know that hypothermia can confuse people so much that instead of walking back to shore they walk deeper into the water?* I waited for him to respond, but he didn't. My phone had 3 percent battery, 2 percent. *Let it die,* I thought, the wind off the ocean damp on my face. Let Caleb call and worry and wish he had called sooner.

I didn't return to Alice, not right away. I was afraid that she would be able to see the dream on my face, that she would turn away from me in disgust. Instead, I passed the nights coming up with rules for being Ophelia: From the moment the ocean came into view at the top of the dunes, I wasn't allowed to stop walking. I had to keep my eyes on the far edge of the ocean, that place where I might be able to tip myself off the rim of the world. My breath had to be a metronome, and the ticking couldn't change until it stopped.

The first touch of the water on my feet felt different on different nights, depending on the temperature of the air or the tides or my internal weather. Sometimes it was a gasp of cold, other times a slap. Sometimes it was the foam of a wave I felt first, an effervescence I couldn't help but think of as celebratory. My feet were the easiest, my stomach the hardest, and then my breasts the hardest, and then my head the hardest. Once I was submerged, the game began: count one, two, three, four, how many moments of being Ophelia could I cling to before my body overpowered my will and I surfaced, hypothermic, gasping. Above the surface, my body made its demands—warmth, air, sleep—and I acquiesced.

On Christmas Eve, I let myself return to Alice. She was building a castle that looked like the Parthenon and didn't seem surprised to see me. "You can work on the columns," she said.

"How?"

"Just let the sand do what it wants," she said, which wasn't an explanation but somehow worked. I ran my hands down the columns until my palms tingled. I felt like I was caressing a horse's neck, like the sand was alive and shivering beneath my touch.

"Do you think gravity works differently for the castles?" I asked.

"I feel like if I think too hard about why they stay up, they'll collapse. I used to hate superstition. I designed a building once for a man who swore rooms with four walls were bad luck. The rumor around the firm was that he'd been imprisoned for political dissent when he was younger. I liked the challenge of that job, all triangles and pentagons. Burned down a few years later. I cried when I found out. I'm still not sure if it was for him or the building. It was an exquisite place."

"My aunt used to say that superstition is a testament to how badly we want to be in control. That it's easier for us to take responsibility for disaster than to acknowledge something is out of our hands."

"Your aunt sounds smart. Architecture has always felt like a sort of god delusion to me, at base. A desire to construct one's own world. But look at this"—she gestured toward the columns, stretching up around us. "If there's god here, it belongs to the sand."

I wanted to tell her that regardless of control, her castles were a form of genius, but I didn't know if it was what she wanted to hear. "I used to think studying physics would let me control time," I said instead. "That if I was smart enough, I wouldn't have to be afraid of death. After Einstein's best friend died, he wrote that the death meant nothing, that the distinction between past and future was only an illusion. I want to feel that way. But I'm failing my physics classes."

"I've heard Einstein was kind of an asshole."

"All the geniuses are monsters," I said, though I wasn't sure if I believed it.

When the castle was finished, Alice ducked between two of the columns and I followed her inside. We lay side by side on the moonlight-striped sand, our bodies not quite touching.

The nights settled into a rhythm, castles rising up out of the sand before they were swallowed by the ocean, the two of us retreating to our separate houses once the sun appeared on the horizon. The cold and the digging exhausted me so that I was able to sleep through most of the days. I couldn't remember the last time I'd seen someone other than Alice and I liked it that way. I hoped she was sleeping through the days too. I hoped I was the only person she talked to. My dead phone stayed in a drawer in the kitchen. My bruises faded from purple to green to yellow to memory; I wanted it all to be like that.

"You know, I looked up Ophelia," Alice said as we worked on a castle that looked like an enormous snail shell. I imagined her sitting on a dated floral couch like the one in my aunt's house, thinking of our conversation, thinking of me.

"And?" I said.

"She never actually walked into the water. She was trying to hang garlands of flowers in a tree over a river and the branch broke."

"That doesn't make any sense."

"I guess that's why they say she's crazy."

I dug my fingers into the sand until I felt grains push themselves up under my nails. "Where did the whole debate around suicide come from then?"

"It was about whether she tried to rescue herself after she fell in. Whether she'd tried to swim."

I felt a disappointment that verged on betrayal. I closed my eyes, and I could see her, Ophelia, in a white dress with a crown of flowers, walking into the water. Was it possible I'd painted the image myself? Why was Alice unbothered by the way Ophelia had been trapped inside a man's words, allowed no agency beyond that single question, *sink or swim*? "That's bullshit," I said. "She wasn't crazy. She wouldn't have been in a tree."

"You'll have to take it up with Shakespeare," Alice said, and I was doubly betrayed by the amusement in her voice. We worked in silence for the rest of the night, and I kept waiting for her to say something that would mean she understood why all of this mattered, but the silence stretched and the tide came in and the day broke.

A

The castles consumed Alice, swept like a magnet through the iron filings of her thoughts, turning them into a single dense nodule of attention. She spent the nights building, the days sleeping or sketching, waiting for the sun to set. Even her dreams filled with digging. And then, like a fever breaking, one afternoon she woke and the desire was gone. That night, she couldn't bring herself to go down to the beach. Instead, she sat on the bench at the top of the dunes, looking out at the empty expanse of sand. Raffi would show up soon. What would she make of Alice's absence?

Alice heard a cough behind her and startled hard enough to send a flash of heat down her spine. Henry's hair was sticking up in all directions, his beard scruffy. He sat and put his arm around her shoulders. She leaned into him, the red flannel she loved soft against her cheek, the familiar scent of his Head & Shoulders shampoo. Henry, who'd approached her at their firm's holiday party, walking over as though she'd always been his destination. Who would never understand her, and bless him for it, Alice thought, the oddly religious language appearing from nowhere, bless him for his steadfast lack of understanding.

"No castles tonight?" he asked. She opened her mouth to say she was spent, that she had nothing left. Then she closed it.

"You've been watching me?"

"I just came out a few times to see where you were."

"You're not my nursemaid."

"Is it because I brought you to the hospital? Is that why you're mad at me?"

She shook her head. "What else were you supposed to do?"

"Then what? Can you at least tell me what I did?"

She shrugged, looked out at the ocean. It was a gray day, gray sky, gray water. What answer could she give? She hated the boxy prefab house he'd rented them. The way he'd said *the ocean always makes you feel better.* How he lined her pill bottles up on the bedside table with every label facing forward, how the tendons in his neck relaxed when she swallowed the pills. They had been married nine years, together twelve. They had been, for the most part, happy.

Alice saw Raffi's shadow in the distance. "Let's just go home," she said.

Henry tightened his arm around her shoulders, and she fought the urge to claw away. "Will you please talk to me?"

The thing about Alice's rage, or her intimacy with Raffi, or her love for the castles, was that she didn't trust any of it. Emotions were chemicals and the chemicals inside her had proven themselves untrustworthy. "Imagine you're working on an interior," Alice said, uncertain whether she was trying to answer or distract him. "You visit the house, sketch out dimensions, mark the doors and windows. You're meticulous, unlike in real life."

He smiled. "I forget one door one time, and you never let it go."

"You take all these measurements and then you go back to the office and you work and work and you know it's coming together, it's going to be beautiful." She could feel the intensity of his gaze; this was the most she'd said to him in weeks. Out of the corner of her eye, she saw movement on the beach. "You go back to the site one day, just to double-check a few things. And you find out—not that you've missed a door or mixed up a measurement—but that there isn't any house at all."

Before Alice could find out if Henry understood what she was trying to tell him, he noticed Raffi. She saw it in the straightness of his back, the tensing of his muscles, knew, without looking away from him, that Raffi was walking toward the water. He stood up, and she grabbed his hand.

"She's okay," Alice said, and for a moment the words held him. Then the water reached Raffi's shoulders and he yanked his hand out of hers and sprinted toward the ocean.

It was impossible to know if Raffi would have reappeared on her own—Henry was there, pulling her out of the water, cradling her in his arms like a child. He strode back toward shore, and Alice felt sick, furious, though she couldn't say with whom. Raffi writhed out of his grasp where the water was a liquid gleam over the sand and ran.

Henry didn't look at Alice until Raffi disappeared, and when he did, there was something that might have been disgust on his face. "In what universe is she okay?" he asked. Alice lifted her shoulders, the aphasia of the past weeks settling back over her. He was quaking with cold or maybe with anger. He shook his head, then turned his back on her and walked toward the house.

R

I told myself not to go back the night after the man dragged me out of the ocean. That I'd humiliated myself or been humiliated, I couldn't decide which. That I didn't want to see Alice again. That she wouldn't be there anyway. But I did go back, and there she was, digging. I didn't know what to make of it.

"I'm thinking something surrealist," she said when she saw me. "Can you work on an octagonal foundation?"

The finished castle twisted in on itself, walls connecting in ways that confused my eyes. I ducked inside, sat with my knees pulled to my chest. The roof was open to the sky, a three-quarter moon draped in tatters of cloud above us. Alice sat beside me, and I waited for her to bring up the night before or to move us past it, but she didn't say anything. "Was that your husband?" I asked, though the answer was obvious. Alice nodded. "What did you tell him about me?"

"Nothing," she said. It was the answer I'd thought I wanted, but I felt worse.

"I was fine," I said. "I didn't need some man with a savior complex grabbing me."

Alice reached a hand out, ran two fingers down my jawbone,

so gently I could hardly feel them. "I know men are terrible, but Henry isn't the enemy here."

I could have laughed at how wrong she had it. As if Caleb had been the instigator, the source of violence. As if I hadn't been the one to beg him to walk to the park with me, that night before winter break.

I'd wanted, ostensibly, to apologize for avoiding him, but the apology was hollow. There was nothing inside it except the desire to be forgiven. He knew it and I knew it and when I started to cry in that empty playground he said, *Can you just stop trying to be the victim for once?* He had never been cruel before, and as soon as I tasted the words I was ravenous. *You hate me,* I said. I pushed him, both hands on his chest. I was somewhere I'd never let myself go before, far beyond control, no separation between impulse and action. *You hate me, you hate me,* I pushed him again and pushed until he stumbled and pushed back and I tripped over the merry-go-round, landing awkwardly on my side. He was the one crying now, his face contorted and ugly. *Hit me,* I told him, *I know you want to,* and when he wouldn't I begged him, and when he wouldn't, I said, *You're just using me to feel better about having wished that your sister was dead,* and then he did. The feeling of his hand against my jaw was pure relief.

"No," I said to Alice, thinking of Caleb's face after he hit me—confusion bleeding slowly into horror. He spent his weekends volunteering at an animal shelter where he was responsible for socializing kittens. He was the gentlest person I knew. "I made him do it."

"Raffi," she said, her voice so tender it infuriated me. "You can't make someone hit you any more than you can make the tides not come in. Any more than I can control the sand."

"You do control it." I gestured at the walls reaching up around us, the miracle of them nearly normal after so many nights. "You made this."

Instead of looking at the castle, Alice looked down at her hands, as if contemplating their role. "We're leaving tomorrow," she said.

For an instant I heard it as an invitation before the truth of the pronoun caught up to me.

"Okay," I said. "Thank you for telling me." The words were too formal but they were steady and I held myself there.

Alice didn't say anything after that. She didn't tell me to stay out of the water, didn't ask for a promise she must have known wouldn't hold. The different words I might say layered themselves atop one another until they'd reached incoherence, and then it didn't matter anymore. Alice was near enough that I could have reached out my hand and touched her, but I could barely see her through the memory of her, already more real than she was. Instead, I reached for the wall of the castle, pushed my hand into it—softly, slowly—and the sand gave way, matter displaced by matter, until I felt the air outside the castle touch my fingers. Nothing collapsed, nothing moved. It wasn't until after, until I pulled my hand back, that the castle came down around us. I brought it down. By the time the tide rose over us, there wouldn't be anything left that mattered for it to wash away.

A

Alice packed the car while Henry worked at the dining room table, pointedly ignoring her. His anger was fresh air after the suffocating staleness of his concern, after the months of being treated like an expensive houseplant gradually losing all its leaves.

She'd become a risk statistic to him. Each time he looked at her, she saw the question on his face: Are you going to try again? Are you? Are you are you are youareyouare. And maybe she would or maybe she would live to be 106 or get hit by a bus or win the goddamn lottery. Her life was as vast and unpredictable as anyone's.

And maybe there was an element of truth to Raffi's illusion of control. For all that Alice couldn't explain the castles, nor claim ownership over their magic, it was true that they wouldn't exist without her hands, her digging, her sleepless nights. So after she loaded the last bag in the car, she sat down at the table beside Henry. When he looked up from his work, she felt a rush of tenderness for this man who wanted so badly for her to live. She tried to put all that tenderness into the kiss she placed on his forehead and then she leaned back and said: "I don't think this is working."

R

Instead of going back to the house, I walked along the beach until the darkness bled into day. I walked to the convenience store where my aunt used to buy us chocolate chip cookies the size of my face. On a dusty shelf, I found a bubblegum-pink phone charger for $16.99.

Back at the house, I paced in circles while my phone turned on, thinking about proving Alice wrong, and the wording I'd use to say so if I ever saw her again. The phone trilled. I had six texts from Caleb. I left them unopened and typed "Ophelia Hamlet drowning" into Google. Then "Ophelia walking into the ocean," then "Ophelia stones pocket." I read the original text. I looked at John Everett Millais's painting, which was ugly. I read an article from the Tate about how Millais's model caught pneumonia after months of posing in a bathtub. *The matter was settled and Miss Siddal recovered quickly.* I googled "Miss Siddal" and read about how Elizabeth Siddal was a painter in her own right, how "recovered quickly" meant: developed chronic illness, an addiction to laudanum, death by laudanum overdose at thirty-two. An accident, they said. I read "Drowning in Womanhood: Ophelia's Death as Submission to the Feminine Element." I threw my phone across the room, but not hard enough to break it.

I retrieved it and opened the messages from Caleb. *Your phone keeps going to voicemail please let me know you're alive.* And: *I'm sorry I didn't pick up just call me.* And: *Raffi, where are you?* And: *Please call me. I love you.* And: *This is fucked-up, Raffi, you can't treat people like this.* And what I felt: pleasure.

I closed the messages and let myself do something I'd never done before—I typed Britt's name into a search bar. *Promising young sculptor wins the Rhode Island School of Design's prestigious Dorner Prize.* And: *Behind the winning work: Britt Mason on queering the boundaries between human and environment.* And: *In this exclusive interview, Mason talks about what they plan to do next.* On Facebook, Britt was smiling, her—their?—head shaved, an arm draped over another girl's shoulders. The photo had 137 likes, the top comment: *you two are disgustingly cute <3.*

I took the phone into the bathroom with me, propped it against the mirror. I used my aunt's kitchen scissors to cut my hair off. It was salty and tangled and it fell in clumps onto the tile floor. By the time I was done, the person in the mirror was unrecognizable.

I left who I'd been behind me and walked back to the beach. It was full daylight, but I stripped my clothes off and left them in a pile on the sand. I walked toward the water and Ophelia walked with me, and Britt, and Alice, and other women, ones whose names

I didn't know, all of us walked together toward the freezing water. It hurt and I moved into the hurt and then the water closed over my head and I was alone. My breath was a steel box, my body was the entire ocean. I unclenched my fists, relaxed my muscles. I let the salt water lift me back to its surface. I let myself float.

* **II** *

CHAPTER SEVEN

The Person in the Mirror

The summer of the octopus—the same summer Raffi's aunt
is diagnosed with terminal lung cancer, and a hurricane
floods Raffi's bubbe and zeyde's house, drowning their photographs
of parents and siblings killed in the camps, and the news is filled
with stories of two dead women found inside a Utah hotel's water
cistern—Raffi has a sudden desire to be submerged. They've never
liked baths, always too aware of all the feet and dead skin cells and
pubic hairs that have passed across the bath's porcelain floor, but this
summer they don't care anymore. Or maybe that's not quite right,
because they still shudder as they lower their body into the water, but
they lower it anyway, that strange *it* of their body, desire overpow-
ering revulsion. When the water—a degree or two colder than their
blood—closes over their head, they feel a strange sense of commu-
nion, as though the borders of their body are giving way. They wish
they could explain to their grandparents, distraught over the loss
of their photographs, that it isn't such a bad thing to be drowned.

When Raffi first notices the octopus, Kay is lying on their emerald velvet chaise with her feet in Raffi's lap. It is summertime—

all bad things happen in the summer—and Kay is wearing a silk slip and nothing else. Their third-floor walkup has no air-conditioning and the climate is breaking and the apartment is staggeringly, astonishingly hot. Kay glistens with sweat. She looks like a work of art, like Millais's *Ophelia* or some other half-drowned woman. She looks, Raffi realizes, quite pregnant.

Raffi stops rubbing their wife's feet. They try to remember what Kay looked like yesterday or last month, but when they close their eyes all they see is their own paintings: Kay fractured and refracted across universes, a multitude of Kays, Raffi's imagination so vivid that their process sometimes feels closer to recollection than invention. They open their eyes to the silhouette of their wife's new curves, the shadow of her nipple visible through the silk, her hands rested atop the rise of her stomach.

"I thought we said we weren't going to have children," Raffi said.

"I wondered when you'd notice," Kay says. "Don't worry. It's not a child, it's an octopus." She says it in the same steady tone she uses to soothe Raffi's fears when they wake from nightmares where Kay has been murdered or mauled or died of cancer. *Don't worry*, she says, *here I am, not even a little dead.*

Raffi's fears do not feel soothed. "But octopi are as smart as children. And they have so many more legs."

"Only eight." Their wife smiles, and it feels like an invitation. But Raffi doesn't know how to accept. Their own octopus-less stomach clenches.

When Raffi is beneath the water, nothing is allowed to change. The octopus inside Kay stops growing, their aunt's cancer stops proliferating, the ice caps stop melting—all of it pauses. And the other things too, the ones Raffi doesn't know about yet, all the damage this summer and the ones to come will inflict on them and everyone else, all the damage they will do to the people they love and the people they love will do to them. All of it holds its breath in the silence below the surface of the water.

Raffi tries not to look below their wife's lovely clavicles. They try not to look at their wife's side of the studio, the half-formed tree, cracks filled with pale-green resin, carving knife perched haphazardly on the table like it might be picked up at any moment. They try to avoid thinking the word *octopus*, which works as well as these things always do, which is not at all. *Octopus-octopi-octopode, octopus-octopi-octopode*, their brain chirrups.

Raffi sits on their own side of the studio, pins a fresh piece of heavy, hot-pressed paper to a board, and takes out their watercolor palette. It's an unforgiving medium—unlike oil or acrylic, which are opaque, allowing you to paint over mistakes, watercolors are translucent. Every brush stroke leaves its trace on the final painting. The series Raffi is working on is called *Deformations*. Like all of Raffi's work, the paintings feature Kay. Or more accurately, they feature a multitude of Kays. The paintings are layered, and each layer is a different imagined life, one slightly deformed Kay atop the next. If Raffi plans the layers ahead of time, the paintings come out stilted, muddy. They have to let each image come to them, however long it might take. In the piece they finished yesterday, the one they've been referring to as *work-wife*, Kay is bent over a workbench. In one layer, she's applying gold leaf to a fatal wound, in the next, sculpting the tree Raffi can see across the studio. She's butchering a sheep. Building a table. Swaddling a baby. The layers cohere so that from a distance, they look like a single outline. But in other paintings, the versions of Kay stretch and warp away from one another—Kay as a murder of crows atop

Kay as a mountain lion atop Kay as a pair of twin ghosts—so the overall effect is entropic.

On the blank page, Raffi begins to draw Kay's outline. They are trying something new: instead of moving across lives, they want to move across time, overlay all the versions of Kay they've ever known until they have a map to show them how they've arrived at the present moment. They try to sketch Kay as she was at twenty, when the two of them first met. Raffi, a broke art student, living in a house with most of a men's intramural rugby team and Kay dating one of the boys. What Raffi remembers most about their first encounter was how they couldn't stop watching Kay—the way she pulled her hair back into a ponytail, how she'd half close her eyes when she smiled, the small skip in her step. Raffi, who had spent their life feeling both observed and inadequate, had become the observer. They try to put all these recollections into their drawing, but in every sketch, the octopus bulges beneath the surface.

When Raffi leaves the studio, they find their wife lying on the chaise again, fanning herself with one of Raffi's sketchbooks. "How come you're not working?" they ask.

"I'm not in the mood," she says.

Octopus-octopi-octopode. "How could you make this decision without me? What about marriage meaning that we're a team?" It had been Kay who wanted to marry, Kay who'd wanted the stability marriage implied.

"It wasn't a decision." Kay's voice lingers on the border between earnest and defensive. "It was more a gradual coming to terms with something that's always been present."

"You've always had an octopus inside you?"

"Maybe in some form or other. Remember that trip we took to Flathead Lake the summer between sixth and seventh grade?"

"I didn't know you then," Raffi says.

"Oh," Kay says, shaking her head. "Right. I was with my best friend Norah. Her family was rich, or they seemed that way to me then, and they rented a place with one of those outdoor showers, the kind with a floor like a boardwalk. I had my first bikini, red with white polka dots. I felt so grown up. Norah and I locked ourselves in that shower after swimming and stripped down to our jelly sandals and danced around under the water. I remember feeling something wriggling inside of me."

Raffi thinks of lying nose to nose with Britt in her bed. Of Britt's arms around them on Calypso's back. Of the shiver that had moved through them at her touch. Is it possible that this is what Kay is describing? "Are you saying you have an octopus inside you because you're queer?"

Kay lets out a disappointed huff of air. "No," she says, "not at all. Were you even listening?"

Raffi is failing their wife by not understanding and their wife is failing them by not making herself understood. Their entire relationship was one of looking and being looked at, seeing and being seen. When did the two acts come to feel so different?

Next to Kay and Raffi's claw-foot tub, a mirror with an elaborate gilt frame and a crack creeping across the bottom left corner leans against the wall. Kay rescued it from a sidewalk in Alphabet City, but Raffi avoids its gaze. They have never liked looking at their own reflection. But lying in the bath, they want to see themself. The mirror is tall and narrow and they rest it over the top of the tub like an imperfect lid. Under the water, they open their eyes and their own distorted reflection stares back at them, light leaking in around the edges.

* * *

Raffi avoids their wife, which is made easier by her continued absence from the studio. It's not that they don't want to be near her, but they don't know how to be near in the way she seems to want. At night, Kay goes to bed hours earlier than normal, so Raffi doesn't have to decide whether to avoid their nighttime ritual: a lit candle, soft music, mugs of lavender-lemon tea to help Raffi sleep, something they've never been good at. The first night, Raffi makes themself tea, but they feel so sad sitting on the love seat alone that they gulp a mouthful before it cools and scald their tongue. They pour it out and go back to the studio.

After that, they give up on tea and sleep, spend their nights staying up late doing graphic design work for an ad campaign. Without meaning to, they keep adding tentacles to things like soda cans or televisions. On the other side of the studio, the unfinished tree seems to be wilting. They work until they have erased so many tentacles that their paper tears, and then they give up and go to bed. Their wife doesn't stir when Raffi slips into the bedroom, but the octopus does, undulating their wife's skin in a way that makes Raffi's own skin prickle. They sleep as close to the edge of the bed as they can, back to their wife.

If only Raffi had gotten into the bath earlier, stopped the flow of time sooner, maybe the octopus would never have squirmed its way into existence and they wouldn't need to be in the bath at all. But wasn't marriage itself a long bath? That's what Kay had told them, more or less, when they'd asked why she wanted to marry. That she wanted a steady surface to sink beneath when the world around them grew chaotic or cold. That their relationship could be warm water to ease the things in life that ached. They think of all the bad summers they've survived under their marriage's steady surface: the strange numbness that overtook Raffi's body one summer; the horrible day in June when their best friend got mauled by a bear, the months of caring for him afterward, the nightmares where they'd been too slow with their shouted warnings. When Kay holds Raffi's gaze, the whole world goes quiet. Even the word *wife* a kind of reassurance.

After a week, Raffi walks into the studio to find their wife sitting in her normal spot, staring at the half-finished tree. They feel a leaping kind of joy. They will go over and kiss the top of her head, like they have so many mornings. They will bring her coffee milky with cream and hand it over saying, *happy wife happy life*, and they will return to the small, silly rituals that together form a relationship. But Kay doesn't look at Raffi when they walk over, not even when they're standing beside her, and the space between them solidifies so it's impossible for Raffi to go any closer. They turn and slink out of the studio.

Raffi is the one on the chaise this time, heavy with sleepless nights. When their wife sits down on the end of it, Raffi startles back to wakefulness, and for a moment they forget the octopus, forget the fact they've barely spoken with their wife in a week, and they smile up at her—their beautiful wife, their favorite person— and she hesitates before smiling back, a deep dimple appearing in her right cheek.

Octopus-octopi-octopode, Raffi's brain says, and they stop smiling, watch the change mirrored on their wife's face, feel a kick of guilt. They shift their focus to lines and shadows the way they do when they're painting. To see as an artist is to forget meaning, abandon memory. Their wife's face is a crescent of darkness and a circle of sun. Delicate, curved contours in smooth surfaces. It is entirely unique; it has nothing to do with the person Raffi knows and loves.

"I've never held it against you when you can't work," their wife says, snapping back into familiarity. She is talking about the heavy days, the times when it is impossible for Raffi to get out of bed let alone make art. The days that Raffi has worked—for Kay—so hard to avoid, becoming disciplined about boring things like sleep and exercise and therapy.

"It isn't about working," they say. "If you want to take a break, fine. I already told you I'd do more graphic design."

"I moved to New York with you. Even though everything here costs a million dollars and the people are mean and it takes me three fucking planes to see my mom. Even though it's hotter than hell and we don't even have air-conditioning because you want us to *save the planet* by which you actually mean we can't afford the electric bill." Kay is breathing hard, her voice rising. Has she been carrying around a list of resentments this entire time? Raffi thinks *calm calm calm*, pulls the soft parts of themself inward.

"You were the one who said we should move. Who insisted."

"Because I wanted what was best for you."

"If you hate it here, fine. I hate it too. Let's leave." Raffi will prove to Kay how little they desire her sacrifices, if that's what this life is to her. They will clear their shared world with the swipe of an arm across a desk.

"Are you upset because I'm changing or because you can't?" Kay asks. The words resound inside of Raffi, their body become an echo chamber.

Raffi holds their breath underwater and looks up at themself in the mirror. They try to imagine how Kay sees them. What they look like to her with their brow furrowed, squinting at a canvas or sketchbook. What they look like laughing at her jokes or contorted with pleasure during sex. What they look like sleeping beside her. They come up for air, and it is like they are coming in for a kiss.

Raffi flinches when Kay walks into the studio. They're sitting on the floor, back against the wall. They are trying to name shades of blue: Prussian, cerulean, phthalo, ultramarine, cobalt, indigo. Can they count Payne's gray? Kay sits down next to them and holds out her carving knife. Raffi takes it, confused. "If you want the octopus gone, you can cut her out." She offers up her arm. It's not quite steady. Raffi stares at it, the subterranean rivers of veins—cerulean blue. They don't know if this is a real offer. They don't know if it means some part of their wife wants to return to sunny days in the studio, lavender-lemon tea, sleeping with their bodies tangled, or if it's another sacrifice their wife would make and resent them for, or if it's a test. They don't know what the after of an octopus would look like, how it would be possible to remove it without hurting Kay.

"That's not where the octopus is," they say, instead of doing anything. They mean it to be a statement, but it lifts itself into a question.

"It's where her tentacles are."

It makes sense, Raffi thinks, that there wouldn't be room for all of them in Kay's stomach or uterus or wherever it is the octopus lives. Octopi have so many legs. Raffi loops their fingers loosely around their wife's wrist, acutely aware of the points where their fingers touch her skin. They lift her arm up to their face. It smells of vanilla from her lotion, and talc from the powder she dusts her body with, and seaweed from the octopus. The skin is puckered into small divots where the suckers must be. "Is it painful?" they ask.

"No," their wife says. "It's like being embraced, but from the inside."

"I'm scared the octopus will hurt you." They think of the tumor growing in their aunt's lungs, of all the ways a body can betray itself.

"I feel good," Kay says. "I feel strong."

They let go of her arm, put down the knife. They don't want to cut the octopus out. They want the octopus never to have existed at all.

Raffi starts locking the bathroom door when they take their baths. They don't know if they are afraid that Kay would try to join them or if they're afraid she wouldn't. They lie flat enough that there is room for an imaginary version of Kay to lie on top of them, also beneath the surface—of the water, of the mirror—knees and breasts and bellies squashed together, the octopus imaginary too. Raffi talks to their imaginary wife. It doesn't matter what they say: the words don't make any sound beneath the water; Kay can hear whatever she needs to hear. But the words Raffi is saying are *who are you who are you who.*

Raffi understands that since their wife has offered to let them cut the octopus out, they are no longer allowed to be angry. To prove they aren't angry, they decide to make Kay dinner. She has stopped cooking. Raffi assumes that this, like the lack of woodworking, is because of the octopus. They don't ask about it because if they do, she might give them that look again, the one that means *don't you know me at all?* They don't ask because if they do, she might say that she has never liked cooking, that this, too, was a sacrifice she made for Raffi's sake.

Raffi is a mediocre cook—they try to be the opposite of their mother in every way—but they do know how to make one good stew. They mince clove after clove of garlic, simmer onions until they're translucent, dice jalapeños. They pour in billowing clouds of coconut milk and globs of peanut butter, slosh in half a can of crushed tomatoes.

They sweat and sweat. It is a terrible time for stew. Maybe Kay will laugh with them about this. And even if she doesn't like the stew, Raffi has tried and is thus allowed to be mad again. The air is thick with heat and garlic, but still they can smell the octopus, the brine that lives in their apartment now. The carving knife glints on the counter. Raffi wipes at their eyes, but this is a mistake. The oil from the jalapeños lingers on their hands, lights their skin on fire.

Raffi yelps and their wife appears, but when she reaches a hand out, her skin is rippling. Raffi trips backward and lands hard on their tailbone on the kitchen floor. Their whole body throbs.

"Let me help you," Kay says, and she sounds so much like herself, the concern so familiar, that Raffi's burning eyes water more. They don't want their wife to touch them with her alien, rippling hand, but they want her to care for them again. They stay very still. Their wife gently tilts their head back and pours the rest of the canned tomatoes over their molten face. The tomatoes are slimy and cool and make soft squishing noises as they slide off Raffi's cheeks onto the floor. They ooze away the pain. Raffi's vision blurs into amorphous blobs of red. Their wife wipes the tomato juice from their eyes, the pad of her thumb tracing the top of Raffi's cheekbone. For a moment, it is just the two of them. Then their wife's thumb suctions to Raffi's cheek, and their reaction is visceral, they jerk away, their stomach heaves. Their wife pulls her thumb off with a slight popping noise, and Raffi scrambles backward until they hit the wall. They wrap their arms around themself, close their eyes.

"They're just suckers," Kay says, and Raffi can hear the hurt even with their eyes closed. By the time they open them again, they are alone in a puddle of tomato juice. They stand slowly, turn off the burner. Leave the stew bubbling its way to stillness in the pot.

The paradox of the bath is that even though it is unchanging, still eventually it is over. The mirror unlids the tub, the plug unstoppers, the solid body of water fractures and drains. Life resumes its normal pace, everything rushing fast as it can toward its own end. The long quiet months of winter cede to the commotion of spring. Raffi must pull their body, its boundaries and edges become porous after so much soaking, out of the water and back into the furious caress of the summer heat.

That night Raffi doesn't stay up late. They sit on the chaise, googling octopus facts until the sun sets. When they walk into the bathroom, their wife is there too, and it is almost like a normal night. While Raffi brushes their teeth, they offer up the facts they've learned. "An octopus's skin is like a giant tongue. They can taste with their whole body." They speak through a mouthful of toothpaste foam that tastes like mint-coated algae.

"She likes the taste of vanilla best," their wife says, sitting on the toilet and patting moisturizer into her skin. She seems unimpressed by Raffi's new knowledge.

Raffi spits out the foam, trying not to gag. "They have three hearts."

"One for eros, one for philos, and one for agape."

"How do you know that?" Raffi says. Kay has never been the type of person who cares about Greek classifications of love.

"She's inside me," their wife says, as though this should be obvious. "We know everything about each other."

Raffi stares at their wife in the mirror. "Octopi don't live long," they say, frustration creeping its way back in.

Their wife doesn't flinch. "They live long enough," she says, voice indifferent as a stone wall, and walks out of the room.

Raffi stays in the bathroom, brushing their teeth over and over, trying to get the taste of brine out of their mouth. They brush until their gums are bleeding, but it's still there, metallic now.

By the time they enter the bedroom, their wife is asleep. All the windows are open and two fans are running, but the air is hot and viscous. A bee is buzzing somewhere in the darkness. Kay's body is dimpled with a thousand small indentations, the curve of her shoulder pockmarked into strangeness. An octopus has more than two thousand suckers. It wriggles beneath their wife's skin. An octopus—unlike a wife—is nocturnal. Watching the way it pushes their wife's skin up in thick, winding cords makes Raffi's own skin feel too tight. Their heart thuds in their ears—or are they hearing the octopus's three hearts?—and sweat trickles off their body and they are so itchy, their skin is so tight, that they dig their nails into it, scratch hard enough to leave welts. They climb out of bed, pace around the bedroom. Through the windows, sirens wail.

The carving knife is lying on Kay's nightstand—*why?*—and they pick it up. It is solid in their hand, so deliciously cold that they press the flat of the blade to their cheek, lean into it, and look up at the painting that hangs over their bed. Kay, reclining on the chaise, holding her hand up. There is a ring on her finger and an expression on her face that is somewhere between confusion and joy. Raffi painted it in secret, hung it on Kay's side of the studio late one night. In the morning, Kay had looked at the painting, then at Raffi, then at the painting again. When she looked at Raffi a second time, they held out their hand, a ring resting in their palm.

They get back in bed. "Kay?" they say. They can't stand it anymore, sitting here alone with the octopus. "Kay," they say again, louder. Their wife makes a sound of annoyance, rolling away from them.

Raffi tells themself that their wife gave them permission that day in the living room. They tell themself they are only trying to understand, only trying to see the things that Kay wants them to see. They tell themself no one could be expected to live this way. They nudge their wife softly, but she keeps snoring, the daintiest chain saw. Raffi loves her and they hate her and they hardly know her in this moment. They understand what they are doing is a betrayal.

They press the blade of the carving knife gently into the flesh of their wife's calf. The skin parts easily; it is like cutting a ripe peach. It feels horribly, perversely good to breach the barrier their wife has erected around herself and the octopus. A line of red wells up, and for an instant there is only this: a thin streak of their wife's blood, dark and opalescent, quivering in the breeze from the fans. And then: something like a vein bulges beneath the skin, pushing up up up, until the tip of a tentacle noses its way out from between the lips of the cut. It sways back and forth, probing the air, covered in pulsing suckers. It looks like an alien; it looks like the calamari Raffi and their wife shared only a month ago, a celebration dinner, oil and lemon juice coating their hands. Raffi reaches out their finger and the tentacle grabs on to it with so many little mouths and it is like nothing Raffi has felt before.

The tentacle tugs at them, as though it wants to drag them down so that they too can live inside their wife's body, a different sort of submersion. Raffi lets it pull them forward for a heart-beat, two. Then the tip of their finger touches their wife's blood and they yank their hand back, recoiling from what their wife contains, from what they have done. The suckers pop off reluctantly. They stare at their finger, the angry marks the suckers left behind, the tip dipped in darkness. When they look up, the tentacle has retreated and Kay is looking at them.

"Oh Raffi," she says, pity in her voice, and Raffi understands that the moment is irreversible. Not the one they're in, but the one that is already over. All this time they have been wishing the octopus gone so they could have their wife back, the Kay they've known and loved. But now that it is too late, they understand that all along this was the wrong wish. That instead of wishing for a different Kay they should have been wishing for a different self.

They don't want to understand it, though, so they run to the bathroom, come back, and kneel over Kay's legs. It takes them three tries to tear the foil off the disinfectant wipe they pull from their little first aid kit. They press it as gently as they can to the wound they have made in their wife. Kay doesn't flinch at the sting, just watches, her skin still for once. Raffi's hands are shaking so hard they can barely spread a layer of antibiotic ointment over the cut. If only Kay will say something, then the two of them can talk and they have talked their way through so many hard things in the past. Raffi smooths down the edges of a Band-Aid. There's nothing else for them to do with their hands then, so they force themself to meet their wife's gaze. Tears drip silently off Raffi's chin, and maybe those are tears in Kay's eyes too, or maybe it's light from the street making them glimmer. Apologies clump in their throat, blocking their airway, but they can't figure out how to force them out into the silence, so they sit and stare at Kay's beautiful face, feel the air from the fan cold as a knife on their cheeks. The moment stretches tauter and tauter until it seems like it might snap into anything. Kay half shrugs, half shakes her head. Then she pulls the sheet up over her body and rolls onto her side so that Raffi can no longer see her face.

Under the water, Raffi keeps their eyes open. The absence of air in their lungs aches like a penance. They've left the tub unlidded, the mirror in its corner, but they look down at their own body, pale and bony and unfamiliar. Under the water, their edges blur so that their boundaries become mutable, so that it is impossible to tell where they end and the water begins. Under the water nothing is allowed to change, not even them, but something is breaking the rules, rippling softly just beneath the surface of their skin.

CHAPTER EIGHT

A Solid Body, Fractured

My mother is a horde of bees. There is one bee for each part of her. My mother of truth-telling, my mother of discipline, my mother of affection. They all look the same—have you ever tried to tell two bees apart?—so I never know which mother I am talking to until she responds. This is the worst part, the moment of uncertainty. Some of my friends say they can tell their mothers apart. Maybe they can. Maybe if your mother is a horde of wolves or cats or lizards you can recognize her different faces. I wouldn't know; my mother is a horde of bees.

Every mother fractures at the birth of a daughter, but not every mother is so angry over her fracturing. As a child, I ask my mother of truth-telling what it is like and she hovers in front of me, buzzing until I regret the question. "Once I was whole," she says at last, "and now I am multitudes. When it's your turn, you'll understand." I tell her I won't, that I don't want a child, so I will never fracture. She laughs at me. It sounds like buzzing. "We all say we won't have children, but it's never true."

* * *

Kay's motherhorde of falcons stops by for dinner, though it's sixty miles from Paradise to Missoula—more if you need roads. My own mother lives 2,400 miles away; it's been years since my last visit. Most of the time, it feels easy enough to share Kay's motherhorde, who calls herself my mother-in-law, though Kay and I haven't bothered with marriage. At dinner, the falcons bow their heads before we eat. "Dear Lord, thank you for this food and this family," Kay's mother of devotion says, and Kay says, "amen," and I say nothing, but keep my eyes down and try to look respectful.

After we eat, the falcons scatter around the living room to settle on wooden perches Kay made. I sit on our emerald velvet couch and Kay lies with her legs draped over the armrest, her head in my lap.

"I wish you two could've seen the bear I passed on my way over. Two cubs cuter than cute," Kay's motherhorde says, and I'm pretty sure it's her mother of persuasion who's talking. "I'm telling you, there's nothing like flying. Maybe if you had kids, one of you would end up with wings. I could imagine you as hawks, Raffi. Such smart birds they are."

"I'd probably fracture into slugs," Kay says. "Show the world my inner laziness."

"Hard to use a table saw as a slug," I say. The tone of the conversation is light, but I'm sure Kay's told her mother that we've been arguing—or whatever the word is for a discussion where both people cry without anyone being angry—about having kids. I know too that on this topic, they're a unified front. "I'll go grab dessert," I say.

In the kitchen, I pull out the polished walnut bowl Kay made for my great-aunt Zlata for her seventieth birthday, returned to us after she died. Each time I use it, I feel her presence, followed immediately by her absence, joy and grief entangled, and I wonder for the millionth time whether it was a mistake to have left for college while she was sick. She'd insisted I go, becoming, for the first and only time, furious with me when I'd tried to refuse. "People try to say family above all," she'd said. "But education is what will keep you safe." I pile strawberries in the bowl, fill another with sugar water for Kay's mother.

Back in the living room, Kay is talking about our plans to camp in the Sawtooths over the summer, and I let out my breath.

I am six years old, sitting at the top of the stairs. It is past my bedtime and the house is full of shadows, but the shouting and buzzing from downstairs have pulled me from bed. I watch as my mother stings my father. I watch as parts of my mother die, as my father grits his teeth and clenches his fists, as if he could hold himself in so tightly as to not be hurt. Even now I understand: this is my fault. They fight over my fear—the way I beg my father to check on me after he puts me to bed, the way I panic when they try to go out at night. I am the one who runs to my father—who loves me entirely rather than in fragments—after a nightmare or scraped knee. I can't help myself. It is hard to love a horde of bees.

Three days after dinner with Kay's mother, the world changes. A woman fractures outside of childbirth. She's a meteorologist, predicting the weather on the nightly news, and then she's a horde of chameleons, scattering across the green screen, her cohost agape, the approaching storm forgotten.

The story makes all the headlines. At the university, my colleagues talk of nothing else. Fracturing, everyone agrees, was meant to be the cost of having daughters, not the cost of existence. At home, Kay acts calm—shows me pictures of the table she's working on, tells me about the epoxy resin she's using to fill a crack with ocean waves—but I can hear the tension in her voice, see it in the way she can't sit still. I know she must be thinking of the children she wants to have, how fracturing before childbirth would take that possibility away. I know too that the best way to comfort her is to help her think of other things, so I ask questions about epoxy, about the new bookshelves she's making for the local library. It's a relief when Graham, Kay's childhood friend, lets themself into our apartment, announcing their presence with a *helloooo* yelled down the hallway.

They hug me tighter than normal, tousle Kay's hair. "What's for dinner?"

"You tell me," Kay says.

"Sometimes I think you only keep me around for my cooking," Graham says.

Kay tosses a pillow at them from where she's sitting on the couch. "You're not *that* good of a cook."

"Dry toast for your dinner, then. Raffi and I will dine on risotto alone." They put on the apron we got them for Christmas last year, printed with bears wearing chef hats and brandishing spoons. Graham and Kay usually cook together, but Kay stays curled on the couch, looking at something on her phone with a crease between her eyes, so I head into the kitchen to offer my admittedly mediocre sous-chef abilities.

While I chop leeks, Graham says in a low voice, "Well? What do you think?"

"I just wish we knew if it was a fluke," I say.

"Do you think she could've been pregnant without knowing? Could a miscarriage count as a birth?"

They're the same questions everyone at the university is asking, but something—intuition or only inherited pessimism?—tells me it won't be that simple. "I'm scared," I admit. "I know that

fracturing doesn't make me any less, that not everyone who fractures is a woman, etc. etc. But I don't want to, Graham. I want to
stay whole."

"Does fracture have to compromise wholeness?"

"Isn't that essentially the definition?"

"Sometimes when I'm wishing I could fracture, I imagine my
body is a house that contains rooms for each part of me," they
say. "A house can be both divided and whole." Graham's feelings
around fracture are as complicated as my own. After their sister
was born and their father, a trans man, fractured into a horde of
antelope, Graham had demanded to know when they could fracture too.

I try to imagine it: a room for the part of me that wants to
stay whole at any cost, a room for the part of me that would risk
anything for the people I love. "The House of Discontent," I say.
Graham quirks their head. "It's what my aunt used to call that out-
let in Missoula. The House of Discounts, it was actually called."

Graham stops stirring long enough to drape an arm over my
shoulder. "You don't seem so discontented to me," they say.

I am seven years old, cross-legged under the kitchen table. It is Friday evening, which means my motherhorde is buzzing instructions at my father while he cooks Shabbos dinner. Before I was
born, my parents cooked together each week, making my bubbe's
dishes—kreplach and shlishkes, cholent, chocolate babka. My
bubbe cooks from memory, but my mother wanted to preserve the
recipes so they could be passed down. I found the cookbook they'd
started to make, behind other books on the shelf in the living
room. My mother's script, unfamiliar to me, and my father's careful photographs of the finished meals. The last recipe dated from
three weeks before my birth. It is hard for a bee to cook. Now she

directs, buzzing and swooping, dipping antennae into bowls while my father stirs and measures and mixes. Sometimes—sometimes, sometimes—dinner emerges from the oven just as my mother envisioned it, and my father helps me light the candles and we say kiddush and hamotzi and my mother tells me to stop mumbling and sit properly and instead of arguing I uncurl my legs and my father says very little and my mother of complaint says the food is good but perhaps a little overdone and my father says nothing but sighs and eats so slowly that I think he is hoping we will all finish and leave him to eat alone. These are the good nights.

Tonight, my father adds a tablespoon of paprika when my motherhorde had asked for a teaspoon and she asks what he was thinking and he says that she should have spoken more clearly and their voices rise and under the table I watch what falls to the ground: dishes, bee-bodies, words.

Another woman fractures: she is eating dinner with her lover when she begins to cough and cough. Her lover pats her on the back in the way we all do when we feel the need to act in spite of our inability to do anything useful. He pats once, twice. At the second slap of his hand against her back, her whole body ripples. An instant later, a horde of ladybugs is swarming in the chair where the woman used to be.

Another random fracture and another, until stories are replaced by statistics. Theories bloom and multiply like cancerous cells—it's an effect of pollution, it's because of vaccines, it's God's punishment for our heathen ways. The White House's official stance is silence. Women take to the streets demanding answers, government funding for research, a promise that somebody somewhere is doing something. The language of the protests—and the country's response—is predictable: this is a woman's problem, a mother's problem. When Kay wants to go to a protest, I use this as an excuse for why I want to stay home.

Graham texts saying that the human rights org he works for has printed signs: NOT ALL WOMEN FRACTURE, NOT EVERYONE WHO FRACTURES IS A WOMAN. *You two want to come to the rally on Saturday?* they ask, in our group chat, and I'm forced to tell Kay the truth. That I heard three people fractured at a rally in L.A. That each time she walks out the door, I imagine her returning as a horde of moose or porcupines or octopi. Imagine never again feeling her intact body against mine, never again falling asleep with her singular head on my shoulder. "I'm afraid," I say, my new refrain.

For so long, I've prided myself on my willingness to move toward the things that frighten me. Now I can barely bring myself to leave the apartment. I imagine a new room unfolding inside the house of my body, a room for the part of me who hides. My mother of caution, my mother of cowardice.

Kay crinkles her forehead. Maybe she's as unsettled by this change as I am. "Okay, Raf," she says, wrapping her arms around me. "Let's stay here. Will you read me another chapter from your book?"

I am eight years old, lying in bed. My mother of storytelling sits beside my head on the pillow. Some nights my father reads books to me, but other nights my mother tells me stories about the universe motherhorde, with her thousand different worlds. I love these stories, love my mother of storytelling whose buzzing sounds gentle, like a lullaby hummed under one's breath.

"Once upon a time, there was a universe with no motherhordes," she says. "Once mothers didn't fracture when they gave birth to daughters." I make a noise of disbelief. "It's true," my mother says. "But in this universe, when a mother gave birth to a daughter, she had to place a curse in her daughter's heart to start it ticking. The curse could be anything at all, but no matter what it was, no matter how good it sounded, it would always turn out to be a curse, never a blessing."

"What if the mother cursed her daughter with niceness?"

"Then the daughter might be so nice that she allowed any mean person to take advantage of her," my mother of storytelling says. "The mothers who gave their daughters beauty saw them pursued by vicious men, hungry for their bodies. The mothers who gave their daughters intelligence saw them torn apart by their understanding of the world's cruelty. Eventually, most mothers learned to curse their daughters with small miseries, the kind a person could live around: weird toes or a terrible singing voice or an allergy to dust mites."

"Like my allergies?"

"You get those from your father," my mother says. "The point is, once there was a mother who refused to curse her daughter. She loved her unborn baby so much that the thought of doing any harm to her, of putting any curse no matter how small into her daughter's heart, was intolerable."

"So how did she start the baby's heart ticking?"

"She put a promise inside it: she would split herself into a thousand pieces before she would let any curse touch her daughter."

"And it worked?"

"Like all births, it caused a splitting. In one universe, nothing happened at all. The baby's heart wouldn't tick, the mother died of grief. But in another universe, in our universe, the baby's heart started pounding and the mother fractured into a thousand wildcats, each snarling and ready to protect her baby."

Would my mother rather fracture than curse me? Is this the moral of her story?

* * *

Even Paradise, its population smaller than a high school, isn't immune from the fracturing. "Marta was carrying a stack of about twenty plates," Kay's mom says, "you know how she is. And then all of a sudden, crash! And the place is lousy with beavers." Marta was sixty-four with two grown sons, owner of Paradise's only restaurant, a twenty-four-hour diner. "She said it felt like sneezing. Wish I could say the same about childbirth." Kay's motherhorde laughs her squawking laugh.

In bed that night, Kay says, "It just sounds so *weird*. I can't think of anything weirder that can happen to a person's body."

"Weirdness isn't a reason to do a thing."

"If we had a kid, it wouldn't be the way it was for you," she says.

"You don't know that. Nobody says, hey I bet this is going to be a disaster, let's do it."

"I mean, probably somebody does."

I grin, then suppress it, but Kay looks triumphant. "What's wrong with the life we have now?" I ask, the question that hurts the most.

"Nothing," Kay says. "It's not about something being wrong, it's just the chance for a new sort of right. To make a family."

Are we not a family? I want to ask, but I can't make the words leave my mouth.

I am nine years old, at my bubbe and zeyde's house. We're sitting at the table in their kitchen playing kaluki, a card game with elaborate rules. We wager with a handful of pennies from the tzedakah box, my zeyde winking at me, saying, "No one will mind if we borrow these for a little time." It's hard to hold all thirteen cards in my hand, but after a few rounds I win a game. "Who taught you to play so good?"

my bubbe asks. She is a horde of muskrats, soft-looking but hardy. *Your bubbe has survived things the rest of us can't imagine,* my mother has said to me, many times. I know she means Auschwitz, and in spite of the statement, I imagine my bubbe's muskrats forced into cattle cars, shoved beneath the gates that say ARBEIT MACHT FREI. But, of course, my bubbe wasn't a motherhorde then. Just a girl.

My mother talks with my bubbe and zeyde about her child-hood, about nieces and nephews and cousins I can't keep track of. They switch back and forth between English and Yiddish. I look at the photos lining the walls, new ones in color and old ones in sepia tones. I've been told who the people in the old photographs are—my bubbe's and zeyde's parents, grandparents, siblings—but I can't remember their names. All I remember is that almost everyone in these photographs is dead.

In one photo, there's a girl who looks just like someone from my kindergarten class. When I'd asked if she died too, my zeyde said, "Not died, killed. Shot by the Nazis." My bubbe had hushed him, saying, "She's only a little girl," but he said that I needed to remember, that it was never too young to remember. But sitting in the kitchen, the dark pressing in on the windows, I want to forget.

I'm at the university when the news breaks. It's almost nine, and I've been telling myself to go home for hours, but I can't bring myself to leave the comfort of my office. A standing lamp fills the room with a warm yellow light, books line the walls like ramparts. The desk Kay built for me—a present when I got the job—glows golden, the wood burnished to a soft shine. I'm trying to figure out how to answer my students' questions, ease their fears: *Do you think it will keep accelerating until we all fracture? Won't this intensify the pressure on women to have babies young? How can you talk about bodily autonomy when apparently we have none?*

My phone vibrates and I assume Kay wants to know when I'm going to come home, but her text says *have you seen the news?* I click over to *The Guardian* and read: POSSIBLE GENETIC RISK FACTORS FOR FRACTURE. My pulse speeds up. Ever since the random fracturing began, I have had a hummingbird heart, and while I wait for the article to load I try to imagine a future with wings, a self composed of so many tiny, vibrating bodies. Try to see it as something other than a threat. *A new study suggests that certain epigenetic alterations are associated with an increased risk of non-natal fracturing. Researchers found a strong correlation between cases of random fracture and familial trauma in the matrilineal line.*

Numbness spreads through my body. I imagine it a topographical map, fault lines marked in red. I read article after article, trying to estimate seismic risk. In Kay's mind, are we standing together outside these articles looking in? Or does she see us separated by the news, the fact of my grandparents' history—hidden beneath the protective mantle of my atheism—become suddenly relevant?

I am ten years old, sitting at a desk in my fifth-grade classroom. I go to a Jewish day school, and each year on Yom HaShoah different students' survivor grandparents are asked to come and talk. This year, my bubbe sits on a chair at the front of the room, her muskrat selves clustered together as if for warmth. I do not know her well enough to know which muskrat is speaking.

The whole class is watching her, but I am watching my motherhorde, who came with my bubbe. My mother's bees are in a tight knot; she is the smallest I have ever seen her. She hovers near the jug of soda can tabs that we have been gathering all year. We are trying to understand what six million looks like, though so far we only have 23,042. What it was like for my mother to fracture her mother? Was it a relief for my bubbe to change shape after all that she had been through? Did she love my mother more for it, or less? In the corner of the room, my motherhorde is a dense, pulsing thing. She looks like a beating heart.

Finally a breakthrough: a test is developed to check whether someone has the genetic alterations associated with increased risk of random fracture. It requires blood drawn from both parent and child. My motherhorde calls while I'm eating dinner with Kay—butternut squash and apple soup by candlelight. She leaves a voicemail and I play it on speakerphone. Her voice is chipper and strident. "Does this mean you're going to come visit?" she asks, before I press delete.

"What do you think?" Kay asks. "Will you go?"

For once, I don't want to think. "I don't know. Probably not."

"Because you don't want the test or because you don't want to see your family?"

"Does it have to be binary?" The word *family* presses on a bruise and the question comes out sounding bitter. "Why bother if I can't do anything anyway?"

"Probably the test will come back negative and you'll feel so much better."

This is one of the things I love about Kay and will never understand: her belief that everything will work out for the best. "Uncertainty can be a place of possibility," I say. "And measurement isn't neutral. It affects the system." I imagine my body a house again, but this time it is made of cards. In the class I teach on superposition, I have my students brainstorm all the ways that a measurement might alter the system being measured, have them try to imagine the least invasive methods, then show how even these can cause collapse. I wish Kay and I shared this language. "You're going to get tested?"

"Once the tests are available in Montana. They're saying it'll be a while. The new assistant at my studio is planning to drive to Denver, but I'm not in that much of a rush." We sit in silence, and I can't bring myself to eat any more soup. "I wouldn't be a different person," Kay says. "Not if I fracture, not if I have a baby. It wouldn't change the way I love you."

I want to respond to her sweetness in kind, but I know too many people who have felt like strangers after fracturing, to me and to themselves. "Every change changes everything else," I say.

I am eleven years old, hiding behind some azalea bushes and watching my father drive away. A temporary separation, they tell me. The couples therapist they have been seeing could not resolve their differences. I am fairly sure that I am their differences and I do not know what it would mean for me to be resolved, but I hate any outcome that means I will be left to live alone with my motherhorde. I don't come out from under the bushes until it is late. As I sneak upstairs to my room, I hear a strange noise coming from my parents' bedroom. I wonder if it is crying, but I do not know what it sounds like when a horde of bees cries. I curl up in my bed with the lights on. Nobody comes to tell me to turn them off. I lie awake and listen to the peculiar buzzing.

I spend the next week at my father's new house. It is small and different, the outside an odd pink color, but I have my own room and we eat dinner next to each other on the couch and there is no shouting or buzzing. We go on long walks to explore the neighborhood. We find a lighthouse and climb up its 223 stairs. We go into an ice cream store with an old husky lying by the door, and my dad holds my hand until I become brave enough to pet the dog's head. We find a house with a big yard where a silvery gray horse eats grass, her tail swishing, and watch until a girl comes out and calls the horse over to her. In an instant, the week is over.

"Why can't I stay with you?" I ask, staring out the window as we drive back to my mother's house. "I could go to school here. I could walk myself."

"Your mother would be too sad," he says, and somehow I understand that this is true even though I don't know if I have ever in my whole life made my mother happy.

My dreams fill with fracture and brutality. I fracture into butterflies, and men in uniforms pin my different parts to a corkboard. I fracture into bears and devour the rabbits I find near the house before I realize they are Kay, that it is Kay's blood on my teeth and claws. I fracture into deer and am herded into a pen with hundreds of other animals packed so tightly we can hardly move, and I am trying to figure out which horde is Kay, what animal she has fractured into, but then I see her: she is standing outside the pen, still a person, and I try to shout her name but my voice comes out as incomprehensible lowing. I fracture into horses and see Kay and Britt sitting across from one another on the grass, staring into each other's eyes. They don't seem to realize I'm there. I try to walk over to them, but as soon as I move, I become a stampede—my mother of jealousy, my mother of despair. I trample them both, wake flailing so wildly that I smash Kay in the nose with my arm.

"What's wrong with you?" she hisses, grabbing at her face, half asleep and bleeding.

"You wouldn't understand," I say, the words buzzing out of me.

Kay reaches for a tissue, holds it to her nose. "You can't keep existing like this," she says, voice nasal. "Get tested. Go to therapy. Do something." For so long, I have thought of our relationship as bedrock, but lately it keeps occurring to me that we are only two people who have chosen to be together, who could choose otherwise at any moment.

* * *

I am twelve years old, sitting between my parents on a couch at the therapist's office. Even though they are separated, they have not given up on resolving their differences. Today the therapist wants me to join them. I don't like her voice, which makes me think of the time I accidentally drank syrup instead of orange juice, or the way she asks "and how does that make you feel?" I want to respond that all of it, everything in the world, makes me feel bad, but I know this is not the right answer, and I am very invested in right answers, so I don't say anything at all.

Today she wants to talk about my parents going out at night, about the way I sob and cling to them and *make things very difficult*. "It's important for people who love each other to get time alone together," she says, in the voice people use when they think they are much smarter than you. "But them leaving doesn't mean they don't love you." I want to tell her that it has nothing to do with love or its absence. But I don't have words for the fear, which is as big as the night sky. I can't talk about the images that flood into me as soon as their car pulls out of the driveway, can't even think the word *dead* because if I do, the nothingness will come into the room with us and destroy the world.

I shrink into my dad's side, bury my face in his shirt, and he wraps an arm around me. "This is the problem," the therapist says, and when I look up, she is pointing straight at me. "If displays of distress are consistently rewarded, children learn that this is the way to get what they want." My mother of told-you-so buzzes victoriously.

Kay's eyes bruise and blacken. Each time I look at her, I think of the welts left by a bee's sting and wonder if this violence too is written into my DNA. I stay late at the university every night, try to prove to myself I'm not a bad person by caring for my students.

One night, I get home to find Kay's hand bandaged. She's on the phone with her mom and I wait until she gets off to ask what happened.

"Just an accident with the router. It's fine, I still have all my fingers." She holds them up in front of me.

"Did you go to the ER? Why didn't you call me?"

"It wasn't a big deal, Raf. Just a few stitches. I didn't want to interrupt your work, I know how stressed you are."

I take her damaged hand in mine very gently, look at the bandage someone else wrapped with such precision around her middle and ring fingers. The fog that has been clouding my mind for months burns off at last and I see the path forking in front of me. I can stay and figure out how to live with the possibility of fracture, or I can leave. I won't live my parents' life. Won't stay when the staying is a form of mutual harm.

"I want to get tested," I say. "Will you come with me?"

"Of course," she says.

I am thirteen years old, at the dining room table in what has become my mother's house. My father is sitting in a chair and my mother is hovering. Her bees are energetic, the whole horde is in a state of flux.

"We have some news," my mother says, through several bees at once. "Your father and I are getting back together."

I look at my father, who smiles at me. I know I am supposed to be happy. I imagine the therapist saying "and how does that make you feel?" and all I can think is bad, bad, bad. I make myself smile anyway, because I know it is the right answer, but I can't stop myself from asking, "Why?"

"We couldn't stand the thought of spending your Bat Mitzvah separated," my mother says. I look at my father again, and this time he isn't smiling, just watching me, tenderly, and I know nothing has changed.

I can't remember the last time I went home. Most winters, my dad comes to visit Kay and me in Montana, the cold enough to dissuade my motherhorde from joining him. He sleeps on the pullout in our living room. When I have to go to the university, he goes with Kay to her studio, and they come home discussing joinery or wood finishes, show me pictures of whatever it is they're working on.

It takes fourteen hours, two planes, and a rental car to get to my parents' house. The closer we get, the heavier I become; by the time we pull up in front of the house, I am dense enough to sink into the ground or collapse in on myself like an old star. Kay tried to book us somewhere else to stay, but the prices were exorbitant and I said no, it would be fine, this would be hassle enough without us wasting money. Now I wish I'd let her do it.

My motherhorde is abuzz with excitement, the air busy with bees that fly circles around Kay's head. "Is that a new haircut, Kay? It's lovely. I wish Raffi would let her hair grow long like yours." The first time I shaved my head, my mother of truthtelling said, *It makes me think of cancer and the Holocaust.* "It's been so long," my mother says. "I wish the two of you would visit more." The first time I told my mother Kay was my girlfriend, she seemed delighted, which surprised me until I realized she thought I was only saying I'd made a friend. When she'd realized what I was actually saying, her delight vanished. *Tell me at least she's Jewish,* she'd said, and when I told her Kay wasn't, she said, *I don't need to hear about your lifestyle. Just don't tell your bubbe and zeyde.*

She leads us into my childhood bedroom, now an apiary where she makes gourmet honey that she sells at the local farmers market. "We've got the air mattress all made up for you. Why don't you drop your stuff off and we'll go for a walk. We can show Kay the marsh." But I tell her we're exhausted, we just want to shower and rest. "Well, you know where the bathroom is," my mother of disappointment says.

That night, she guides us through elaborate meal preparations, staying upbeat even when I lose track of how many cups of flour I've added. When the food is in the oven, we sit in the living room and Kay flips through old photo albums from my childhood. My motherhorde flits from page to page, alighting on the different photos. "This one is from when Raphaela was six," she says, "we made a Cheshire cat cake for her birthday, but her dad and I were on a health kick and we didn't use any sugar. It was disgusting!" By the time the oven beeps to tell us the food is done, even I'm smiling, but I feel the mood shift as my mother checks the time. "Your father should be back by now. He knew you were getting in today." When he walks in ten minutes later, she says, "You're late," before he can take his coat off. "Dinner's getting cold."

He wraps his arms around me, murmurs, "Hey, Giraffe. Good to see you." Exhaustion has etched new lines in his face since I saw him last.

We sit down to eat, all of us quiet. After dinner, my motherhorde mentions dessert, but I shake my head.

"Don't be so glum," my mother tells me. "I'm sure your results will be fine. And even if they're not, fracturing isn't the end of the world. Maybe this is the universe telling you to have kids. Children are a gift." I stare at her. It's hard to tell if a bee is being sincere.

I am fifteen years old, and I am leaving. I hardly know what it means—I have never spent time away from home, even sleepovers make me panic. But some part of me that knows more than I do has taken control. A boarding school in the mountains, not so far from where my aunt lives. A full scholarship, a life without motherhordes or synagogues or soda tabs or therapists. My father cries when we say goodbye. My mother of affection lands on my wrist, stings me a final time. It almost feels good.

Alone in my tiny dorm room, I unpack my bags, put my books on the shelf. I push the bed around the room, stepping back to see how it looks against one wall, then the other. I make the bed, sit down, get back up. I rearrange the furniture again, position the bed so that the snowcapped mountains will be the first thing I see when I wake. This space belongs to me. It is a home I can make myself. I am a home I can make myself.

The day I'm supposed to get the test, I wake at five in the morning. The beehives are dark shapes, huddled and staring down at us. The smell in the room is strange, not quite sweet, a little musky. I nudge Kay. "Can we get out of here?" I say, and after blinking her eyes into openness, she nods.

We walk across the dew-damp grass to the car, and I drive us away from the house without a plan. The appointment isn't until the afternoon. Kay dozes in the passenger seat and I feel the calm of early morning settle into me, that time before expectation or obligation.

I think I'm driving aimlessly, but I begin to recognize the neighborhood. We pass a dilapidated house with a large yard, a few strands of wire fencing it in. There's no horse in the yard, no couch steaming in the sun.

I drive us to a nearby park, deserted at this hour of the morning. We meander along a dirt path, past a playground like the one where I'd once gotten into a terrible fight with my college boyfriend, Caleb. The path winds through gnarled oak trees, which give way to fields of flowers. The sky lightens gradually, the day sneaking up on us. Eventually, Kay settles onto the grass and I lie with my head in her lap, breathing in the scent of her favorite laundry detergent, fresh-cut grass, wildflowers. I watch a bee dart from bloom to bloom, doing its best to kiss each flower. Put a hand on it and it will sting you, even though there will be no winner. It will sting you when it is afraid and both of you will be hurt and there is no way of phrasing this to make it less damaging.

Sitting there in the sunshine, I tell Kay about the moments that weren't in the photo albums. Memories of hiding at the top of the stairs, sitting in a classroom or on a therapist's couch. Images of myself at five, eight, eleven that I have refused to look at for years.

"We are a family," Kay says, when I've finished laying my memories out before her. "Baby or no baby, fractured or whole." If the word *family* has any meaning, she must be right. It must be this, here, her body curved around mine, her fingers in my hair. Graham letting themself into our apartment, my dad's voice on the phone saying "Hey, Giraffe," Kay's mother of love digging her talons into my shoulder.

I find a new door in the house of my body and rest my fingers on the knob. How horrifying it is to be mortal and to love someone, in this world whose brutality I have run from but never forgotten. How much easier—and emptier—to refuse the possibility of loss. *How do you bear it?* I ask the self inside that room.

Nearby, the bee hovers in front of a vermillion flower. It is stationary, untethered from gravity, but the stillness is an illusion created of constant change. The bee's wings are twisting in figure eights, beating two hundred times a minute, spinning the air into a vortex that holds them aloft.

CHAPTER NINE

The House of Discontent

Raffi finds the physical manifestation of the House of Discontent on an evening in October when the shadows are stretching. They've been hiking for hours through the forest outside Paradise, the kind of long, punishing hike whose sole purpose is to make sleep possible. They're not carrying bear spray, which is more invitation than oversight.

The house is hidden by Ponderosa pines, but even in small slices—even though, prior to this moment, the house had lived only in Raffi's mind—they recognize it at once. Their legs go wobbly and then they are kneeling on the ground, making fists around pine needles. They count to steady their breathing, focus on physical sensations: the pine needles are sharp and silky against their palms, a small rock is digging into their left knee, the cold air burns the back of their nose.

Once Raffi can stand again, they approach the house. They move slowly, as if it might startle, turn tail, run away. The path leading to it is overgrown, and at first Raffi doesn't notice the FOR SALE sign, propped haphazardly in the hard ground, bird droppings speckling the red letters. When they see it, they stop. Look back and forth, house to sign to house. The house is so familiar that Raffi wants to embrace it, press their body up against its walls, curl up on the porch and sleep until the ghost opens the door and welcomes them in.

They don't have their cell phone or anything to write with, so they read the number on the FOR SALE sign out loud once, twice, three times like a spell. Then they turn and walk away. Raffi feels the house watching them go. When they reach their car at last, they enter the number into their phone with a shaking finger. They press send, but the call fails. *Fucking Montana*, Raffi thinks, not for the first time.

At the top of a mountain pass, Raffi finds service. The number rings and rings. They've given up hope by the time a woman picks up. *Hello?* she says, sounding tired. *Hi*, Raffi says, *I want to buy your house.*

Raffi doesn't have the money to buy a house. Before the attack, they were a snowboard instructor in the winter and a hiking guide in the summer. (Before that, they were a physicist, but that life is so far away now that it belongs to someone else entirely.) After the attack, they are a server at the diner in Paradise. They like the job because it requires them to put on cheerfulness each day like the black apron they tie around their waist. They smile at the people who come in, ask how they're doing and whether they'd like coffee and if they're done with that. It's a small town—everyone knows how the ghost became a ghost. The customers are gentle when Raffi forgets the cream for their coffee. Marta, the owner of the diner, doesn't yell when she finds Raffi staring off into space, just pats them on the shoulder. But neither waiting tables nor teaching snowboarding results in the kind of money that lets you buy a house, even a falling-down old one in the middle of the woods.

What results in enough money, it turns out, is loss. The

ghost—before he was a ghost—left the girl a small inheritance. When Raffi found out, they tried to give the money back to the ghost's parents, but the ghost's parents said it wasn't what he would have wanted. So Raffi left the money in a separate bank account and tried to forget it existed. Using the money felt like accepting it as a fair trade for the ghost's death.

Parked at the top of the mountain pass, Raffi hangs up with the real estate agent. They close their eyes to visit the House of Discontent. It is instinctive, this retreat to the home that lives inside them. They want to visit the Room of Difficult Decisions, with its elaborate brass scale, taller than Raffi. Around the edges of the room, pros and cons of all sizes for them to label and set on the scale's plates to see which way it will tip. But when they close their eyes, all they can see is the house in the woods, and its door is locked. They squeeze their eyes tight enough to see spots of light. *Please*, they think to no one in particular, to the universe or the mountains rising in the distance or their own mind, *I can't lose anything else.* But they know the universe doesn't care about what they can or can't do. Both the ghost and the house he helped them create are gone.

Raffi buys the house without ever going inside. *You sure you don't want to see it?* the real estate agent asks, and Raffi has to repeat their answer several times before it is accepted. The only person they tell about buying the house is their dad. They make him promise not to tell anyone else, by which they mean their mother, who would call this delayed grief or erratic behavior or some other term born in a self-help book. Their dad sounds worried, but he is 2,400 miles away, and it isn't so hard to sound okay from that distance. Raffi tries to put a chirp in their voice. They end several statements with exclamation points. Raffi's dad needs them to be okay, so he believes them. He asks how much work the house needs, and Raffi doesn't tell him that they haven't been inside. They say, *well it's a fixer-upper!* They ask him for a list of tools to buy. He is a mechanical engineer who knows about these things. He sends them a long list.

A month after finding the house, Raffi walks up to its front door. Three months and seven days since the ghost died. Five years, plus or minus, since their aunt died. Do all griefs age their way into blurriness? Raffi hopes not. They want their grief over the ghost's death to stay sharp as a razor.

Their senses are unusually acute as they approach the house: the wind through the trees is a roaring; the sharp, sweet scent of pine sap overwhelming. They drop the key twice before managing to unlock the door. They step over the threshold into an empty room and they realize that some part of them had believed the house would look the same on the inside as it did in their mind. The mudroom in the thought-House of Discontent had a large workbench on which a variety of dissection tools were arrayed. It was the place where they assessed their emotions, figuring out which ones would become rooms. It had a rainwater shower in one corner for washing off lingering confusion. The mudroom of the real house is just a small square, with dirty floors and a cracked window looking out into the overgrown yard. *Okay*, Raffi thinks. It has become a habit to think *okay* when nothing is. *Okay, so it's a skeleton. The flesh and blood are up to me.*

They spend the day pacing around the house, making plans, panic prowling after them. The house is in a state of tremendous disrepair. Its boundaries have become porous: moss creeps in through the broken windows to carpet the floor, a tree reaches its branches through one of the living room windows, mold mottles the bathroom walls. There is an entire family—or perhaps village?—of raccoons residing on the second floor. Many of the rooms are empty, but others are home to a strange assortment of furnishings. A claw-foot tub stands alone in the center of one room. In another, a taxidermied buck hangs slightly crooked on the wall, one of its antlers broken off. Raffi finds a box of yellow notepads, strangely pristine. An old fur coat, moth-eaten, in a closet. A surprising number of broken mirrors. There is a study whose floor is papered in books and magazines, as though victim of a small, localized tornado. In one room, there is a bed that looks as though some enormous creature ate a few bites of it like a sandwich. Beside the bed, there's a nightstand on top of which Raffi finds a book of poems. The house feels both eerie and familiar. They keep thinking they will know what is behind the next door. Mostly they are wrong—mostly there is nothing but dusty air—but sometimes they are right.

The house tries to help Raffi. It closes doors softly behind them, it warms the light that slants through the windows. The house loves Raffi—how could it not, when it knows them so entirely?

It was the ghost who dreamt up the House of Discontent after Raffi's aunt died. Of course, that was before the bear attack, before the ghost was a ghost, back when he was just Graham. Raffi—who was a niece then—had moved to Paradise to be near their great-aunt, who was dying. It was a decision they couldn't entirely explain. They had always been terrified of death, but when their mom told them about the cancer, said she didn't know how Zlata would cope, out there in Montana with no one to care for her—*no Jewish community at all, and her so private she'd starve before asking for food*—Raffi said, *I'll go.* They'd finished college a few weeks earlier and they could already tell it was going to be another bad summer. *Are you sure?* Raffi's dad asked later, and Raffi was surprised to find they were. They packed up their old Civic, quit their job in the observational cosmology lab, broke up with their boyfriend, Caleb, presenting the decision as a mutual one—*neither of us wants to do long-distance*—and he'd acquiesced to this version of things, as they'd known he would. To their aunt, they let the move be a favor they were asking of her: a place to reset, to reassess the shape of their life.

And for a while this view of things held. Aunt Zlata weakened incrementally, so that the change was hard to notice until some measurement of daily living quantified it: a fall going down the stairs, a new difficulty opening pill bottles, a sudden inability to understand clocks. Raffi made themself useful—got a lift installed on the stairs, found an automated pill dispenser, learned about portable oxygen concentrators and different brands of nasal cannulas—but this still left them with more free time than they'd ever had. To fill this time, they learned to snowboard, got a part-time job at the nearby ski resort, met Graham, found the perfect recipe for a flourless chocolate torte, ate roughly a hundred slices with their aunt, who'd developed an astonishing sweet tooth as a side effect of one of her meds, and fell into deep and lasting love with the mountains. Even when Aunt Zlata slipped out of the house at 3:00 A.M., thinking it was morning, and fell on the ice; even when Raffi had to restrain her as she tried to climb out of her hospice bed, whispering in languages Raffi couldn't understand; even when the doctor said, in the euphemistic hospital phrasing that Raffi hated, that they ought to prepare themself; even though they'd come to Montana for this very reason—even then, Raffi didn't truly believe their aunt was going to die.

Afterward, they couldn't bring themself to go back to her house. Instead, they went to Graham's couch. That first night, when he heard them crying, he lay down next to them and held them so tightly that the sensation of floating untethered in outer space eased. *I don't know what to do with all the sadness*, Raffi said. *There's no room to live around it.*

Maybe we need to build the sadness its own place to live, Graham said. *What would its house look like?* And when Raffi closed their eyes, there it was, fully formed, looking like any normal house until you stepped inside. Together, Raffi and Graham walked through the door and began imagining the house's architecture.

The next night, Raffi said, *Will you sleep with me again?* They didn't know if it was an appropriate thing to ask. They were friends, not lovers, and Raffi didn't want to change that. But he nodded, padded into the living room later that night and lay down next to them. *Maybe there should be a room for forgetting*, he said, *not permanently, but a place to go when you need a rest.* Raffi listened to the steady rhythm of his heartbeat. *A room where memories can lose their sharp edges*, they said.

It became their nightly ritual, lying side by side, imagining new rooms until sleep came. Even after they'd built enough rooms for Raffi's sadness, even after Raffi could fall asleep without crying, they held to the routine. The house got a Room of Unexpected Joy, for the feeling of driving around a bend in the road and seeing the mountains appear, for discovering that it's possible to invent a relationship that doesn't have anything to do with the drop-down menu life presents you. Its name remained the House of Discontent, but it didn't mind. It knew that whatever its name, it had enough rooms for every sort of emotion.

The most significant limitation of the physical-House of Discontent is that its space is finite. Raffi is both relieved and alarmed by this limitation. They are already daunted by the work in front of them. But how are they supposed to fit all their sadness into a bounded space?

The rooms on the first two floors will have to be fluid, they decide, changing from the Room of This to the Room of That as necessity dictates. The attic, with its sloping ceilings, will be for daydreams, wishes, and aspirations, which itself feels like an aspiration—the idea that someday such a space might be necessary. The bears will go in the basement. Raffi doesn't want any bears in the house at all, but that's not how the House of Discontent works. So Raffi will put them in the basement and lock the door.

Raffi thinks they know the house. It's lived inside them for so many years, but containing something isn't the same as understanding it. Raffi doesn't know that the bears aren't the only ones who live in the basement. Raffi doesn't know that the ghost lives down there too.

The years between Aunt Zlata's death and the ghost's death have a golden hue to them now. In grief, Raffi found themself asking, for the first time in their life, what it was that they wanted—not in the way of goals or aspirations, but in a day-to-day, moment-to-moment way. In grief, they couldn't care anymore about what people thought of them. Couldn't care about genius or success. They searched out small joys to help them get through the days: alpenglow on the mountains, a moose snacking on the tree outside their window, the first snowboard run of the day in fresh powder, the meals Graham cooked without ever expecting Raffi to do the dishes. They discovered they could build a life out of these small joys: moving in with Graham, teaching snowboarding for money, painting and reading and hiking, falling in love with Graham's friend Kay, falling back out of love, but gently. Ending each day sitting on the couch in front of the woodstove, dreaming up new rooms for the House of Discontent.

Maybe there's a universe where Raffi's whole life unfolded this way. Where Raffi never suggested mountain biking, that morning up near Glacier. Where the ghost never careened around that tight twist in the trail, whooping with delight, crashing full speed into the bear. Where Raffi had remembered to grab the bear spray that was sitting on their counter. Where the attack became a story they told each other for the rest of their long, entwined lives. Instead of the destruction of the world.

The ghost likes the bears, which is surprising, since they're the reason he's a ghost. He has the sense that this is not the first time their paths have intersected, not the only time he has died in this way. In death, the ghost has become philosophical; he finds it difficult to blame the bears. They each followed the path a zillion small choices and chances set them on—blue sky, the scent of berries, the joy of rushing wind—and when their paths intersected, when the ghost rode his mountain bike around the path's bend and directly into the bear, they each did what they had to do, which is to say, the bear attacked and the ghost died. It doesn't hurt him to think about it now. In campfire stories, ghosts have many regrets. But in reality regret is a heavy emotion and the ghost is insubstantial. Anytime he tries to hold on to regret, it falls straight through.

What the ghost wishes is that Raffi would walk down the basement stairs, so he could tell them that none of this is their fault. That whatever story they're telling themself is the wrong one. He would tell them it isn't so bad being dead. He would say, *I'm sorry I've left you all alone, but you're going to be okay,* and Raffi would shake their head, and they would both cry, but the words would plant a seed inside Raffi that would eventually blossom into truth. The two of them would sit together, overlapping slightly, speculating about how the singular bear who killed the ghost had turned into a multitude of bears. They would laugh at the bears' antics—even Raffi wouldn't be able to help themself—and the future in front of them would be a promise instead of a casket.

The ghost doesn't know that Raffi doesn't know that he's in the basement. Still, he doesn't blame them for their continual failure to walk down the stairs. He knows that sometimes surviving is the harder end of the deal. That guilt can be a tumor, a curse, a locked door. Unlike regret, pity is light enough to stay in his body. Sometimes it fills him so entirely that it lifts him off the ground like a helium balloon, and he can't come down until the emotion fades. It's never buoyant enough to lift him all the way through the ceiling though, not even when he spends whole days thinking about what it must have been like for Raffi to watch the attack, to decide to go for help, to bike so hard and fast that afterward their calves cramped into solid knots of muscle. To have been too slow anyway.

Raffi has never built anything before. When they were dating Kay, they liked to sit in a corner of her woodshop and watch her work, but they never so much as held a drill. This is going to change. They drive to the nearest Home Depot, an hour and a half away, and put everything from their dad's list in their cart. They don't even look at prices, though prior to this they were the sort of person who considered fruit a luxury. They wander through the rows of stacked lumber, running their fingers across the boards, breathing in the cut-wood smell. They call their dad. *How do I pick good lumber?* they ask. *For what?* he wants to know. *I'm not sure*, they say and hear the hesitation that means he's wondering if he should be worried. Each time they hear this silence, they try to decide whether they want him to intuit the real answer, get on a plane, come take them home. But where is home? Not anywhere he could take them.

He tells them to check the wood for warping, so Raffi hangs up and lays different lengths of wood on the smooth concrete floor. They squat, tilting their head upside down so that the boards are at eye level. They find the pieces so warped they're like tiny teeter-totters. They begin to put these ones back, then change their mind. There will need to be a Room of Warping, a room for the way it feels to deform so gradually you don't even realize it until you lean up against some flat surface.

When they try to check out, their card gets declined. The total is more than they make in a month at the restaurant. They use the card attached to the other bank account. Soon that money will run out too.

Raffi lets the house tell them what to work on. When they're not working, they feel raw and irritable. Cheerfulness becomes increasingly difficult to put on. They cut their shifts at the diner, try not to think about the dwindling numbers in their bank account. At night, they work until their eyes blur, and then they go up to the attic and sit in the little twin bed and watch YouTube—time-lapse videos where men moving at the speed of sandpipers build tiny houses in twenty minutes, DIY guides about how to repair molding or install a floating wall or use a router. One night, they come across a TED Talk called "Impossible Design." The architect is a woman named Alice, who reminds them of someone, though they can't think who. They get in the habit of falling asleep to her careful sentences. They like how she doesn't smile, doesn't seem to care what the audience thinks of her. Raffi's dreams fill with buildings that twist and curve in impossible ways, houses like enormous sandcastles that wash away with the tide.

The rooms in the physical-House are not the same as the ones in the thought-House. That version of the House of Discontent was co-constructed with the ghost. This house they build alone, their internal architecture remade by new grief, new solitude. They hear Alice's voice as they draw up plans. *It is tempting to frame possibility as an objective characteristic, but that is an oversimplification. Possibility is less an innate characteristic than an invented one.* Raffi sketches and erases, sketches again.

They dedicate an entire wing of the house to regret. They build a Room of What You Should Have Done. Inside, a labyrinth of plywood. No matter where you enter, which way you turn, you end up at a dead end. A Room of Missed Opportunities, a Room of Wasted Moments.

In the Room of Secret Shames, Raffi paints a silver-gray horse, a copse of trees, a little pond whose light glimmers golden. They take the crate of glasses they found in the pantry and throw them against the walls until the painting is fractured and the floor glitters with glass. They cover the windows with dark red tissue paper, and when they finish, they turn around and there is the shadow of a girl standing beside the horse. When they walk closer, she disappears. They return often, catch glimpses of her out of the corner of their eye. They sit on the crate that had held the glasses and talk to her, sometimes. To her and to the girl they used to be.

They work in that wing until they are sick with regret and then they head to other rooms. They try to create a Room of Loneliness—paint the walls and windows black, carpet the floor in dark blue velvet—but it shifts of its own accord to become the

Room of Stars. A lamp projects constellations onto the walls and ceiling. Raffi sets up speakers, which play NASA recordings of binary stars that make them feel like they are listening to the universe's heartbeat.

The ghost teaches the bears to walk through walls. He doesn't do it on purpose, but they are always watching him, and he is always trying and failing to walk through the door at the top of the basement stairs. (He passes through it without a problem but ends up exactly where he started.) One day, a bear nudges him aside—knocks him out of the way, really, with one enormous paw, but everything feels gentler when you're mostly incorporeal—and walks through the door. Unlike the ghost, the bear does not end up where it started. Humans are easy to contain. Bears are not so easily put in boxes.

The ghost hurls himself after the bear. He ends up where he started. *Wait*, he shouts, *stop, take me with you.* He runs pointless loops through the door. He tries to pound his fists against it, but of course they go straight through. When the ghost was alive, he'd tried to distance himself from men who yelled and punched and threatened their way through life. Now he wishes for just an iota of that violence. Just one solid blow against the door's infuriating facade.

Eventually, he gives up and sits at the top of the steps, waiting for the bear to return. Another bear lies on the stairs next to him like a babysitter for an unruly cub, its body liquid, its big head resting on the top step. The ghost ranks his emotions for the bear:

1. Worry for what Raffi will feel if they see a bear wandering through their house

2. Envy that the bear went so easily where he, for all his trying, could not
3. Hope
4. Pity

The bear looks deeply bored by his enumeration. The ghost knows by now that bears do not think in lists, nor do they feel any need to name their emotions. But he lacks a more sympathetic audience.

The boundary-crossing bear returns. The ghost throws himself over its back and thinks a question at it so loudly that the bear growls and rolls onto its back, as if it could crush the ghost. But death by bear is like chicken pox—you can only get it once. The ghost passes through the bear so he is lying on its stomach. He props his chin up and looks at the bear. *Well?* he says, and the bear lets out a big whuff of air through its nose and begins answering the ghost's many questions.

Raffi turns the master bathroom into the Room of Submersion. They fill the enormous tub and squeeze in a few drops of food coloring until the water is seafoam green, then add handfuls of salt for good measure. They buy blue lightbulbs and paint the sandcastle from their dream on one of the walls, its top brushing the ceiling. They paint sea creatures, fish, anemones, a giant octopus reaching one of her tentacles toward the lip of the tub. They buy a sound machine that fills the room with ocean waves, and maybe this is why they don't hear the bear approaching. Or maybe it's because bears, in spite of their bulk, are silent by nature. They are painting suckers onto one of the octopus's tentacles when they sense the bear behind them. They don't turn around. When has looking at bears ever made things better? They don't scream or move or breathe. They wait and wait and the crashing of the waves sounds like *so—rry, so—rry* and then, all at once, a certain easing of the air tells them the bear is gone.

They turn and walk out of the Room of Submersion, out of the Room of Stars, out of the House of Discontent. It is a clear, cold night, and even though the sky looks very far away, Raffi screams their rage at it. They are not scared. They are furious. They will burn the house to the ground. They will make the bears suffer for what they have done. Instead of going up to their bed in the attic, they grab their tent and sleeping bag. It's too cold for camping, but they don't care. They set their tent up, climb inside it, and lie there, shivering. The woods around them creak and moan. Every rustle is something with teeth and claws. Even the wind growls.

Huddled deep inside their sleeping bag, they research how to burn down a house. It is surprisingly easy, according to the internet. A house, they read, can go up in flames in under five minutes. The autoignition temperatures of common building materials are between 595 and 740 degrees Fahrenheit; the ambient heat of a house fire can reach 1,100 degrees. Behind Raffi's eyes, the rooms of the House of Discontent burst into spontaneous flame. It hurts them to think about. The night passes slowly. A roof can collapse in as few as six minutes. A bear can run at thirty miles per hour. A human is a fragile object. A bike helmet cannot protect a head from a bear's jaws. The House of Discontent will burn faster than a normal house because Raffi has filled its rooms with food for flames. Once it is gone, what will Raffi have left?

By the time the sun rises, Raffi's rage has burned itself to ash. They go back inside. As they walk through the house, two things strike them: how beautiful it is, this place they considered destroying, and how many of the rooms are something close to finished. They'd thought they might feel a sense of accomplishment, a lightness like the sun streaming through the windows in the Room of Unexpected Joys, but there is no Room of Unexpected Joys in this version of the House of Discontent, so maybe they shouldn't be surprised that what they feel is another permutation of panic.

Raffi goes into the smallest bedroom on the second floor, which they haven't begun working on yet. They lie down on the floor. They breathe in the emptiness. There is still so much work to be done, they tell themself, and after the main work is finished, there will be improvements to make. Rooms that will need to be turned into other rooms. *And then what?* Raffi asks the house. *Then you will have a home*, the house wants to say. *Then you can unlock the basement door.*

Raffi doesn't hear the answer. They have caught sight of a bear standing outside the open door, watching them. They stare and breathe and everything is quiet. The bear doesn't approach, just watches and watches and then turns and lumbers silently away.

The ghost can't help himself: he sends the bears to check on Raffi and report back. He knows this is wrong. Probably he's frightening Raffi, haunting them even. *Maybe I can't help myself because that's what ghosts are meant to do*, he thinks, but he doesn't believe it. He swears to himself that he will stop. Each time is the last time and so is the next and the time after that. The desire to know how Raffi is doing, what they are doing, is like a hunger, insatiable, though he doesn't eat anymore. The bears tolerate his requests, he doesn't know why. The bears can't tell the ghost if Raffi is happy or not. The ghost shows the bears a smile—though it feels like a ghastly impression—and the ghost shows the bears crying. *Yes*, the bears say to both.

Occasionally the bears leave without the ghost asking, walk

through the walls of the house into Outside. They don't go far, just far enough to smell the air, feel the sky and trees. When a bear returns from Outside, the other bears gather around, press their bodies together, revel in the way Outside-air tastes of damp earth, of the snow that will fall tomorrow. There is a part of the bears—small and quiet but ever-present—that can still feel their origin bear. When he digs into the damp earth after the rain, pulling up sweet-vetch roots to gnaw on, their claws twitch. When he crunches ants and beetle larvae, their teeth ache. When he catches the scent of a newborn moose, their noses crinkle. When the bears go to sleep in the basement, they can feel the rightness of a well-dug wallow, the way the dirt and leaves cradle their sleeping bodies.

The bears don't know why Raffi put them in the basement. Raffi's smell is familiar to the bears, but it is muddled with fear and pain and the overwhelming scent of the ghost. The bears miss Outside, but bears aren't the sort of creatures who wish for what isn't. They live here now, and Raffi is a part of them, like the origin bear, like the ghost, like the smell of snow.

Raffi decides they will work more slowly. They make rules. In the morning, if they can't sleep, they will read until the clock says eight. In the middle of the day, they will pause for lunch, and if they can't make themself eat, they will at least drink an entire mug of tea. (They throw out the box of tea the ghost gave them last Christmas, then pick it out of the trash and put it back on the shelf, but drink a different one.) At night, they will stop working when the sun sets.

The last rule is the problem. Evening becomes an abyss, the vacant hours filling themselves with memories of the ghost: reading next to each other in front of the woodstove, snowboarding through powder so light it felt like surfing on a cloud, pulling their face masks down to smile at each other. The way the ghost had shown them that family wasn't about blood. All of it irreplaceable. They run into the brick wall of that word over and over, and it never hurts any less. And with each collision they face the same fact: it was a single moment. That was all it took to catapult Raffi into this new universe. All they need to do is go back and say *let's bike later,* say *how about a hike,* say *slow down.* And they can't.

The ghost gets depressed. He would have thought depression was too dense to fit inside him, but he should have known from his past life: depression doesn't go inside you, it becomes you. *Who knew someone intangible could be so heavy?* the ghost thinks as he lies on the basement floor. He can barely stand up now, forget about floating toward the ceiling. He tries to fill himself with pity to see if it will lift him up onto his feet, but it only makes him feel worse. *This is my fault,* the ghost thinks. *I suggested mountain biking, I went too fast, I'm the reason there are bears in the basement. I asked the bears to check on Raffi, knowing it would scare them, what kind of a person am I?* The ghost's vision dims, and he realizes he is sinking slowly into the floor. He decides it's no more than he deserves. He will disappear into the ground. He won't send any more bears to bother Raffi.

The bears are concerned about the ghost. They take turns lying next to him. They can sink into the floor too if they want; heaviness comes naturally to bears. The ghost only wants to talk about the mistakes he made, and the bears don't understand mistakes. *It's when you do the wrong thing,* the ghost says. *Wrong?* a bear asks. *The opposite of right,* the ghost says. *Right?* a bear asks. The ghost sighs. He tries to think of an example that would make sense to a bear. *Imagine there are two bushes*, he says, *each filled with berries. Like berries*, the bear says. *I know*, says the ghost. *So imagine one of the bush's berries are poisonous and the other ones aren't. Now assume you don't want to die* (the ghost doesn't think there are suicidal bears, but once he might have scoffed at the idea of a suicidal ghost, so he covers his bases). *Can you figure out which berries are the right berries to eat?*

The bear cocks its head exactly like the poodle the ghost had as a kid. The ghost feels a certain pleasure in having been killed by an animal who so impressively integrates ferocity and adorableness. *Right berries are good-smelling berries?* a bear asks. *Sure*, the ghost says. He's lost track of the metaphor, but the bears' solicitousness warms him. He lifts himself out of the ground and drapes his body over the bear, who is half buried in the floor next to him. *Good bear*, he says, like he used to say to the poodle.

To make the evenings bearable, Raffi turns their attention to the attic. Though they've been sleeping up there, they haven't done anything with the space except sweep and put sheets on the bed. It's meant to be the place for aspirations, for wishes, but their only wish is to change the past, and that sort of wish is just another name for regret. *Possibility is an invention*, they remind themself. They fill an entire cart at Home Depot with green and growing plants that they perch near the windows. They hang paper lanterns from the rafters, cover the floor in brightly colored rugs, stack pillows to sit on. They let the architect's voice guide them: *to truly innovate, we must reach beyond ourselves, beyond what we can know or see.* They try to make the space feel like an embrace. Like being held.

The attic is the farthest place in the house from the basement, and Raffi feels safe there, until the night the bear climbs the ladder. Its nose appears first, pointing up through the hole in the floor, then a paw appears followed by another, and the bear hoists itself up in the way bears have of being both graceful and clumsy at once. The light in the attic is a wishful light, warm yellow with hints of rose, and it haloes the bear. They watch each other, Raffi's heart settling back to its normal rhythms. Then the bear turns and climbs back down the ladder—more clumsy than graceful in this direction—and Raffi is alone again.

The basement is the one part of the house that remains unchanged from its original state: a dark, dank space with a concrete floor and exposed wooden joists overhead. There is a large worktable in one corner, fluorescent lights that are never turned on. Sometimes the ghost imagines his own body laid on the table, a figure bent over him emptying his insides out, but when he looks, it is only ever the bears he sees. The bears don't seem to mind the bleakness of the basement, but sometimes they dream about where they came from. Their origin bear catches salmon, and the bears talk to one another of the quicksilver flash, the slick squish, the rough of scales against their tongues. The feeling of standing amidst the river's roar and roil. The ghost listens and realizes, with a rush of love that makes his whole body blur, that he wants the bears to have the things they miss.

The next time the ghost sees a bear heading off to Outside, he says, *Could you bring me back a few things?* The bears are used to the ghost's strange requests by now. The Outside-bear drops a clump of snow quilled with pine needles at the ghost's feet a few hours later. The ghost has only the vaguest idea of what he wants to do. *Help me?* he thinks to the house, which pulses with enthusiasm. It has been waiting for him to ask.

* * *

The next night, Raffi watches the top of the ladder, waiting for the bear to reappear. They are trying to remember how to make wishes that look forward instead of backward. This used to be as effortless as breathing, so habitual that the ghost joked that Raffi's favorite hobby was grandiose planning. They wanted to climb mountains and learn languages and understand the entire universe. Now Raffi's imagination is a muddy lens, the future they see through it grimy and shapeless. What is left for them to wish for? And where is the bear?

To name something impossible is to limit our own imagination. An architect's job—any artist's job—is to seek out ways to see past our own limitations.

Raffi climbs down the ladder, walks past the Room of Letting Go, past the Room of Difficult Decisions, down the stairs. They stop at the basement door. They can't explain what they're doing. Thinking is unbearable, the only way to live is through action. On instinct. They unlock the door. *Possibility.* Then they make their way back up to the attic where the architect's steadying voice waits for them.

When the bear climbs up the ladder a second time, Raffi tilts their head in a way that is almost invitation, and the bear takes it. It pads over to them, settles down on the floor by their side. Carefully, so carefully, Raffi reaches a hand out and rests it on the coarse cold fur between the bear's ears. Then, they try to imagine new futures. They make lists: Here is what I used to love, here is what I love now, here is what I might love in the future. Here is what I am left with.

What happens is unexpected—not a construction but a deconstruction. A self-portrait in retrograde, a shedding of skins and selves, of all the people they have tried to be, all the stories they have told themself about who they are. Deep in the woods with a bear by their side, they dream new possibilities into existence.

Down in the basement, the ghost cups snow in his hands, blows the flakes carefully into the air. They float, flout gravity, fall slowly to the ground. The snow builds up, layer upon crystalline layer, until it crunches in a familiar way beneath the bears' paws. The ghost plants pinecones, and Raffi dreams of trees and the house strings stars among the rafters in the basement, where the cobwebs used to be. Raffi can almost see it: what the house might become. The basement door open, the bears roaming freely. *Who decides what is possible?* A kitchen filled with sunlight, and there, sitting at the table—

CHAPTER TEN

Self-Portrait in Retrograde

Alice is waiting for me, but before I get out of bed I catalog my body. My morning routine for almost a year now. Tap a finger against my feet, knees, sternum. A little call-and-response. Are you there? No. Are you there? No.

Here is what I can still feel: the hollow between the heel and ankle of my left foot, the pad of my right index finger, a crescent along the side of my left breast, the smallest corner of my mouth. Here is where I am numb: everywhere else. Soon these last hold-outs of feeling will be gone, and I will float through the rest of my life untouchable.

In the kitchen, Alice has set a cake on the table next to a vase of flowers. "Happy birthday, love," she says, kissing me on the cheek—I know this from the movement of her body, the quiet sound of lips on skin. I am trying to replace feeling with my other senses. Here is what I am left with: The way Alice's outline glows in the morning sun. The scent of coffee. The birds outside chirping *scary-feet-scary-feet-scary-feet*. The flamboyance of the flowers. The words IN THE KINGDOM OF THE SICK printed painlessly across my left forearm.

"Breakfast cake?" I ask.

"I made it myself, so you have to pretend to like it or I'll be gravely offended." She lights the candle on top. "Make a wish."

When I close my eyes, I don't wish for a different ending. I don't wish my body unbroken, this moment or this life anything other than what it is. Here is what I wish for instead: not a different ending, but a different beginning. In the kaleidoscopic dark behind my eyes, I can almost believe such a thing is possible.

"Tell me about the first time we kissed," Alice says.

"How old were we?"

"Fifteen." Freshman year of high school. Year of it no longer being enough to beat the boys at four square. Year of staring in the mirror trying to discover the trick to being beautiful.

"I had braces and thought they were the ugliest thing in the world, but you said you liked the colors I'd picked out. Alternating blue and purple. It was the best compliment I'd ever gotten." I smile, pausing to think of details. "You invited me to sleep over at your house, and I convinced you we should stay up all night. I didn't have a goal in mind exactly, just this sense that there was something, somewhere I wanted to go with you where I'd never been before. And the only way to get there was to suspend all the real world's rules."

"It worked too."

"It must've been what, three in the morning?"

"At least. I pretended I heard a noise downstairs, that I was afraid of ghosts, but it was just an excuse to get close to you," Alice says.

"When I felt you pressed up against me . . . it was like my body was a house and for the first time the lights were turned on, all at once." I will my body to feel even the quietest echo.

"I can see you like that," Alice says, "blazing with light."

* * *

A month before my birthday—back when I can still feel Alice's lips against my cheek—she suggests the support group. "I think it would be good for you to have community," she says. "Make you feel less alone, offer some different perspectives."

"All I ever talk about is the numbness," I say. "I would rather talk about literally anything else."

"Fine, then join a book group or a cribbage club, I don't care. But you need to leave the house. You haven't showered in a week."

She sounds tired, and I feel like a petulant child. I should apologize, but I can't force the words out. I don't know if I'd be doing her a favor by ending things. If she's still in the relationship because she wants to be or only because it seems cruel to leave. I do know that whatever I say next will make things worse, so I grab my keys from the kitchen table and leave without saying goodbye.

The support group meets in the basement of a church, in a room that smells like stale coffee and old Bibles. I add this to the list of reasons why coming was a bad idea. I linger in the doorway, too aware of my greasy hair, the odor emanating from the T-shirt I've been wearing for days. Maybe twenty people stand in clusters or sit on folding chairs, the youngest at least a decade older than me. The thoughts I have been refusing burst their dam: it isn't fair, I'm too young, the treatment should have worked. Alice, twelve years older, was meant to be the first one to take up residence in the kingdom of the sick. I hate every wrinkled stranger in this room, I hate Alice for making me come here, I hate myself most of all, for my self-pity, for believing there is such a thing as fairness. For thinking that any of this counts as real hardship. I'm almost relieved when a woman with a name tag that says CINDI with hearts over both *i*'s walks over and introduces herself as the organizer.

I had imagined something like AA, all of us sitting in a circle, going around telling our same stupid stories, but it's less formal than that. Cindi introduces me to a few people, and I say something about coffee and meander toward the table with its half-empty box of powdered doughnuts. The coffeepot has a name tag that says DRINKING TEMPERATURE.

Around me, people are talking about logistical difficulties: burns and cuts gone unremarked, falls caused by not being able to feel the ground, inexplicable bruises. About precautionary measures, alternative therapies, new theories. "I swear my hand has gotten a little less numb since I started taking ashwagandha," a man who looks like my grandfather says, holding up the hand in question for examination. "We installed temperature guards on all the faucets." "I heard they think it's a genetic mutation." "My cousin sliced her hand open on a jar and didn't notice until she slipped on the blood." Close to the coffee table, a tall woman, younger than most of the crowd, is saying to a brunette, "It's not like we can't still have sex."

"What's the point though?" the brunette asks.

"I like watching Joe's pleasure. It's not the same, of course, but it's like . . . mentally arousing." I save the phrase to tell Alice later, before remembering that I'm mad at her.

"I don't know, it doesn't seem very fun to me. I told Dave he should go on the dating apps if he wanted. Though the man can barely manage email, so we'll see."

The tall woman sees me watching and smiles. "What about you?" she asks.

I feel caught, unprepared. "My girlfriend and I have always had an open relationship." It doesn't answer the question—I don't even know what the question is—but the fact of the girlfriend seems to satisfy their curiosity.

"Well, aren't you two ahead of the curve," the brunette says. I shrug, gesture vaguely at my coffee cup, and duck away.

Outside the church, I suck in a lungful of cool, hyacinth-scented air. I can't bring myself to go home. I walk in a random direction, waiting for the anger to dissipate, but every time I think of the church it flares. I don't want the support of these strangers, don't want help figuring out how to live with what we've been given. I don't want Alice's lectures on ableism and perspective, the books she keeps leaving on my desk. I want to walk until I've found my way back to the kingdom of the well, where illness is a thing that belongs to other people.

"Remember the time I got chicken pox?" Alice asks. "And you told me you'd already had it."

"We were sixteen! Everyone's had chicken pox by then."

"Which was why I believed you. You skipped school to hang out with me. We must've watched a dozen movies."

"I made you take a calamine bath so that you wouldn't keep itching."

"I remember the pink water. And making you read out loud to me, so I wouldn't get bored."

"Always so impatient," I say, laughing.

"And then two weeks later, you had chicken pox too. I couldn't believe it. You looked so pleased with yourself. Exactly the same expression as my cat after he stole an entire stick of butter."

"It was worth it," I say. "It was all worth it."

* * *

Before my birthday, before the support group, before picking fights with Alice just to see if she'd stick around—before that, I convince her to seed her yard with wildflowers. The little cob house she built after she and Henry divorced feels like a physical representation of her person. I like the idea of painting myself into the frame, showing up as a riot of color, sometimes hidden by the snow but always returning in the spring. I'm surprised when she agrees, I promise to help with the planting. But now that the time has come, I lie on an un-hoed patch of grass and watch her work.

When she walks past, I grab her ankle and pull her down into the grass on top of me.

"You're not helping," she says.

"I'm not trying to."

I kiss her, gently at first, then deeper, sliding my right hand— the one that can still feel the warmth of her skin—up the back of her neck until my fingers are tangled in her hair in the way that makes her body go soft against mine. I can still feel the way that kissing her pulls at something deep in my stomach; I try not to wonder for how long.

Lately we've been fucking with a kind of frenzy, our bodies crashing into one another whenever we're alone, her teeth leaving bruises on my skin that I can only sometimes feel, her fingers insistent inside me, saying again again again, and my body responds, and it is like she is trying to give me enough pleasure to last for all the years to come, as if desire were a thirst that could be sated once and for all.

But here on the grass, our movements are slow and tender. We kiss, and I keep my eyes open so I can see the blue sky above us, the curve of Alice's cheek, the branches of the nearby oak tree.

Because my eyes are open, I see the exact moment Alice's face changes, a crease furrowing itself into her forehead. She looks down and I follow her gaze and it is only then that I realize she has slipped her hand inside the waistband of my jeans.

"Nothing?" she asks.

"Keep going." I wriggle out of my pants right there in the yard without worrying about whether someone will peek through the fence or spot us from a high window, because I need to see what is happening. I need to know. I watch her finger disappear inside me and I feel nothing. She's watching my face and so I close my eyes. "Keep going," I whisper again, and try to remember the times our bodies have been here before, try to exist inside the memories, but instead I see Caleb and the men who came after him, my body forgetting the desire that is so newly learned, forgetting Alice, and then I do feel something and it is her hand on my cheek and I realize I am crying.

"Come on," I say, and lead us inside to the bedroom. I open the drawer next to the bed, pull out the strap-on we bought together— this, at least, I remember, the way I laughed at the sheer number of options, the way Alice insisted on the color purple.

"Are you sure?" she asks.

And I nod, yes, yes, because I want to believe that we can still make love, want to have something be a part of my body that I am not supposed to be able to feel. I push myself into her and she pulls me closer and we both pretend, as hard as we can, that this is working, but it is so clear that it is not. I stop moving and she holds me and we try to wait the sadness out.

Alice watches me as though I'm a house on the verge of collapse, as though she's trying to see her way back to solidity. "You could get a tattoo," she says.

"Excuse me?"

"It wouldn't hurt at all."

"That's a pretty half-assed silver lining," I say.

"You could get a lot of tattoos."

We both laugh, and because this becomes funnier and funnier, two hours later, Alice is driving us to a tattoo parlor that takes walk-ins. I have never wanted a tattoo—my family's history with them too fraught—but I like the idea of marking my body, reminding myself it belongs to me. Of extracting a silver lining with needles.

The tattoo artist has a shaved head and a mountain-scape across their collarbones. "I want words, like from a typewriter," I tell them, holding out my forearm and tracing a finger across it. "Can you have it say IN THE KINGDOM OF THE SICK?"

"You read the Sontag," Alice says.

The tattoo artist comes back, cleans my arm, presses the transfer paper against my skin so that the words are left behind in faint blue ink. They pick up the tattoo gun, and Alice takes my other hand as if this will hurt me, but it feels like nothing at all.

"How about a favorite memory?" I ask.

"From when we were how old?"

"Eighteen."

"Easy," Alice says. "The year we went to prom together. The school was scandalized and my mother refused to take pictures of us, kept calling you my friend. Said I wasn't allowed to leave the house in a suit."

"She'd gotten you that pink tulle dress. You would've looked like a cupcake."

"All the fighting was worth it though. You were so damn sexy in that tux. I fucked you in the girls' bathroom because I couldn't wait until we got home."

I smile, run the pad of my right index finger down the side of her face, trace it over her lips and feel the slight ridges. The fact that I am allowed to do this still feels like a revelation. That she shivers beneath my touch, more so. She slides her own fingers over the crescent of feeling along the side of my left breast. Cups it and squeezes, gentle at first, then harder. I am a constellation of desire, a few burning points of light amidst so much darkness.

Before there are words printed across my skin, we go to the beach, which is empty. It's a warm day for January, but a cold day for swimming.

"I regret this plan already. Is it too late to bail?"

"Definitely," Alice says. "Besides, it's balmy out."

"Great, so you're coming in with me?"

"Absolutely not." She waves the towel she's carrying. "I'm too old for that sort of nonsense. I'll be here to warm you up after."

She spreads the towel out and we sit facing the ocean, watch a wave wash away the remnants of a sandcastle.

"When I said the ocean, I meant in summer," I say. We've made a two-pronged plan: assume the worst while trying to stave it off. A compromise between our preferred coping mechanisms. It was Alice who came up with the list—all the things I want to feel while I still can. Hot springs, a salt scrub, a kitten's belly, a deep tissue massage . . .

"You'll feel it more dramatically right now," she says, and we laugh, though I know we're both thinking about how summer might be too late. The numbness is spreading inconsistently, randomly— stable for a week or two, then devouring three new areas in a day.

"Fortification," Alice says, pulling a handle of Fireball out of her bag.

"Too old for skinny-dipping, but not for Fireball, the favored libation of high schoolers everywhere?"

She elbows me. "Fine, I won't share."

I grab the bottle and take a swig. The cinnamon burns its way down my throat. We pass the bottle back and forth, listen to the arrhythmic crashing of the waves. I dig my feet into the sand, feel the damp grit of it.

"Okay, enough dawdling. Get in the water."

"Come with me," I say. "Please?" I kiss her, taste cinnamon on her tongue.

"I hate you," she says, and pulls her shirt over her head. We strip quickly, looking around to make sure there's no one in sight.

"Go go go!" We hold hands, charge forward, high-stepping into the waves, and I have a sense of déjà vu, as if we've done this many times before. The cold is a solid object with sharp edges. I feel it everywhere except the places I don't. It's so cold that I laugh through my chattering teeth. I take a breath, plunge under the water. Come up gasping, tasting salt. My whole body tingles.

"Tell me about the first time we went to the beach together," Alice says.

"How old were we?"

"Thirteen."

Summer of the pink house, summer of the horse. Summer of Britt, cowardice, the closed door. "Let's see . . . I used to go to my aunt's house on Long Beach Island every summer, back before she moved to Montana. You were staying next door, your parents asked my aunt if she'd mind watching you one night. I didn't want a stranger to come over, but once I met you, everything changed. We saw each other every day after that, I cried when it was time to go home."

"The beginning of our pen pal era. I used to check the mail every day. And the sheer number of gel pens I went through . . ."

"That was the year my parents divorced. I kept having nightmares where the lights went out and when they came back on the whole world was empty."

"I told you that when it happened, you should picture the two of us at the beach together in the sunshine."

"I don't know how I would've made it through that time without you."

Before the beach—before I've given up hope, before the creep of the numbness feels as inevitable as aging—Alice finds me sitting naked on the bathroom floor, looking at myself in the mirror. When I close my eyes, my hand disappears. So does my right shoulder. I open my eyes and stare at the missing places, order them to return, order my body to obey me.

Alice sits on the floor next to me, holds her arms out, and I collapse into them. She is such a solid, certain person. I feel her waiting for me to tell her what's wrong, but I don't want to. I want comfort and I want to be alone and I want her to ask what's wrong so that I'll have to get the moment over with, but she doesn't. She waits.

"My shoulder," I say. I still have four days of antibiotics left, but we both understand what this means. The doctor made it clear—if the drugs worked, the numbness would stop spreading, possibly even reverse course. If they worked. "There's no guarantee," the doctor had said, "but young people do seem to have better results."

Alice lets a breath out. "Antibiotics aren't the only option. I've been reading about alternative treatments."

I pull away from her. "I'm not some poorly designed building for you to problem solve," I say. "Why do you keep acting like you can fix this?"

"I'm trying to help."

"You don't want to be with someone who's broken."

"That's your language, not mine," she says. "You don't get to decide what I want."

We sit in silence until my anger gives way to sadness and I let my body sag against hers. She pulls me closer. "I wasted so much time," I say. All those years I spent running away from my own desire. Letting men use my body like it was something that belonged to them because that felt safer than owning it myself. "I wish we'd met earlier."

"A twelve-year age gap gets creepy pretty fast when you start moving back in time," she says, smiling, but when I don't smile back her face turns serious. "You know, my mom had me when she was nineteen, but she always said she'd have been a better parent if she'd waited a decade. I bet there's a universe where you and I are the same age."

I shake my head. "I'm trying not to live in alternate worlds anymore."

"Imagination doesn't have to be avoidance, Raf. It can be a tool to help you imagine new futures." When I look unconvinced she says, "Come on. Give me an age."

I'm not in the mood to play games, but I know I've been unfair to her, so I say, "Seven."

She pauses for a long moment. "Okay," she says, "when you were seven you hadn't told anybody else yet, but you'd told yourself, started noticing the way your best friend chewed her pencil and wore her butterfly clips just so. When the other kids talked about who was sitting in a tree K-I-S-S-I-N-G, you thought about her and it was like a delicious secret you were keeping with yourself."

I picture myself at seven, the bowl cut that lives on in photographs. The lessons I was already learning about who and how to love. "Seventeen?"

"We sat next to each other in English class," she says, quicker this time. "We'd write each other notes inside our books, swap them back and forth under the desk. I asked you to the Valentine's Dance in the margins of *Madame Bovary.*"

I let the image bloom in my mind, let it overwrite my memories of drinking until my head spun, a boy whose name I barely remember groping at me under a blanket.

"Thirteen?" I close my eyes and I'm in my dad's house, watching Britt knock at the door, and in this world of Alice's creation, I say, *of course I'll help you*, and just like that, anything becomes possible.

"Nine," I say. Then, twenty-two, fourteen, twenty-six. I listen as Alice rewrites my history, writes us a history together, until it spools out behind us so bright and beautiful that I can almost believe it is real.

On the morning of our one-year anniversary, I wake in Alice's bed. It is the last day of August. A year since we first met. Since I went to Alice's lecture on "Impossible Design," asked if I could buy her a drink sometime, the words tripping over themselves but somehow making their way into the world, creating a whole new universe.

The sun is shining in through the east-facing windows and I think: *one year one year one year.* I have never been the type to acknowledge anniversaries, I don't even like the word, but dating a woman, dating Alice, has changed all the rules. Alice is lying on her back next to me, her head flung across my left arm, the covers pushed down so I can see the rise of her breasts, the curve of her rib cage. The lines of her body are still astonishing to me. My arm is asleep beneath the weight of her head, but I don't want to wake her, so I ignore the prickling and drift back off, my body hot with sun.

When I wake again, it's to Alice's kiss. "Happy anniversary, baby," she says, and I smile up at her, a goofy, uncontrollable grin.

"Happy anniversary to you too." I wrap my arms around her, pull her closer. My left hand is still tingling, but I hardly notice it. I kiss her again.

"Is this my anniversary present?" she asks.

"One of them." I run my right fingers down over her breasts to the heat between her legs. She bites my lip as I push a finger, then two, inside her. Her eyes close, her breath quickens. The whole world narrows to the two of us, I exist nowhere except here inside this body electric with desire.

Later, I sit at the kitchen table in my boxers and watch as Alice puts a pot of coffee on. Underneath the table, I flex and unflex my left hand. The prickling has abated, but the feeling hasn't come back.

"The mint is trying to destroy the basil," Alice says, poking at her window box herb garden.

I think of saying: my hand is numb. The thought is a window into another morning. There, Alice would drop the mug she's using to water the herbs, forget about the coffee brewing, say, *for how long?* Say, *but maybe it's just asleep?* In that morning, we would leave the coffee to burn itself bitter and go to the ER, because both of us have seen enough of the news lately to know what this might mean, and a man with gloves and a mask would examine me, and he would say, *there's nothing to do but wait and see.* In that morning, by the time we got back to Alice's apartment, all the light would have left the windows. It wouldn't be the same place anymore.

"You'll find a way to save it," I say instead, and the words are my real anniversary gift, a doorway to a different universe. Here, my love, take this beautiful, sunlit morning. Sit with me and we will drink coffee and look out at the flowers and I will rest my hand against your cheek and I will feel your skin, so soft beneath my fingers, I'll feel all of it, every last thing.

* **III** *

CHAPTER ELEVEN

A Different Beginning

I / VIDDUI

Insofar as the dead know anything, they're probably omniscient. In which case you already know that I didn't miss your calls that night. That I wasn't sleeping like I'd told people (my mother, yours, various therapists). Human memory is highly susceptible to suggestion, I've heard, and for a long time I hoped that if I repeated this lie enough, eventually I might believe it. Might remember being asleep, which is to say, nothing. But, of course, the phone call was the end, not the beginning.

In the beginning, I was thirteen years old and Jacqueline shut the door in your face and I stood there staring at it, oblivious to her chatter, which had become unintelligible to me. I lived somewhere else already, I no longer spoke the same language. "I think you should go," I said, and waited for her to be gone. Alone in the house, I retrieved the envelope of money from beneath my mattress, and walked the blocks to your house, where all the lights were on and out in the yard I found you and your mother walking

Calypso in circles. You barely acknowledged me, your attention entirely focused on Cally, as though you could keep her alive by sheer force of will. I gave the envelope to your mom, handing it over wordlessly, then fled back to the relative safety of my father's temporary home. Leaving you to face the night alone. Waiting to see if Calypso would live.

It was your mom who reached out to me after Calypso died. "Britt won't get out of bed," she said, "she could really use a friend right now." I was dizzy with gratitude for the chance to redeem myself. Do you remember those afternoons I spent, sitting on the floor beside your bed, reading aloud? I could never tell if you knew I was there or not, if I was helping or making things worse. I read you kids' books about magical worlds where nobody died. I skipped the paragraphs that had to do with horses. I stopped hanging out with Jacqueline, sat alone at lunch, ignored the whispering. Soon, my parents would reconcile, I would move back to the town where I'd grown up, switch schools again. Soon, you would get out of bed, a different person than you'd been before, and I would once again become uncertain how to exist around you. But for a little while, I sat by your bed and read until my mouth was dry and my throat aching, and on my way out your mother would squeeze my shoulder and thank me for stopping by, and I would walk home in the dark illuminated by the knowledge that I was doing the right thing.

After Calypso died you became sharper, harder. There was no more mind reading. Once, we were watching TV and a commercial came on for something like tampons or body wash, a tall blonde riding a horse bareback on the beach, and I watched as your face shut like a door. You changed the channel without a word, barely spoke for the rest of the night. I never pushed on this silence.

Your dad moved out, taking your brother with him, and your mom picked up another job and you took care of your baby sister, like you always had, never complaining about it, or at least not to me. When I stayed at your house, we'd walk down to the Sunoco that was a block away, where the cashier let you buy six-packs of Smirnoff Ice even though no amount of makeup made you look twenty-one. He flirted with you in a way that made my skin crawl and also made me jealous. One time I saw you with him, in the food court at the mall. You were perched in his lap, feeding him Burger King fries. After that, he started calling you *babe* when we went to the Sunoco, and I wondered if this nickname sufficed to displace the others that had been hurled at you over the years, whether kids at your school had stopped coughing *dyke* at you when you walked past.

"Do you actually like him?" I asked once, brave on half a bottle of Smirnoff Ice.

"He's sweet," you said, "even though he doesn't look it." As if he were a pit bull, misapprehended, and not a twenty-six-year-old dating a high school sophomore. As usual, I let it go. But I was relieved when you said one night that you didn't want to go to the Sunoco anymore.

I was the one who called you, the night before you died. It was February, and I was the only one of my friends without a date to the Valentine's Dance, and I'd overheard a boy I liked saying he'd take me as long as I agreed to wear a bag over my head. I was sixteen and this still seemed cataclysmic, though within twenty-four hours it would be nothing, forgotten except insofar as it led me to calling you. It had been a few months since we'd spoken. This was one of the ways I was unfair to you—disappearing when things were going well, then reappearing when I was at my lowest.

"What's up?" you asked.

"I hate my life," I said.

"Join the club," you said, as I'd known you would. I wanted this reassurance that I wasn't alone. I hadn't yet realized there might be consequences to hating one's life. It was almost eleven, but when you asked if I wanted to meet you at the park, I agreed, surprising both of us. "Look who's grown a pair," you said. And it was true: mostly I abided by the rules. I didn't sneak out at night or have sex with boys or smoke cigarettes or marijuana. I'd never drunk more than one of your hard-won Smirnoff Ices. I didn't skip school. I got perfect grades. And all of it for what? I hated my life. So I said yes and I stuffed some pillows beneath my comforter and I skipped the third step from the bottom which creaked. I was giddy with my newfound power by the time I got to the park and saw you sitting on the swings.

Here is another truth: you were beautiful to me, that night on the playground. Wearing a hoodie so big you must have stolen it from a boy's closet, your eyeliner smudged, a new piercing glinting from your bottom lip. You handed me your Nalgene, dark with some mix of soda and alcohol, and I wanted to live up to you. I forced myself to take a sip, felt my stomach heave.

"So," you said, "tell me everything."

If there are a million universes, I think there are 999,999 where I didn't go after you the night Calypso died. Where we never spoke again. Where I couldn't call you that night. Where you are alive still. Therapist #2 told me I'm giving myself too much power, when I think like this. That you were ultimately going to do what you were going to do, regardless of my actions. But I don't believe that.

I think, for some of us, there will be moments in this life when we stand balanced on the knife's edge between here and gone, and which way we tip has little to do with decision or desire or fate and everything to do with circumstance. Which way the wind blows. Whether someone we love says something unbearably cruel. If a friend picks up the phone when it rings and rings.

Two years after you died, I met Alice. I'd started volunteering at an LGBTQ center—therapist #4's idea, which I was desperate enough to go along with. Before my first shift, I parked my parents' old minivan five blocks away, walked up to the building feeling as though there was a spotlight on me. But after a few weeks, my anxiety gave way to routine. My job was to sit behind the front desk and say hi to people when they came in and answer their questions: the bathroom was the third door on the left, the center was open until nine, the youth meetup was every second Thursday. One of those Thursdays, I parked at the center at the same time as another girl, around my age. She was taller than me, with sharp cheekbones and black hair.

"You here for the meetup?" she asked.

"No," I said, "I'm just a volunteer. I work the front desk."

"Ahh, the great-ally-to-gay pipeline," she said.

"Excuse me?"

"Give it three months," she said. I held the door open for her, and before she headed down the hall she said, "Well, Ally, I'm Alice. Nice to meet you."

It only took me two months to join her, but it was three before I'd acknowledge why I was there. In therapy, I obsessed over what it meant to decide I was queer, given how I'd treated you. I knew it wasn't meant to be a decision, exactly, but it felt that way. It was a decision to join Alice at the meetup, a decision to walk through that door, both literal and metaphorical. I could have chosen otherwise. "It makes me feel like a monster," I said to therapist #4, "like a hypocrite."

"Do you think there might be another way to look at it?"

"Like what?" I asked. She was a different sort of therapist than I'd had before. She would answer questions sometimes. In one of our first sessions, she told me she'd also lost a close friend to suicide.

"Have you considered that one of the reasons you weren't always kind to Britt is that you weren't ready to face certain truths about your own sexuality yet? Sometimes we're cruelest to the people who most remind us of our own selves."

The viability of this narrative relied upon my newfound, still tenuous queerness, which in turn depended on what my truest, most authentic desires were. All my actions became an answer to this question, but particularly Alice. Of course, this destroyed any possibility of having a real relationship with her. A person cannot be an answer to a question. A person is a person.

For a while, my relationship with Alice existed primarily in my mind, where the damage I could do was limited. I assumed her friendliness was a form of volunteer work. When she started inviting me to do things outside the center, I thought, how generous, how kind. When she invited me to prom, it was so offhand that I could have missed it, had I been less attentive to her every move.

She was talking about her mother—a woman who wore heels even inside her own home—who'd been trying to convince Alice to go dress shopping. "As if I've worn a dress once since she stopped being the one to pick my clothes," Alice said. Then: "You should come with me."

"Dress shopping?"

"No, to prom."

"Like a date?" I asked, startled enough to say what I was thinking.

Alice smiled. "Sure," she said. "Like a date."

"Okay," I said.

I was deliriously happy walking home, deliriously happy shopping with Alice at the mall, trying on boys' tuxedos, laughing, Alice saying, "Don't you make a handsome fourteen-year-old boy," watching her in the dressing room mirror as she slipped into a men's suit—she was too tall for boys'—and the jacket was enormous on her, but it looked incredible, buttoned over her black sports bra, it made my breath catch, was it queerness, that sudden hitch?

Deliriously happy all the way up to the evening of prom, my dad driving me over to Alice's, where I was planning to spend the night, and I felt the first flickering of anxiety, like static breaking through a TV show before the image snapped back into place.

I didn't know what my dad thought about all of it, whether he assumed we were only friends—were we only friends?—but I knew he was relieved to see me leaving my room, laughing at his ridiculous jokes. After you died, sometime in the morass of those early days, he came into my room and made me promise not to follow you. That was the phrasing he used, and I love my dad more than anyone in the world, even now, so far away, but I hated him in that moment for loving me so much that I was forced to stay in this life that had become intolerable.

* * *

It took Alice a little while to answer when I knocked and the anxiety crackled again, got louder when she opened the door looking furious, her cheeks pink. "It's an embarrassment," her mom was saying. "It's an embarrassment and I won't have you leaving the house like that."

"Come on," Alice said, taking my hand—a small thrill—and pulling me up the stairs. "Don't pay attention to her."

"I am your mother and you will not—"

But Alice shut the door on whatever it was she was not allowed to do and the music from her CD player drowned out the shouting. I thought she might cry, but she shook herself like a dog at the beach and smiled at me. "Best night of our young lives," she said.

After Alice drove us to the school and tried to take my hand and after I shied away from her like a skittish horse and after they stared at us—not just the other students, the parents and teachers too—and after I hid in the bathroom so I wouldn't have to face the eyes and after Alice came to find me, said, "fuck them all," and after I still couldn't force myself to do it, to take her hand, to say fuck them all, after that, we went back to her house and we must have looked as miserable as I felt because even Alice's mom stopped yelling. "Well," she said, "I don't know what you thought was going to happen."

In Alice's room, I sat on her bed with my knees pulled to my chest while she inflated an air mattress for me. "Did you even want to go?" she asked.

"Yes," I said. "I think so. I don't know."

She climbed onto the bed, sat down next to me. Her knee bumped into mine. I was shaking and I didn't want her to notice, but the more I tried to control it, the more intense the tremors became. "Hey," she said, "easy." She put an arm around my shoulders and the shuddering moved through both of us. She squeezed harder and I let myself topple into her, felled, and she held me so tightly that whatever had been moving me quieted. "What are you so afraid of?" she asked.

I rambled to therapist #5—the last one I had before I came to the City of Refuge—about you, about Alice, about what it meant to be a bystander to wrongdoing.

"It sounds," she said, "like you're drawing a parallel between yourself and Nazi sympathizers."

"A Nazi sympathizer is just a Nazi," I said.

"Okay. Between yourself and Nazis."

I shrugged. I was taking a philosophy class on ethics, and we'd been talking about the banality of evil.

"Do you think that's a fair parallel?"

"I think a lot of Nazis thought of themselves as good people," I said.

Another week, she read me the symptoms of childhood PTSD. "This isn't a diagnosis," she said, "just something to think about." Recurrent distressing dreams related to the traumatic event. Prolonged psychological distress at exposure to cues that symbolize or resemble an aspect of the traumatic event. Avoidance. Hypervigilance. Sleep disturbance. Substantially increased frequency of negative emotional states (e.g., fear, guilt, sadness, shame, confusion).

"Wait," I said. "What's the traumatic event here? My friend dying or the Holocaust?"

"I don't think we need to pick one," she said.

* * *

We spent the summer together, Alice and I, swimming in the ocean until our skin was tight with salt, then building elaborate drip castles while we talked about our plans for college, for the future, architecture, physics. We were the same in our ambition, both of us determined to claim spaces that too often belonged to men. We talked until the heat became too much and then we ran into the ocean together, holding hands, ducking under the waves. The first time we kissed, I was treading water in the Atlantic, and her lips tasted of salt and sun.

A summer inseparable and then the rending of fall. How was it possible that I spent all those years regretting how I'd treated you, then replicated the pattern the first chance I had? I'd thought my behavior with you was a mistake, $1 + 1 = 3$, that to change I only needed to recognize the wrongness. But the mistake wasn't a math equation, it was more like a word I'd been mispronouncing my entire life. If I didn't pay attention, I would echo it again and again.

I met Caleb during freshman orientation. He was funny, unafraid of taking up space, sweet in a midwestern way. Everybody liked him and he liked me, which was so implausible that at first it didn't feel like I was doing anything wrong when I let him buy me drinks at the bar on campus, which never checked IDs, found excuses to touch him, borrowed my roommate's low-cut shirts and dangling earrings. After these nights, I'd call Alice and we'd talk for hours while I walked endless loops around the quad. She was at a women's college a few hours away, where she said the student body was so gay that the straight girls had to form their own support group.

"Should I be worried?" I asked. "No," she said, "none of them look as good in a boy's tux as you."

I didn't mention Caleb to her—what would I have said about him?—and I didn't mention Alice to anyone at school, either. When we talked, I called her Al, partly for the intimacy of nickname, partly for the androgyny, the ambiguity it afforded me. Soon, I told myself, I would come out, officially, to everyone, but first, for a little while, I wanted to be someone else, someone I'd never been before. Popular, desirable. I drank until my head spun and I didn't think of you. I was thinking of you less those days. To my detriment.

The morning after going home with Caleb, I woke in his dorm bed, his roommate snoring loudly across the room. In the nauseating clarity of dawn, I understood your decision better than I ever had—the only solution to an impossible equation. The facts fanned themselves out before me and I lined them up like I was learning to do in my class on philosophical logic. If a, then b. If not b, then not a. If I loved Alice, then I wouldn't cheat on her with Caleb. If I'd cheated, then I didn't love her. If I didn't love her, I wasn't queer. If I wasn't queer, then the way I'd treated you had been only, entirely, my own fault.

I got in the car, started driving, though I didn't know where I was going. It was four in the morning, a day later, when I got to my aunt's house in Montana. I didn't knock on her door; I didn't want to scare her. Instead I called and asked if I could visit. "Of course," she said, "you're always welcome here, Raffi, you know that."

"Great," I said, "then could you open the door?" A few minutes later, she did. She was wearing a red silk dressing gown, which reminded me there was a lot I didn't know about her. Her eyes traveled the length of me and maybe she was thinking the same thing. "A shower," she said, "and then we'll talk." When I got out of the shower, she'd left clean pajamas in the sink and there were two mugs of tea on the table in the kitchen, steam spiraling upward. Even inside it was freezing. The pajama bottoms were too short, so I sat with my feet tucked under me. My aunt didn't ask any questions, just waited. She was good at that.

Here's another truth: when I asked my aunt whether she thought there were some wrongs that couldn't be righted, I wasn't thinking of you. I was thinking of Alice, the arc of her back as she dove beneath the waves, the way she laughed with all her teeth showing, the delight of hearing her voice on the other end of the phone. Of Caleb's body suspended over mine, something close to pain on his face, desire and repulsion twinned within me. And yes, if I dug a little deeper, I could find traces of you in each of these. But isn't it also true that if you dig deep enough into human matter you find stardust? And at the end of the day, what does that have to do with anything?

"Teshuva," my aunt said. When I looked at her blankly, she said, "The righting of wrongs. Maimonides wrote a book about it." I forgot, sometimes, how deep her Judaism was. Unlike my bubbe and zeyde, whose home was filled with the evidence—tzedakah boxes, the sound of Yiddish, photos of various family members wrapped in tefillin, the ever-present smell of gefilte fish—my aunt's house was minimalist, austere. There was, too, her decision to live in Montana, a state with so few Jews that my mother claimed it had only a single rabbi.

"Can I stay here for a while?" I asked.

"What about school?"

"I just need a little time," I said. I could feel the pressure building behind my eyes, despair or pure exhaustion. "I'll study. I brought my books." This was true, though only because they'd already been in the car. My aunt looked at me for a long moment, then nodded.

* * *

I went to the Christmas Market in Missoula to get a present for Alice, as though a glass bauble or knitted hat could fix what I'd done. She'd gotten very quiet when I told her about Caleb, let me ramble myself into a silence that stretched long enough for me to wonder if she was still there. Then, voice composed and distant, she said: "I need some time and you need to figure your shit out so you don't keep hurting people." This response struck me as incredibly generous.

The market smelled of holly and mulled wine, the chatter of the crowd overwhelming after two weeks reading books in my aunt's living room. I stopped in a quiet corner, at a table of hand-carved spoons with a sign that read WHITTLE ME THIS! "Nice spoons," I said to the woman behind the table.

"I couldn't figure out how to whittle anything else useful," she said, "and I like useful things. But I didn't want to waste a good pun."

I picked a spoon for Alice, and the spoon-maker wrapped it in red tissue paper. "For you? Or a gift?" she asked.

"For my ex-girlfriend," I said, surprised how easy it was to say the words. "What do you think, do your spoons tend to encourage forgiveness?"

"How can you be mad when holding a spoon like this?"

She told me that her name was Kay and asked if I was from the area, and somehow, an hour later, we were still talking. Before I left we swapped numbers, agreed to hang out again soon. I thought perhaps it was the sort of plan one makes and then promptly forgets, but she followed up a day later, invited me to go on a walk. We saw each other a few times a month after that. She taught me how to whittle, I took her to the diner in Paradise.

I told her about Alice, a little about Caleb. It wasn't so hard, I found, to be honest with her. But this honesty only went so far. I didn't mention you.

* * *

When Kay invited me to a bar in Missoula for her birthday, I assumed I was meeting her alone, but when I saw her at a table of friends, I felt foolish for the assumption. The bar was crowded, too hot. Kay introduced me, told her friends I was in Montana taking a sabbatical from being a genius. The word hit me the way it always did—the flush of happiness at being perceived the way I wanted, paired with the shame of knowing it to be a facade. "On sabbatical?" I said. "I'm a college dropout."

Kay glowed a little in the bar's yellow light, laughing and leaning into her friends. There was an easy physical intimacy among them, a shared ownership of one another's bodies that I'd always envied. I tried to make conversation with a square-shouldered boy in a camouflage jacket named Buck, but his responses were terse. I peeled the label off a bottle of Blue Moon, watching Kay rest her chin on the shoulder of a woman in a black jacket. I wanted to be the only one Kay laughed with, or maybe I just wanted to be Kay, to slip inside her skin and see what it felt like to move through the world so easily.

I kept thinking of excuses to leave, but I stayed, and at the end of the night Kay came over to me. "Would you give me a ride home, Raf? I drank too much and I don't trust these fools."

"I drunk better drive," one of the boys said, and Kay rolled her eyes at me.

In the car, she fiddled with the radio until she found a country station, then sang along off-key, making up her own lyrics. "Take me home, Raph-ay-ela, to the place I belong. Paradise, North Montana, take me home, Raph-ay-ela." I laughed, and the evening's awkwardness catalyzed into an almost painful happiness at being there in the car with her.

When we got to her house, she said, "Don't go," and when I looked uncertain she said, "It's my birthday! Let's go for a walk."

It was a clear, biting night, the sickle of moon sharp enough to slice a finger. I let Kay pull me down the dirt road away from her house, her arm looped through mine. She led me off the road and across a small stream that was mostly frozen, the water dripping from ice a kind of music. The trees opened into a clearing and Kay sat on the snow, patting the ground beside her. When I sat down, she leaned against me.

"Brr," she said. I put an arm around her, rested my cheek on top of her head. My heart was thrumming, I was sweating in spite of the cold. *Closer*, she said, or I thought she did, but when I asked her to repeat herself, she told me she hadn't said anything. I heard it again, though, or saw it, it appeared inside my mind, *closer*. I pushed myself to my feet. "I have to go," I said. "It's late. My aunt is going to worry."

As if to punish me for my lie, my aunt was lying on the couch reading when I got home, a knitted blanket draped over her knees, though it was close to two in the morning. She was a night owl, like me, and I imagined a universe where we were close enough for me to tell her everything, curl up on the couch beside her and wait to be told what to do. But we were in the universe we were in, so I settled for asking, "Will you tell me more about Maimonides?"

She set down her book. "What do you want to know?"

"How do you avoid making the same mistakes over and over again?"

"According to Rambam, teshuvah is about transformation," she said. "You have to become a different person, one for whom it's impossible to imagine committing the same sin."

"But how?"

She stood and walked over to her bookshelf, pulled down a well-worn book, and handed it to me. "The Mishneh Torah's good reading," she said.

I didn't hear from Kay for a few weeks after her birthday. I filled the hours flipping the pages of my physics textbooks, highlighting random passages. I called Alice, who didn't pick up. I called my dad, who did. I told him I was okay, not to worry, that I just needed a few months to study on my own. That I wasn't someone who learned via lecture, which seemed true enough, though I didn't seem to learn any other way either. I read my aunt's copy of the Mishneh Torah and tried to guess her history from the passages she'd underlined. I typed out text messages to Kay—*I'm sorry about the other night it's just that I thought maybe I was reading your mind and that didn't work out great the last time I tried it*—then deleted them. I thought about you.

I tried to tell Kay about you the next time I saw her. She'd invited me to come snowshoeing. "I'm sorry for being weird the last time we were together," I said, to her sturdy, jacketed shoulders. "I can't explain why exactly, but you reminded me of a friend who died when we were in high school."

Kay turned around, though I wished she wouldn't. "Oh Raffi. I'm so sorry."

"No," I said. "I mean yes, but it's my fault she died."

Here is the story I told Kay about our last conversation: That we'd fought. That you'd called me the next night. That I'd ignored your call. That less then twelve hours later, you were gone.

She was quiet for a few moments; I awaited judgment. "I know it isn't the same," she said. "But I lost a friend around that age, too. Graham didn't kill himself, but he went to a place you can't come back from. I still think about what I could've done differently."

"What do you mean 'a place you can't come back from'?"

"There was an accident. He and his brother were playing with their dad's gun, Graham was holding it when it went off. It was supposed to be unloaded. After his brother died, Graham became obsessed with this place . . . the city of something—respite, maybe? A city for people who had accidentally killed someone. I didn't think it was real. I kept trying to get him to talk about other things, to come hang out like we always used to. I thought that would help. Now I think that if I'd actually made space for him to talk about what he was going through, maybe he wouldn't have felt like he needed to leave."

"You think he really went there?"

"I think so. Or at least, he left and didn't come back. And I've never been able to find him. I should have taken him more seriously. But I didn't know. Neither did you. We were kids and we didn't know how things were going to work out."

It was the absolution I'd thought I wanted. But I didn't feel relieved or unburdened. I balled my fingers up inside my gloves, dug my nails into my palms. "It *is* my fault," I said. "I know her. I knew her. She didn't want to die. She was just going through a bad stretch. If I hadn't made things worse, she'd still be here."

"You can't think about it that way," Kay said.

"Can we keep walking?"

She looked at me for a minute, then nodded and turned around.

In a sense she was right: I was young and I was afraid. I couldn't see the future. But I was right too: there is a causal chain linking my actions step by inexorable step to you, alone that night, leaving. Kay wanted to believe what we all want to believe—that good intentions are enough to protect us from doing harm—but you and I both know that's a lie.

* * *

And here's another one. Even in that telling, I let it be a single call. It's so much easier to remember it that way. Not call after vibrating call, so many that I knew something was wrong. I let the first call vibrate itself into silence and the second and the third, and then I started pressing ignore. Ignore, ignore, ignore, ignore. Even in that moment it felt like an act of violence.

What were you calling to say that night, Britt? If I had picked up, would you have asked for help? Would you have said, the way you do in my dreams sometimes, *I'm scared. Not of the dark but of other things.* And if you had, would I have stayed on the phone with you until the fear passed? Would I have found a way to apologize for the things I'd said? Would you have forgiven me?

Deuteronomy 4:41–42: *Then Moses separated and set apart a City of Refuge that the manslayer might flee thither, that slayeth his neighbor unawares, and hated him not in time past; and that fleeing unto one of those cities he might live.* A biblical city for accidental killers, a refuge where we could go to escape the blood debt we'd incurred. If it had been, truly, an accident.

The conversation with Kay wasn't the first time I'd heard of the City of Refuge. I'd found it myself in those early days after your death, when I couldn't sleep, when I stayed awake googling things like *what to do when you don't pick up the phone and your ex-best friend who you still think was maybe the only real friend you'll ever have kills herself.* A modern form of prayer, those desperately specific searches, the hope that someone, somewhere, might have answers. Might have at least asked the same questions. It had been unclear to me, back then, whether the city was real or only a religious myth. But after the conversation with Kay, it became a place like Antarctica—somewhere distant, difficult to imagine, but locatable. A place a person could go, if they tried hard enough. People on message boards argued about the city, how to get there, who was allowed in. Posted coordinates and anecdotes. Some people said that if you heard about it, it was meant for you, but I've always thought there are some things in the universe you can only find if you're looking for them.

2 / THE CITY OF REFUGE

You were sixteen when you died, and I always imagined you staying that way, as though death were amber resin. The woman I nearly trip over on the street in the City of Refuge is not sixteen. She—you—are my age, with a shaved head and delicate tattooed lines crisscrossing your biceps. You're kneeling, trying to lift a crate overflowing with pomegranates. "Could you give me a hand?" you ask, and your voice is both familiar and nothing like my memory of it, which has warped and changed over the years. "Excuse me," you say to my silence, "could you just help me lift this?" You look at me, your eyes deep brown flecked with gold, and I am frozen in time, in space.

An older woman says, "Here, dear, let me." The two of you lift the crate together and you settle it on your hip, smile at her, and walk away. You don't look back.

I leave time for a while, let minutes and strangers flow around me like water around a rock in a river. I have lived in the City of Refuge for eight years. I am twenty-nine years old. But after seeing you I am fifteen again, sitting on the playground, watching you spin your swing in a circle. *Tell me everything*, you say, and I want to cry. Where would I even begin?

It is late morning by the time I come back to myself, the sun high in the sky, my skin hot. As I walk to the barn I ask myself again and again if it was really you, but of course it was you. Who else's asking could so entirely unmake me?

At the barn, the yentas trot over to me, but I only have one treat in my pocket so I don't give it to any of them. Broodmare politics are complex, and it isn't wise to play favorites.

Rebecca, who takes care of the horses, waves when she sees

me. "Your timing is perfect," she says, though I'm hours later than normal. "Dodo and Bird are just back from plowing the fields, you want to cool the two of them off?" I pour buckets of water over the draft horses' broad backs, walk them in the shade. Before Rebecca came here—before she left the stove on and her house burned to the ground with her two daughters still inside—she ran a therapeutic riding program in South Carolina. Now she offers lessons to anyone who wants them. Offered me work, in those early, empty days when I'd first arrived.

After the draft horses are cool, I muck stalls. I stack hay bales. I join Rebecca's partner, Amani, who's cleaning troughs, help her scrub away the soft green slime, carry buckets of clean water. Amani's husband is a not-quite-solid figure, lingering a perpetual half step behind her. "A car wreck," Rebecca had told me early on. A few words, which said enough. Here we are all fluent in the language of disaster.

You always feel present to me at the barn, but today your presence feels literal. I look for you around every corner, hear your voice in every sound. When Graham says my name from the entrance to the barn, I startle elaborately. "Raffi," they say, "you look like you've seen a ghost."

It was Graham who explained the workings of the city to me when I first arrived. I'd promised Kay I would find them, send them her love—a favor, she'd said, but it was a gift. Graham, tall and elfin, with a head of curls and an easy laugh. Graham, who felt like family from the moment we met. They'd helped me get settled in a little house a few blocks from their own, brought me produce from the gardens where they worked, perpetual half-moons of dirt beneath their fingernails.

After my first night, Graham came by to check on me and

found me crouched beneath the kitchen table, hands over my ears. I told them about the ringing that had woken me. The same ringtone as the cell phone I'd had when I was fifteen. I'd stumbled out of bed, searching for it in the dark, certain you were waiting on the other end of the line. But the ringing came from everywhere and nowhere.

"Do you hear it?" I'd asked, and Graham shook their head. They told me there was something like this for everyone in the city, different for each person but always related to the deaths that brought us here. "A punishment?" I asked, and maybe they saw the hope in my eyes, maybe they understood—the way people outside the city so rarely did—that to be punished would be a terrible relief, because their voice was gentle when they said no, that they thought it was more like gravity, just part of the nature of this place. But couldn't gravity be a punishment too? For the child who falls for the first time and learns the lesson of it? For the person who decides, mid-jump, that they've made a mistake?

A week or so later, I interrupted Graham in the middle of an explanation of the city's agricultural system. "I think I made a mistake," I said. Once I spoke the words aloud, they became real, took on urgency. "God, what have I done?" I was twenty. I'd left behind everyone I loved.

"I think most of us feel this way, sooner or later," they said.

"How do I undo it?" I asked, thinking of my dad, my aunt. Of Alice and Kay. I'd known I was leaving them, but the knowledge had been theoretical, thought rather than felt until this moment. "I need to leave. How do I get out?"

"I wish I could tell you. There are a lot of theories, but not a lot of clear answers. We know that on occasion the gates open for someone. But if there's a reason for who and when, it's not an obvious one."

Whatever they saw on my face was enough to make them

walk over to me. They knelt, took my hands, and held them tightly. "You're going to be all right," they said. "I'm not trying to undermine what you've lost or say you'll never regret your decision to come here. But this is a good place, and you're going to be okay."

It doesn't take so much to make a life. A small group of kind people. Work that leaves a body tired enough for sleep. A little house with a bed and a chair. Food grown in the fields or gardens. Letters I write to the people I love, even knowing I can't send them. Graham is right on both counts—it's a good place and I'm okay. But everything feels different, now that I've seen you. Will you always be the divider of my timeline, my before and after?

I still start my days sipping tea with Graham, listening to them rhapsodize about sweet potatoes or the bumper crop of radishes. I go to the barn, bring treats for the yentas and their knobby-kneed foals, rest my cheek on Bird's massive neck. Listen to Rebecca sing old country songs while she works. But the days are inflected by the possibility of your presence. As I scrub water buckets, I practice saying of course I'll help you, yes, whatever you need, whatever I have, it's yours. I whisper the words under my breath like I'm trying to learn the vocabulary of goodness. I watch the way Amani pauses work sometimes to turn and smile at her husband. Will I find a similar ease with you? But you are not a half-corporeal, wordless ghost. You are solid, real, your life seemingly unbound from mine.

I see you at the market, holding hands with a woman I don't know, the two of you laughing. I try to keep you in sight, but you're gone, and then I turn and you're beside me. "Can you pass me that jar of honey?" you ask, and I'm a statue. The woman you're with walks over, grabs the jar of honey off the table, and the two of you walk away together. Do you recognize me? Do I mean anything to you?

You appear when I am least expecting you, so I try to expect you all the time. Inevitably, I fail. You ask me to move out of the way, hold your bag, hand you a basket of figs, give you directions to the market. You say, Would you mind? Could you just? Would you happen to? You act as though I'm a stranger to you. You smile at the people who help you. You have a sunburn pinking the tops of your shoulders. You pick an apricot from a pile, run your thumb over the fuzz of its skin.

It isn't the end of the world, my small and continual failure. Someone else proffers the figs, holds your bag, tells you to walk until the road ends and then turn left at the old lemon tree. No one asks me what my problem is. This is the City of Refuge, and I am not the only one who is haunted. Still, I am witnessed in my failure.

To avoid this witnessing—to avoid you—I spend less and less time in the center of the city. Instead, I explore the outskirts—olive groves, irrigated farmland, sand dunes. On one of my long, rambling walks, I come across a saltwater lake that is a shocking pale pink. Halobacterium and microalgae, Graham says when I tell them about it, but here in this place where the impossible is everyday, I have given up distinguishing between science and magic, I'm letting it all be magic. The water is so salinized that it's easier to swim than sink, which is magic too: a reprieve from the endless pull of gravity. I get in the habit of walking there in the afternoons after I finish work at the barn, floating until the sun sets and the lake's water shifts from pink to lilac-gray.

One morning, after a sleepless night, I go to the lake at dawn. Shed my clothes, shivering, take a step forward and then stop.

Someone is swimming toward me, moving through the water like it is their natural habitat. I watch them the way I might watch a fish or a heron, shamelessly, until they stand in the shallow water and startle at my presence. There is a surreality softening the edges of the moment. We are a similar height, a similar build. I want to reach out a hand and see which one of us is real. "You're a beautiful swimmer," I say, the words plinking into the water between us. They don't say anything, and embarrassment floods in to fill the space their silence leaves. I flush, look away from their nakedness. When I look up again, they are a flash of movement in the water slicing away from me. Instead of swimming, I put my clothes back on and walk in circles around the city until my legs twitch from tiredness.

A few days later, I find the letter waiting on my doorstep. An elegant, unfamiliar scrawl: *I'm sorry I didn't say hello when I saw you at the lake. I haven't spoken in a long time.* They tell me their name is Miko, that they've only been in the city a few months, that they came here after their friend died. That some days their lack of speech feels comforting, the way it insulates them in silence, and other days it feels suffocating, the way it insulates them in silence. They write: *I have forgotten how to be a person around other people. But it might be nice to have someone to write letters to.*

The letters become a part of my life in the city. Every other day, I leave one on Miko's doorstep. Every other day, I find one waiting for me on mine. I put them in a basket on my windowsill. We write about the deaths that brought us here, and it is a relief to write your name, a relief to put my feelings about you into words. It is easier to be honest in letters. I knock on my sentences, try to see if they're hollow. Revise toward truth.

I tell Miko that I wish you'd never forgiven me for that first betrayal. That if you'd been less generous, you might still be alive. I tell them about your requests for help, how I want to believe that in my time here I've learned enough to—at the very least—make new mistakes, but instead I make the same old one over and over again.

In turn, Miko tells me about the friend they've lost, how they are looking for her ghost, how each day they wake and hope she will be here so they can prove to her how sorry they are. They write, *I don't know how to make things right if she's gone.* They ask if I believe it—the rumor that it might be possible to leave the city not for one's old life, but for somewhere entirely new. Someplace where the dead are still living.

I write, *I studied physics because I loved the idea of adjacent universes where every decision was unmade, every choice taken differently.*

I write, *When I hated myself the most, I told myself that this life was only a single data point. That to know if I was a good or bad person, I would need to take the integral of all my parallel selves.*

I write, *I know this doesn't answer your question.*

I write, *Do you believe there is such a thing as good and bad?*

Months pass. The basket fills.

I'm not thinking about you when I invite Miko to come riding. Or if I am, the thoughts are subterranean, too deep below the surface to be visible. It's a moment of exuberance, the delight of being able to offer someone a thing they want. Miko writes that they used to live next door to a man whose daughter had died in a car accident, leaving him with two horses he didn't want. He couldn't stand to be around them, said they reminded him too much of her, so it was Miko who cared for them, until their own life fell apart. They tell me they dream sometimes of galloping across an open field, wake grieving their sudden stillness.

After I leave the invitation on Miko's doorstep—wondering, as I always do, if they're near, if they can see me—I go to Graham's house, let myself in without knocking. They're lying on their rug, reading. "I've done a terrible thing," I say. They raise an eyebrow. "I invited Miko to come riding with me."

They close their book, gasp dramatically. "The pen pals meet at last!" they say.

"Miko might say no."

"They won't," Graham says.

I lie down on the floor next to them, rest my head on their shoulder. "Was it a mistake?"

"It was brave. I'm proud of you."

Miko is seven months of words, a basket overflowing with letters. They are a pool into which I have tossed my wishes, the memory of a face, a body, in the shadowed moments before sunrise. They are a story I have been telling myself and then they are a person, smaller than I remember, their hair grown longer. We hug awkwardly. I don't know how to have a body around them, how to be a body. The moment feels pressurized, though I've been telling myself it isn't a test, just a trail ride. We walk to the barn in silence. In their last letter, they wrote of their fear that in person I would find their quiet disturbing. I want to reassure them, but I can't find the words. Their letters are slow, deliberate, but they walk so quickly that I reach for their arm, take their elbow. "I can't keep up with you," I say. They smile and turn pink. I'm acutely aware of my hand on their elbow, uncertain whether to leave it there.

It's a relief to arrive at the barn, to introduce them to Rebecca, then to the horses. I watch their face as they let Marengo sniff their palm, as they scratch Bird's neck in the spot that makes her whiskers quiver. They smile at me, and I feel it in my whole body.

I hand them Marengo's saddle and our fingers touch. Time passes in peculiar leaps. We're here, I remind myself, this is happening.

I take Miko to a field where the horses love to gallop, thinking of their letter. "Do you want to let them run?" I ask. Miko nods. I loose my reins and cluck at Bird, who takes off at once. I knot my fingers in her mane, hover over the saddle as her stride stretches long and longer. Beside me, Miko's face is fierce and delighted. When we slow to a stop where the path narrows, they're breathing hard and grinning and I swear I can read their face like a letter.

We're nearly back to the barn when I see you walking toward us, leading a dapple-gray mare. You've never come to the barn before and we have no dapple-gray mare, but all I can think is: of course. You walk toward us and we walk toward you and I wait for collision. "Raffi," you say, when we're near enough to hear. "Raffi," you say, though you've never said my name in the city before. "I need help, Cally is colicking."

Calypso's eyes are wide, her nostrils flared. Her beautiful gray coat is lathered with sweat, she kicks at her own stomach, once, then again. "I need to keep her walking," you say. You're soaked with sweat, too. There's hay stuck to your shirt, dirt smudged across your cheekbone. "Help me. Please."

I feel Miko watching, waiting. I am waiting too, somewhere far outside my body. This is your chance, I say to it. To myself. This is your chance to do the right thing. The moment swells, all of us suspended within it, and then Cally tries to lie down, and it bursts. Miko swings themself off Marengo's back, hands me the reins, gripping my knee for a second before they turn to you. I want to say to them, here, now you see who I really am, tell me again how you don't believe in good or bad people. But I can't say anything at all. Together, you and Miko force Calypso back to her feet. Miko takes the lead rope and you hit Calypso's flank, her rear. "Come on," you say, your voice raw, "walk, dammit." I sit atop

Bird's broad back and think how impossible it is, from a distance, to tell the difference between helping someone and hurting them. How even close up it doesn't always get easier.

Back at home, I sit down at the kitchen table and begin a letter— not to Miko, this time.

Dear Britt, I write, *according to the Mishneh Torah, the first step toward repentance and repair is viddui—confession. To say: I implore You, God, I sinned, I transgressed, I committed iniquity before You by doing the following. Behold, I regret and am ashamed of my deeds. I promise never to repeat these acts.*

Dear Britt, I don't believe in God, but I believe in you.

I write out a full accounting of my misdeeds—the ones you know about and the ones I've never mentioned. How I tried to buy your forgiveness, your friendship that first summer. How I sat in silence while others mocked you. I write my way inexorably toward that night, sitting on the swings, crying to you.

I write, *It's been thirteen years since you died, eight since I came to the City of Refuge. I can barely remember my father's face, the silhouette of the mountains through my aunt's window, the lyrics of my favorite song. But I still remember every word of our last conversation.*

I write, *I close my eyes and there you are spinning endlessly on that swing on the playground.*

The memory feels more real than my life does. That's the irony of wishing to forget—the wish itself is a reminder.

"Tell me everything," you say.

"No one will ever love me," I reply, dramatic as only a sixteen-year-old can be. "I'm going to be alone forever."

You look at me like I'm stupid. "I love you."

"I'm not talking about friend love," I say. We're facing each other, our swings twisted, and you lean across the space between us and kiss me. Everything goes quiet and then very loud in my mind.

Dear Britt, I write, *I can still feel my hands pushing you away.*

I push you hard enough that you lose your balance, fall off the swing, and I stand so I'm looking down at you when I tell you that you're disgusting, that I don't want that with you, that I never had and never would. Then I walk away.

I write, *I didn't miss your calls, the next night. I wasn't sleeping like I told people I was. Human memory is highly susceptible to suggestion, I've heard, and for a long time I hoped that if I repeated this lie enough, eventually I might believe it. Might remember being asleep, which is to say, nothing.*

I write, *I don't hope to forget anymore. I hope to remember.*

When you knock at the door that night, I don't startle. I open it, and you walk in as though this is a world where we often show up at each other's houses unannounced. You're calm, composed. Wearing clean clothes, smelling faintly of citrus. I know, looking at you, that Calypso is all right and I could cry with the relief of it, but I settle for handing you the letter. You sit in a chair at my kitchen table, and when you finish reading you set the letter down.

"I'm sorry," I say, before you can speak. "I want to promise I'll do better, but I don't know how. I don't know why I keep freezing."

"Come here," you say, and because you're asking me to, my body refuses to move, but it's all right, you walk over, wrap your arms around me. I let my body lean into yours. "Can't you see the difference?" you ask. I shake my head. "Miko was there. Rebecca, too. Being a good person, it's not something you do alone."

I make us tea. Sit at the table with you and marvel at the mundanity of it. The miracle of it.

"You need to go talk to Miko," you say, after a while.

"You know if you ask me to do something, I can't," I say.

You give me that look again—like you will always know more than I do, and I believe it. "Raffi. I'm not asking for help, I'm offering it."

You start showing up at my house—sometimes to talk, other times asking for help I remain unable to offer. This frightens me, the way that alone, at night, there is no one else to turn to, no one to step in and give you whatever it is that you need.

One night, Graham and I are lying on my roof, watching the Perseids. "One more shooting star," they say, for the tenth or eleventh time. "And then I'll go home."

"What if you didn't?" I say.

"I'll fall asleep on my radishes tomorrow."

"What if we lived together?" I ask. I imagine a house with three rooms—one for Miko, if they ever want it. Sunshine and radishes and a seat always waiting for Britt at our kitchen table. Graham is quiet. "Just something to consider. I don't want you to feel pressured."

"It's not that." For the first time they tell me what the city means to them. A gun that appears by their bed each night, a compulsion, terrible nights that make space for days filled with green and growing things.

I don't ask why they've never told me. Even here it's easy to choose silence over the fear of being too much.

"Come live with me," I say again.

Graham and I slip easily into cohabitation, as though it's a pattern we've practiced in some other life. I gradually stop fearing Britt's knock at the door, get used to the sight of her and Graham laughing together. Miko comes over for dinner and Graham makes them laugh, too. Miko and I keep writing letters, but we also do other things—swim in the salt lake, go on long quiet walks, take the horses out and let them run.

On one of these rides, Marengo spooks at a bird and Miko falls off. They are stoic, nonchalant about it, but by the time we get back to the barn, their ankle is swollen to twice its normal size. "Let me come stay with you. Help out while you heal." Their face is concerned, they make an uncertain gesture. "It will be good," I say.

As is so often the case, I'm wrong. We've never spent more than a few hours together. The first night, we lie in their bed, neither of us sleeping. I'm afraid to relax my body, afraid to bump into them, afraid to breathe too loudly. *I need you to leave*, they write on a piece of paper the next morning. *This is a bad idea, I'm going to end up hurting you.*

I go over to your house, the one you share with the woman I saw you at the market with, all those months ago. We sit outside in the sun. You look feline, as relaxed as I've ever seen you.

"It sounds like the only person who's ever really cared for them is dead," you say. "And they blame themself. This city is filled with egotists . . ." You throw a fig at me and I catch it and eat it, laughing. I know you're right, and I know the common knowledge—that people need to work through their own problems before being ready for a relationship. But I live in the City of Refuge, and I also know that sometimes help freely offered is the only way forward. I think of the steadiness Graham and Rebecca have modeled for me. I think this is something I'm capable of at this moment in my life.

So I go back to Miko's. That night, when they panic, making guttural scared animal sounds, when they write on the pad beside the bed that they can't do it, that I need to leave, to go away, that if I stay they will hurt me and they can't live through that again, they really can't, I believe them, but tell them that I'm not afraid. That

I know them. That we are not repeating the past, we are writing the future. *How can you be sure?* they write.

"I can't," I say. "But I have faith."

One day I get to the barn later than usual and find it deserted. The horses nicker to inform me they haven't been fed yet. I scoop grain, toss bales of hay, check water buckets, try to quiet the worry rattling around inside me.

Amani shows up a few hours later, her eyes red. "What's wrong?" I ask. "What happened?"

"Rebecca left," Amani says. I don't understand, at first, what she's saying. In my years here, no one I'm close to has left the city.

"Oh Amani," I say, hugging her. "I can't imagine what you must be feeling right now."

"We went on our normal walk yesterday," she says. She sits down on one of the bales of hay, shaking her head. Her husband rests his hand on her shoulder and I wonder if she can feel it, whether there's any weight to that diaphanous comfort. "Every Sunday, we walked that path, the one that loops the city wall. Every Sunday, we stopped at the gate and she put her hand on the wooden door, thinking, I knew, of her family. But this time it was different. I saw it on her face before she spoke."

"What did she say?"

"She said she could see it, clear as the city in front of her. A world where her daughters were still alive. She remembered turning the stove off, remembered thinking, thank god I came back to check. She said, they're so beautiful, Amani. They're all grown. She wanted to say goodbye to you, to everyone here. But she said it felt like a door she only had one chance to walk through."

"What will you do?" I ask. It's the wrong question, but it's all I can find.

"What can I do?" Amani says. "Move forward. Reach for gratitude."

I stay late at the barn. Rebecca feels present still, and I'm afraid soon her presence will fade. When I get home, Miko is writing in their notebook at the table while Graham cooks dinner. "You're late," they say, tossing a hand towel at me, but when they catch sight of my face, their expression shifts.

I tell Graham and Miko what happened, try to read on their faces what they make of the news. Graham goes to the cellar, comes back with a jar of the prickly pear moonshine a friend makes. They pour us each a glass and we raise them. "To Rebecca," I say, and Graham echoes me. Miko leans against me, and I wrap my arm around their shoulders and I think, there is nothing I would not do for this person's happiness. The thought comes to me fully formed, and whether it is true or not is beside the point, just the fact of thinking it is enough.

At the barn a few days later, as Amani and I stack hay bales, I ask her the question that's been circling me. "Do you think you could have gone with her?"

"I don't know," she says. "I didn't try." She looks over her shoulder at her husband. He's leaned gracefully against one of the stall doors, the sun shining through him so that he looks lit from within.

"Did you stay for him?"

"Americans want everything to be a math equation," she says, smiling.

I smile back. "Guilty," I say, but I can't let the subject drop. "What do you think would happen to him if you left?"

She lifts her shoulders. "Who can say? I imagine he would disperse back into the air here, into the sand and trees and water."

In the distance, Britt leads Dodo and Bird out toward one of the far pastures. She's been working at the barn with us since Rebecca left. We are settling into a new dailiness together.

"Maybe they're just figments of our subconscious," I say, though I don't believe it. "Maybe that means we don't owe them anything."

"You don't owe yourself anything?" Amani asks.

A story is just a story until it happens to someone you know and then it becomes a possibility. I get in the habit of tracing Rebecca and Amani's walk around the city walls, of resting my own hand against the gate. At first, my heart sparks each time I do, but after a dozen repetitions, the gesture settles into something softer. I press my palm against the wood, and I feel Rebecca there with me and I think of her with her daughters and hope she feels my love reaching to her across universes. I think of my dad, my aunt. Of Kay and her easy smile and her rows of wooden spoons. Of Alice, and how I wish I could show her the life I've created here, wish I could tell her that I'm not afraid anymore, or at least, that I've learned a new fear, the kind specific to happiness. Then I take my hand off the gate and walk home.

There's a pad of paper next to my bed, but Miko writes on my forearm. *Do you think there's a reason Rebecca had the chance to leave?*

I tell them what I learned from my aunt's books: to take a life is to destroy the world. Biblically, the accidental killer had to stay in the City of Refuge until the kohen gadol—the high priest—died. "There were different theories about why," I say, "but the one I liked best said that because there was no amount of atonement that could make up for the destruction of the world, the killer's time in the city had to be random, had to be outside of reason."

Maybe randomness is just another name for god, Miko writes across the back of my hand.

"God doesn't play dice, god is dice?" I say, and they tilt their head at me. "It's what Einstein said about quantum mechanics, why he thought the theory was incomplete. Too much randomness. In classical physics, if you know every detail about a system you can predict it perfectly, but in quantum physics even knowing everything, you still can't know what will happen."

We lie together in silence for a while, Miko's head pillowed on my chest. I hear the gunshot from Graham's room, more reliable than the moonrise. By morning, their head will be healed. How many times will they lift the gun to their temple before the city or god or random chance decides it's enough? They were a child with a child's understanding of death when they shot their brother with their father's gun. A game, a noise, the destruction of the world.

I take Miko's hand, write on their palm: *Would you leave?* It is easier to write the words than to say them out loud. All the letters we've sent and I still don't know the answer to this question.

I don't know, they write back. Then: *I will never deserve to leave.*

I take the pen, shift so I'm kneeling over them. Across the soft skin of their stomach, I write: *I deserve all good things.* They shake their head but smile, the dimple I love appearing in their right cheek, their eyes crinkling, so I keep writing. I make my way up their sternum, write across their clavicles. I cover their body in the story of how I see them and will the words to sink through their skin into their blood, into their bones, into their own understanding of who they are. And when they take the pen from my hand, pull my body against theirs, the ink blurs onto my skin too, until the words belong to both of us.

One day, after work at the barn, Britt joins me on my walk around the city. We walk arm in arm, not talking, but I feel my own happiness reflected back to me, magnified, the warmth of it tangible. I almost don't stop at the gate, but ritual slows my steps and Britt lets go of my arm. I reach my hand out, rest it on the gate's worn wooden surface. I am thinking that Rebecca would be so proud of me, my dad, my aunt, I think they would be proud, I am thinking the word *love*, I am thinking and then I am not, then the I of me fractures into a thousand overlaid selves—

I am remembering a summer spent searching for dark matter, the sky pressed into flatness on a computer screen

I am sitting with Kay in a house full of the strangest statues, staring through the window at a bear with golden eyes

I am standing beneath the spray of a hotel shower, two dead women next to me

I am walking down the darkest road in the cold, my hands held up in front of my face

I am building an enormous sandcastle with Alice, big enough for us to stand inside

I am crouched over Kay's leg, pressing a Band-Aid to her skin

I am sitting with her in a park, watching a bee dart from flower to flower

I am building a house for my grief over Graham's death, unable to see his ghost, reaching for me from the basement

I am watching Alice plant flowers, pulling her body down on top of mine

I am picking up the phone when Britt calls

I am telling her I'm sorry

I am opening the door and running after her

I am waiting to see if she will forgive me

she is alive and alive and alive, in every universe, alive

—and all I have to do is step forward through the gate into one of these lives and it will be mine.

I look back, and Britt is radiant, the sun gleaming off her bare shoulders, and she gestures with her head, I can almost hear her think it: *the gate is right in front of you.* Behind her, the City of Refuge is orange sand and the bluest sky, the smell of citrus and sage, mountain hyssop and olives. It is cicadas singing at night, the sky so filled with stars that I gasped the first time I saw it. It is Graham, laughing at me, saying come for the sin, stay for the stars, an idiom of our personal language now, *stay for the stars.* It is the yentas trotting over to nose my pocket for treats, Amani's soft teasing, Britt and all the ways I can't help her and the ways I can. All the ways she helps me. It is Miko and the sea of words between us. How I would spend my whole life telling them of their goodness. I do not want to say, never want to say, that something good has come of the events that brought me here. But that is not to say that nothing good comes.

I let my hand drop and I am a single self again, the gate is just a gate, the only universe that exists is the one I am in, the one where Miko is waiting by the salt lake for me and Graham is at home cooking dinner with vegetables they've brought back from the gardens and Britt is smiling, holding out her arm, and how can I want any other life than this one?

Isn't that a beautiful, ridiculous thing to say?

ACKNOWLEDGMENTS

Thank you to my phenomenal editor, Ezra Kupor. At least once a day, I think about how lucky I am to have you as a partner on this journey. From the very beginning you've seen this book—and me—so clearly. Thank you for lending me your brilliance, for believing in me and this project, for being not only an incredible editor but also an incredible friend. Working with you is the best part of publishing a book.

To my agents, PJ Mark and Hafizah Geter, who believed in this project from the beginning and who have never suggested I make anything less weird. To everyone at Janklow & Nesbit, particularly Kirby Kim, whose early generosity blew me away, and Ren Balcombe in the UK office. To Ansa Khattak Khan and Charlotte Cray, both of whose edits have made this book better in myriad ways, and to Amy Batley, Ailah Ahmed, and everyone at Hutchinson Heinemann.

To Shelly Perron, the world's best copy editor. What a gift to be read so well. To Elina Cohen and Robin Bilardello, for making *In Universes* into such a beautiful object. To Samantha Lubash and Bel Banta, without whom no one would know this book existed. To Frieda Duggan, without whom the book never would have made it to print. To Jonathan Burnham and everyone else at Harper who has supported this project in ways seen and unseen.

To Danielle Evans, a genius in the truest sense of the word.

Thank you for making this book better in too many ways to count and for your endless support on and off the page. To Peter Ho Davies, whose talk on revision changed my entire philosophy of writing and who is one of the most generous people I know. To Nana Kwame Adjei-Brenyah, whose brilliance is matched only by his kindness. To Garth Greenwell, whose writing and teaching have changed my life. To Pam Houston, who offered me a home and encouragement when this was all barely a dream. To Catherine Imbriglio, my first writing teacher, who let me into her class even though I lacked every prerequisite—I am the writer I am because of you.

To the Clarion Class of 2019, both students and instructors. To everyone at Tin House. To Jenny Xu. To my teachers and peers at Hopkins. To Fonda Lee, Laila Lalami, Julia Phillips, Fenton Johnson, and Hosam Aboul-Ela. To the Wildacres Residency. To the Gulliver SLF Travel Grant. To Lori and Jay Moore, who turned their home into an unofficial writing residency. To *Lightspeed*, *Conjunctions*, and *The Sun*, for publishing pieces of this book in other forms.

To Riss Neilson, my writing soulmate. I could never have made it here without you. Your faith in my work has carried me through. To D and Grey Arthur-Cohen, I could write paragraphs about how much I love you, but instead I'm going to go write your wedding ceremony. To Swetha Siva, my chosen family, always and forever. To Heather Savino, the most moral, empathetic, and kind person I know, how lucky I am to have you in my life. To Lauren Fenaughty, my oldest friend, who has seen me and stayed with me through so many lives. To Eleni Linas, whose advice I rely on in both writing and life. You and Brian are family to me. To Katherine Packert Burke, thank you for never giving up on our friendship and for letting me text you about writing one million times a day. To Emma Dries, thank you for lending me your editorial wisdom time and again. To Dani Blackman, who spent countless hours on the phone with me, cutting unnecessary words. To the many incredible friends who read this book in various forms, some of you more than once: Beatrice Alder, Roseanne Pereira, Alysandra Dutton, and others whom I'm certain I'm forgetting.

To Maya Chesley, my best friend, most trusted reader, language buddy, SOS phone call, partner-in-crime, and so much more.

To my dad, the best dad in the world. Know that I would never make the choice that Raffi does at the end of this book. A universe without you is no universe at all.

To Morgan, my happiest beginning.

To Kyle, everything I am is thanks to you.

ABOUT THE AUTHOR

EMET NORTH has lived in a dozen states over the past decade and has no fixed residence, but they feel most at home in the mountains. In previous lives, they've worked in an observational cosmology lab on a grant from NASA, taught snowboarding in Montana, researched Lie algebras, led wine tastings, waited tables, trained horses, and written a thesis on the many-worlds interpretation of quantum mechanics. They also translate from Spanish to English with a particular focus on queer and trans voices and are always looking for new projects.